Highway Star

The Charlie Caine Story

Keep on rocking!

Neil

Neil Avey

This is a work of fiction. Names, characters, places, and incidents either are the product of the author's imagination or are used fictitiously. Any resemblance to actual persons, living or dead, events, or locales is entirely coincidental.

Email: iamcharliecaine@gmail.com
Twitter @iamcharliecaine

First paperback edition February 2023

Book design by Neil Avey

ISBN: 9798373293518 (paperback)

For Mum and Dad. Thank you for giving me the time and space to write.

Special thanks go to the Long-Haired Lover from Liverpool,

and the Jean Genie.

Preface

When my agent approached me to write the biography of Charlie Caine, I initially rejected the proposal. I had been offered (and, against my better judgment, accepted) the chance to write Cliff Richard's life story. However, whilst I was flattered to be asked, what could I write about Caine that had not already been written? So, I declined and went back to my research on Cliff.

A month later, I began having doubts I had made the right choice. True, Cliff has a long and varied story to tell, but my conversations with his close friends and associates were leading me to the conclusion that they were unwilling or unable to tell me anything other than the fact that yes, he is a lovely chap and that yes, he is a devout Christian who has along the way made a lot of records and made a lot of the elderly generation happy with his uncontroversial lyrics and lifestyle. At the same time as I was losing hope of getting to know the real Cliff, I looked closer at Charlie Caine's life story and read some fascinating published books. His story was one that I felt needed to be brought up to date, so I quietly let the Cliff Richard project slip into the background.

I contacted my agent to say I would be delighted to accept the Charlie Caine offer. At that point, my agent dropped the bombshell that I would be writing the book with help from the man himself. My only stipulation was that I would want to do it properly and

I insisted that it had to be a no-holds-barred account of his career. I told Charlie I would need access to the wealth of journals he is known to have written, and he readily agreed to this.

As a fan, what better way was there for me to get to the bottom of stories such as how Charlie met Elvis and passed himself off as a Beatle? I would finally get to hear who and what started the fight on Juke Box Jury and how he was arrested for nudity in New York. Along the way, I would question him on how he gate-crashed Woodstock, kick-started the punk scene, and find out if the stories of his celebrated rock and roll lifestyle were true. Not forgetting the lowdown on his celebrity battle with Billy Shears.

Charlie set to work on writing a personal account of his life, full of little titbits that I might not have known about him that I could use in the book. We met regularly over a few months, and I asked him many questions about his life, which he readily answered. His journals were surprising because he had written quite a lot of the names in anagram form in case anyone saw some controversial entries. Others are just funny rewordings of celebrity names. I spent quite some time going through these anagrams with Charlie, and most of them are here in their correct form. Some are so funny that I left them as Charlie intended, and others are so obscure that even Charlie could not remember whom he was writing about. For instance, Charlie kept mentioning *Musical Carpentry,* which took some time to work out before I realised it was a reference to Paul McCartney. I shall leave you the reader to judge if I made the right choice between Charlie and Cliff.

Two Chord Wonders

It is said that everyone who attended the Sex Pistols concert at Manchester Lesser Free Trade Hall on 4th June 1976 went on to form a band. Peter Hook, Pete Shelley, Morrissey, Howard Devoto, Ian Curtis, and Bernard Sumner were all there and went on to varied levels of success. Everyone standing at the front during Saliva's performance went home with a laundry bill after I puked up over them on stage. 40-50 people claimed to witness the event which included my ex-bandmate John and I, in Manchester and looking for somewhere to get out of the rain after a day spent drinking.

We headed through the entrance doors to the main hall, where a band called the Sex Pistols were banging out a number to an enthusiastic but sparse crowd. We listened for about ten minutes with a look of bafflement on our faces. Who in their right mind would pay to watch this? We didn't know that the Pistols had been invited to Manchester by a couple of students in the crowd who secretly wanted their band, the Buzzcocks, to be the support act for the night. It was a case of we could do better than that, even though we were slightly the worse for wear.

We were pushed onto the stage after making some bold claims about knowing three chords, and a couple of guitars were thrust at us by a couple of spiky-haired punks to prove ourselves. I looked at my guitar and immediately began to tune it. No wonder these lads sounded so bad. "What key are we in, John?" I shouted over the catcalls and promptly wished I hadn't because playing this kind of music did not require musical ability. Another punk shouted out for the band's name, and I yelled back in a drunken yobbish manner: "We're called SALIVA, and we don't care!!!!"

(Big cheer from the crowd)

We decided to have a laugh and bring an old song up to date by playing it the way the Sex Pistols had just done. I shouted out: "We'll Meet Again. Ask your gran about this one!" We were not out to dazzle these upstarts with anything too technically proficient. So, taking a cue from the Pistols, we played our instruments as badly as we could but better than the act the crowd laughingly called the main attraction.

John looked quite ill after our drinking, but I was worse. At the end of our destruction of the old Vera Lynn song, I leaned out across the front of the crowd to shout something at them but involuntarily puked up over the front row, which is a much quicker way of pissing an audience off than spitting at them.

It wasn't my finest moment on stage, and it brought the show to a sudden finish, but it could have been much worse for the front row. Stack Waddy, a Seventies British blues rock band also from Manchester, are infamous for their vocalist John Knail who urinated on the front row in front of label executives.

We left the building quickly before we could be asked to mop up the mess, but the night's events had piqued our interest. What had we stumbled upon? I mused that a more apt band name would have been Phlegm or Mucus. My life has been a series of happy coincidences and being at the right place at the right time. Unfortunately, sometimes I was there at the wrong time.

Let's Begin From The Top, Shall We?

Jimi Hendrix, Pete Townsend, Eric Clapton...

This story doesn't include these musicians and their musical prowess. Instead, it's the tale of how I single-handedly steered and shaped the course of music history, from Woodstock with the Psychedelic and Progressive Rock era and accidentally created the Punk scene. I influenced MTV and their Unplugged series and got involved in sport before it was fashionable to be Chairman of a football club. Then, I moved on to starting what became the Saturday night monster of talentless entertainers. On the way, I gate-crashed Graceland and stood for election in my local constituency. Most of what I have achieved has been through sheer luck and being in the right place at the right time, but I used it to my advantage and (primarily) for good. You can judge me on my influence on Saturday night TV later.

Who am I? You may know me under a few stage names, but I am Charlie Caine, born Rob Dylan in Pitney, Somerset, on 7th July 1942. So, despite whatever you might have heard or read in unofficial biographies of my birth on the Isle of Dogs, in the East of London, my true roots lie in the West Country. The myth behind my East End upbringing is nothing more than creating the right image of a rough and tough lad from working-class East London. You must admit it sounds better than being a country bumpkin.

The photocopied birth certificate in faded ink that I hold says that I was born at No 15 Stanley Road, Pitney, to Ms. Lucy Dylan. The father's name being blank because Mum didn't want me to go looking for him in the future. The only information I knew of my father, besides the little snippets handed down over the years from my family, was that his name was Raymond. He died in an explosion at an ammunition factory where he was employed, shortly before I was born. Still, he passed on his musical talents to me as I have been told he was an exceptional musician and had a keen eye for the ladies. While he was partaking in these two favourite pastimes, he met Mum. She liked how he played and struck up a conversation with him; the rest is history. Theirs was a brief affair, and Raymond was deceased by the time I made my appearance in the summer of 1942.

From an early age, I was interested in making noise. Be it as an infant banging on my food tray when I was eating, banging empty tin cans together in the kitchen, or hitting saucepans with whatever food utensil was lying around. It's a wonder I never became a drummer. Mum probably sensed this and was trying to steer me clear of what was sure to be a noisy hobby, so for my 4th birthday, she bought me a present to send me on my way in the music world. It was a harmonica and I played it daily for a year or so and must have driven Mum mad, but it kept me occupied and interested in music. It's funny, but if I had kept up the practice, I could have been the next Bob Dylan. Scrub that, I would have been the first Bob Dylan before that American upstart came on the scene.

In 1947 we moved out of Pitney to Edmonton in North London, where Mum could be nearer to her relatives. For the next twelve years, I got what education I could between bouts of truancy. You see, school and I were never great mates and I spent most of my time down by the River Lea, fishing with my schoolmates or just fooling around in the local market doing odd jobs to earn pocket money.

It was in 1955 that I discovered Rock & Roll, and so began a musical education learned from a supply of 45s sent to me by a penfriend in Liverpool. These exciting sounds came from the States, bought over by Americans coming in with their cargo. The first record I received was Elvis Presley singing *Heartbreak Hotel*, followed by 45's by Chuck Berry, Little Richard, and later, Jerry Lee Lewis. Making music or being involved in the music business was all I wanted from this point.

For my fourteenth birthday in 1956, Mum bought me an acoustic guitar. I had seen one in a pawn shop, complete in a case, but the price tag put me off; the paper round would never pay for that because I could barely pay for sweets, let alone a second-hand guitar. Mum must have hoped that providing me with something to do after school would keep me out of trouble and at home where she could keep her eye on me. I had to find out how to string it first because I'm left-handed - about the only thing I have in common with Jimi Hendrix.

Mum bought me a record for my 14th birthday. I was set on having *Blue Suede Shoes* by Elvis Presley to go with the collection I already had of the King. Well, they didn't have that in stock, so Mum took the advice of one of the older assistants as to what to buy and came back with *Whatever Will Be Will Be* by Doris Day. To say I was mortified would be an understatement. I played it on Mum's beat-up second-hand Dansette player before the record met with an untimely end, melting on the radiator in my room. An accident? You decide.

The most significant event of my formative years was in 1954 with the introduction of TV to the Dylan household. We had watched the Coronation the year before, next door, on a tiny black & white screen, and were mesmerised. We needed a television in our home to invite other neighbours in to impress them. In late 1954, Mum started getting secretive about my Christmas present and would not tell me what it could be other than to say I would have to share it. I wasn't keen on this and kept pleading for a present to myself, but she laughed and said wait and see.

On Christmas Day, I awoke to the sound of conversation downstairs, came rushing down to see who it was, and was shocked to see a television in the far corner of the room. All my birthdays and Christmases had come at once, or so it would seem. The only channel available then was the BBC (or Band 1 as the TV showed), but even that had far more to entertain me than I could need. Moreover, TV in those days had peculiar hours and seemed to be forever closing during the day for hours at a time, only to come back at peak hours. I can even remember it shutting from 6-7 pm. I was told this was so parents could get their younger children to bed before settling in for their evening entertainment.

Television in those days was a mixture of news, current affairs, history, and serious drama and I devoured the lot. It is a wonder that I never had square eyes from the time I spent watching television. The one thing lacking was a dedicated show for music fans. Sure, there were orchestras from time to time to keep us entertained, but I felt there was nothing for my age group. I remember the first time I saw *Six-Five Special* one Saturday night. It was a live BBC show, as most were in those days. Launched in February 1957, it was a mix of music and public service in a magazine format. Now, this was something I could get to like. I remember the theme tune to this very day, with footage of a steam train chugging along to the tune of *Six-Five Special.* Pete Murray was presenting the first time I watched the show, and I remember him saying his catchphrase, "time to jive on the old *Six-Five.*" I can remember all this as clear as yesterday. This is the show that introduced me to Lonnie Donegan and was also about the time I saw Chuck Berry on TV.

Good old Chuck. These were the days before he started playing with his *Ding A Ling*, and it made an excellent case for his being the most influential musician of the Fifties. He certainly was for me, and I bought all his records as they were released, even when I had a career of my own. I tried to emulate his Duck Walk, but only one person could pull that off. Little Richard and Jerry Lee Lewis were other contenders for the King of Rock & Roll, I was never wholly convinced about Elvis as he never seemed to be the master of his destiny, with too many handlers and hangers-on for my liking. Tommy Steele was another influence on me. He was a home-grown talent being a London boy, and I could relate to him more than Elvis, as much as I appreciated his music.

It would be another year before ITV challenged *Six-Five Special*'s dominance of the teen music market with their music show, *Oh Boy* which began on ATV, within the ITV network. Both *Six-Five Special* and *Oh Boy* were the brainchild of Jack Good, who managed some of the UK's first rock and roll stars in his time. This included Tommy Steele, Marty Wilde, Billy Fury, Jess Conrad, and Cliff Richard. He was also a local lad, having grown up in Palmers Green. Good carried on working within the music scene and was responsible for *Shindig* and the show became very popular in the States in the mid-Sixties.

I got wind they were going to broadcast the first *Oh Boy* show from nearby Wood Green Empire, and with another music-obsessed friend, we decided to sneak in through the back door. My previous attempt at free entry to a cinema to see *Rock Around The Clock* had not gone very well. I had no money, so on this occasion, I was going to try and sneak my way into the cinema without paying. I saw my chance when the ticket stub checker left his post and made a dash through the double doors into a darkened cinema, quickly followed by cinema staff who were determined to eject me. I dived face-first onto the floor behind some seats near the back row, and my pursuer said something like "I'm sorry everyone but a boy just ran in here without paying and I'm trying to find him". A man replied, "Don't worry mate, I'll pay for his ticket as I leave". I stood up and said "Really? thanks mate, I didn't expect that" and he replied, "Nor this, I don't have any more money with me" and at that point the entire cinema of about forty people erupted in laughter and I was ejected quite forcibly from the cinema.

When it came to the day of the show, I had come up with the simple plan that I would hide in the toilets and then at a suitable time, when there was a crowd, I would casually walk out and hang around and watch the show. My friend gave me a hand outside the cinema to get in through one of the toilet windows, and I waited for the rest of the afternoon for a suitable time to enter the cinema. Unfortunately, I had not accounted for choosing the ladies' toilet by mistake, and when I was caught coming out, I was ejected from the building.

I heard that Chuck Berry was performing in Luton later that year; I had to go and see him play. I bunked off school again with the idea of hitchhiking all the way there one afternoon, not appreciating what a task it would be. Remember, these were the days pre-motorways, and there was the matter of being without a ticket for the show. I made it as far as Hertford before being picked up by a local bobby who wondered where a young lad was going late in the afternoon, crossing muddy fields for a shortcut. I had fallen over once or twice and looked in a sorry state, covered in mud from head to toe. I later learned that Chuck was never even due to play in Luton. I got a right whacking from Mum over that escapade!

Visits by American artists were few and far between at that time, but at least we had Lonnie Donegan providing his own home-grown version of Skiffle. I saw Lonnie perform once live, and he certainly made an impression on me; I wanted to learn how to play the guitar just like him. We even had a local skiffle band in Edmonton, led by a funny little man named Reggie Cramwell. Reggie and his band The Foot Tappers weren't very good, but they were the only ones playing that kind of music locally, so they tended to get most of the bookings in the area. I often saw them when they played in Edmonton and got to speak to Reggie between shows. Reggie was in his thirties and was the senior member of his band by a good ten years.

Along with being the singer, he claimed to be the group manager/leader. All gig bookings were made through him, but even though The Foot Tappers were constantly working, they never seemed to have any money. Reggie was good enough to listen to me practise when he wasn't busy and gave tips and advice along the way. I wouldn't by any stretch of the imagination say I was a great guitarist, but I was getting better all the time.

I decided that if I wasn't going to see live Rock & Rollers any day soon, I would make my own entertainment and get a band of my own. I resolved to form a multi-talented band that could play anything: washboard, jugs, guitar, washtub bass, cigar-box fiddle, comb & paper kazoos, or musical saw, but with a tiny problem: nobody was interested in playing my kind of music. I tried putting adverts in the wanted column of the Edmonton Gazette that read *Band Members Wanted For Skiffle Group*, sat back, and waited for a rush of interest but it never came. I was left with only two alternatives: play solo (which wasn't going to happen because I had barely mastered the guitar) or join forces with an established band. The latter seemed the better option, so I went back to the Gazette and changed the details to *Guitarist Searching For Skiffle Band* and waited for the inevitable rush, but it never happened. This knock back was quite a blow for me until a month later I saw the Foot Tappers show in town and decided to ask Reggie Cramwell what he thought I should do. His answer was quite a surprise. He thought I should join his group, subject to an audition the next day. I did not know that the previous week his guitarist had left the Toe Tappers citing creative differences, which probably meant he thought that skiffle was on the way out and the band ought to play Rock & Roll in the future.

The next evening I arrived at the audition which Reggie decided should be at nearby Enfield. Guitar in hand and feeling apprehensive and nervous, I don't think I had even considered the consequences as to how I would fulfil my commitments with the band should I be successful and still attend school. Reggie confirmed my worries when he came straight out and asked how old I was and sucked in his cheeks when I admitted I was fourteen. True, I was soon to leave school, but playing in a band was a commitment, and wouldn't I want to pursue a lifestyle more befitting a teenager such as going out with my mates, chasing girls having fun and such? I hadn't thought about things that way, but we put that aside for the moment till after I played. I got my acoustic guitar out of its case and tuned up before playing along with Reggie to one of the band tunes that I knew off by heart after having seen them play countless times. I think he must have been impressed because he asked me to play another, and after four or five tunes, he asked what I was doing the next weekend. I never even thought to ask how much I would be paid. The paper round was never going to pay for my travel expenses! So, in April 1957 I joined the Toe Tappers.

When Mum got wind of what was happening, she hit the roof. I had played a few local gigs with The Foot Tappers and got around my absence for two successive weekends by claiming I was staying overnight with a friend. I had forgotten to tell my friend what was happening, and it all came to a head when I got back late one Sunday night to Mum, a look of rage and a broom in her hand, but when she smelt alcohol on my breath, that was the final straw. I got a severe whacking and was told I was grounded for a month, but it was worth it.

I got my first taste of live performance and beer in those two weeks. Reggie attempted to settle my nerves, and it worked, but only in the short term because once I had downed my first pint I felt quite unable to come out for the second show. Finally, mum relented, and we came to an arrangement whereby I was allowed to continue playing in the band, but on the condition that it was only at the weekends and would never get in the way of my schooling. I also had to buckle down and do well at school.

This agreement held good for a few months until I got expelled from school for arson - or at least that's the official reason for my expulsion, but the truth of the matter is that it was just a horrible accident involving electrical equipment the night the Foot Tappers performed (for free I might add) at the 1957 Christmas school concert. It was also the last night that the Foot Tappers were ever to perform for reasons that will become clear.

We were hoping for a large crowd that night or, should I say, I had convinced the band there would be a big crowd. I nagged and nagged for them to agree to play that night, telling them that the whole school was looking forward to some live music. This was a bit of a fib because only fifty tickets had been sold up to the point the Foot Tappers walked on stage that evening. You can just imagine the shock on the band's faces when they walked out to a light smattering of applause and right there in the front row of chairs was a line of teachers and the headmaster Mr. Leonard Skinhead. Not a man to suffer fools gladly, he had already decided that this would be the last time he would allow live music and instruments into his school.

I had found an electrical socket for Reggie's microphone at the back of the stage and ran the lead across to the front where Reggie liked to stand. Somebody pointed out that the lead might get tripped over, so I helpfully put a rug over it and left matters at that. I could hear a faint buzzing sound from the microphone, which couldn't be explained, but it seemed otherwise okay.

We played for fifteen to twenty minutes and during that time I could smell something similar to burning, but as I couldn't see anything untoward, I continued playing. The others must have noticed too because they kept looking over towards the centre of the stage and mouthing "What's that smell?" or something similar. Then out of nowhere George Turpin, the washtub bass player suddenly jumped up and began dancing around. This wasn't in the script and I looked across to the front of the stage with a puzzled look.

All hell was now breaking loose as it became apparent that the dancing bass player was trying to put out a flame that was licking at his washtub. Being the ever-resourceful chap that I was, I instinctively reached for a glass of water that was within easy reach and flung it over the flames, but this made things even worse because it was Reggie's vodka and as the washtub exploded into flames, everyone leapt from the stage. The hall was plunged into darkness and all that could be seen was a bonfire in the middle of the stage and everyone was quickly ushered outside.

In the aftermath the cause of the fire was quickly established as the frayed wires of the microphone, not helped by the rug I had placed over it that caught fire. The hall was gutted by the time the fire brigade put out the flames, but the rest of the school was untouched. At the start of 1958 I was called into Headmaster Leonard Skinhead's office with Mum for what was no simple disciplinary matter and told that I was to be expelled from school permanently for arson. My actions in attempting to put out the fire with alcohol were seen to be premeditated and despite my protests of innocence, that was to be the end of my education. It was also the end of The Foot Tappers who lost most of their instruments on the night and went their various ways.

Not Fade Away

After the school fire disaster, I was without a band. No more free beer and money from the Toe Tappers gigs. I also had no school to attend, which was no bad thing to be honest, but Mum was decidedly unhappy about my job prospects. I kept telling her that something would come up and that I would be able to contribute something towards the bills, but in my heart, I only wanted to play music to enthusiastic crowds. I had the performing bug, and it had bitten badly.

Playing in a band sharpened my playing, and I debated whether I should join another band or even go solo. I started playing in pubs and local youth clubs wherever I could get a booking; my age was not causing me too much of a problem until I asked for a performance fee. But at that age, it was the experience I was looking for. I played a set every Sunday night at the William IV in Lower Edmonton, featuring folk and contemporary chart numbers, and occasionally would venture further afield to Cheshunt or Stamford Hill. Mum always raised an eyebrow when I said I was off out for the night but never complained. Lonnie Donegan was still part of my set list, but I was now playing Eddie Cochran numbers, something I couldn't do in my previous band and was an indication of how my musical tastes were expanding.

I found part-time work in the Summer of 58 at Battered Platters, a record shop in town, working primarily mornings. This arrangement gave me ample time to prepare for my evening gigs. The job had the bonus of supplying me with plenty of free records from pluggers and the like who were only too keen to hear their artists' music in the shops. I was checking out the latest chart sounds and new market trends. The owner of the shop we called Bob, though I never did find out his surname. I do remember him talking about visiting Liverpool and, in 1960 hearing of a new band called The Beatles. "But they'll never amount to much," he kept saying, "they've not even cut their hair for a year!"

Battered Platters was so much fun to work at that it didn't seem like work at all. I got to meet lots of girls, and if one took a shine to me, I could supply her with the latest release of her favourite artistes for free and even sometimes manage to meet after work. I met John James, who also worked part-time, had a way with the ladies, and knew the right thing to say to get their attention. He was also into his music as well and played bass. He had an extensive collection of singles which I assume he liberated from the shop over the months he worked there. It was only a matter of time before we would pool our talents and perform together. He was also a couple of years older than me and had wheels (or so he said).

At Platters my initial task was to keep the shelves well stocked. Artists like Elvis and his rock & roll peers shifted their fair share of LPs and I was kept busy. John and I were always up to mischief in the stock room with the records and occasionally with girls. In fact, that's where I had my first sexual experience with what was my first serious girlfriend. There, wedged between a box of Cliff Richard and Little Richard LPs, I had my first knee trembler. Goodness knows how I wasn't caught, but to this day, when the name of Cliff Richard gets mentioned, my thoughts go back to Agnes of the buying department.

I never really got into Cliff and took enormous pleasure in occasionally scratching his singles during dull moments. Mum loved the Inkspots, a 1930's vocal group who presaged an early doo-wop and ballad style, and I used to smuggle some home under my jacket for her. I could not understand their popularity; every song had the same introductory guitar sound, and if you don't believe me check them out on YouTube.

Christmas Eve 1958 is a date I will never forget because I had a strange dream that it was winter, and I was watching the skies as a plane took off on a snowy runway. The aircraft had been in the air for a minute when it flipped upward and crashed behind a row of trees. There were a few seconds gap, then an almighty explosion. Fireballs of wreckage rained down on the snow, I began to run, but then I knew I was dreaming and awoke. Later that day, I heard of Buddy Holly's death in a plane crash. I occasionally had dreams like that, but the Buddy Holly dream was the most vivid of all.

With some money now coming in, I could keep Mum happy and buy a better guitar. I bought a 1958 Gibson Melody Maker on hire purchase and an amplifier because I couldn't get heard over the shouting and noise in the pubs. Lugging all this gear around was a nonsense until John suggested we play gigs together. I don't know why I hadn't thought of it before because it made sense, as he had a van.

I'm no singer, so John took vocals, and I provided harmony where I could. We called ourselves The John James Trio when we couldn't think of anything else. It would mess with people's heads why we had called ourselves that, but we were always looking for an extra person to come along, such as a drummer. In the end, we just stuck with the two of us. It wouldn't be until the late Sixties that three-piece bands came into popularity with the likes of The Jimi Hendrix Experience and Cream, so we were ahead of the curve there. We were no Everly Brothers by any stretch of the imagination! We both lived locally and continued with the same venues I had been using. Just a couple of guitars and some rock & roll numbers.

On the subject of which, it was about this time that I became obsessed with building my own guitar. This is the same Rob Dylan who never created anything with his own bare hands before or since. I'm not going to bore you with the details of how John and I did this, but the simple fact of the matter was that we hadn't followed the instructions to the letter and what went down should not have been too much of a surprise.

We used to go down well with the local youth club on Hertford Road, where we knew we would get a few of my ex-school friends in attendance. In those days, this was where teenagers would go because there was not much entertainment for people our age that we could get entry to. There was nothing on television for our age group. The TV stations had not cottoned on to the market for the kind of entertainment teenagers were into (other than *Six-Five Special* and *Oh Boy*).

One occasion we didn't fare so well was when we were booked to play at an event at one of the church halls in town. I'm not quite sure what they had been expecting that afternoon, but when I asked where to plug in our instruments, I'm sure there must have been raised eyebrows, but not half as much as when we blew out the electrical circuits with my home-made guitar after beginning our performance. We left in a hurry after checking we had not left any contact details!

National Service ended in 1960, and the minimum age for joining up to that point was 18. For quite a few of my teenage years, I was afraid of the call-up. I often wonder how I would have coped doing National Service. A friend once told me the following story:

During training exercises, a Lieutenant was driving down a muddy back road and encountered another car stuck in the mud with a red-faced Colonel at the wheel.

"Your car stuck, sir?" asked the Lieutenant as he pulled alongside. "Nope," replied the colonel, coming over and handing him his keys. "Yours is."

As 1962 dawned, I was still living with Mum and performing solo. It could be quite a struggle at times and quite frankly, I was wondering if I shouldn't just jack it in and get a more respectable job that would bring in some regular money. I was going to turn 20 in the summer, and I was entertaining thoughts of finding my own place or moving in with friends. Unfortunately, I couldn't do this with the odd jobs and irregular bookings we were getting at the time.

At this point, I ran into my ex-bandmate George Turpin from the Toe Tappers. I hadn't seen him since the band split up and it was good to hear that he had formed a new band and they were doing well around London. I knew George would do well, and I congratulated him on his success. George wasn't happy with the band name, though I told him in an off-the-cuff manner that he ought to call them the Highwaymen because of his name, which made him laugh. We swapped numbers and agreed to keep in contact this time.

Two months later, I got a call from George. Would I be interested in seeing his band perform? They were playing in St Albans at the weekend and oh, would you bring your guitar with you as well? Their guitarist had left suddenly, and George remembered our previous meeting. I met the band that Thursday and we went through a few of their stage favourites which were standard numbers of the time - and all was arranged for the weekend. I was also informed of the new name change. They were now the Dandy Highwaymen, having taken my suggestion seriously enough to make the switch. I asked about the details of a record deal the band intended to sign but all they would say was "oh, Reggie has taken care of all that." Good old Reggie Cramwell was now into music management and looking after a couple of other bands simultaneously.

I was shocked to say the least when on the night of the gig, 150 screaming fans turned up. I just hadn't appreciated how big a draw the band was. There had already been discussions regarding signing to a record label, and they had a loyal following, judging by the audience size. I wondered how I would fit into the band and how having a new guitarist would upset the fans because the one I was replacing was quite a popular chap.

All kinds of thoughts were going through my head as I played, but thank goodness there was no adverse reaction when I was introduced midway through the set. The gig passed off without incident. It must have gone even better than I expected because, during the week, I was asked what I would be doing the following weekend. After a few more weeks of playing with the Highwaymen, I was officially asked if I wanted to join the band and jumped at the offer. John didn't mind my splitting up the duo because he needed a break from the constant travelling. He had a new lady in tow and wanted to spend more time with her. We remained in touch.

My new bandmates seemed like a friendly bunch. George Turpin had moved on from his washtub and now played bass. Dapper Dave was on drums, alongside a rhythm guitarist/vocalist named Pete Stuart, who wasn't much of a guitarist and an awful lot worse as a singer. At least that's what we used to tell him to get him stirred up before a show. We all lived in or close to London and George had a white van that he drove with the equipment to our gigs. George was the only one of us who had a driver's licence till Dave passed his test and after that, they shared duties on longer journeys.

Aside from my debut in St Albans, we were gigging in the Southeast or wherever Reggie could find us to play. Mainly at the weekends, but there was an occasional evening venture to Hertford, where Reggie lived. The record deal? We provided backing to artistes that were touring from the USA, and every so often, this would involve recording backing tracks in the studio. These were the days of solo artistes using session musicians on their latest recordings.

At one point, much to my chagrin, the band was bottom of the bill on a Cliff Richard package tour. Oh, the shame of it! If you saw Cliff at Croydon's ABC or the Southall Dominion, you were right at the start of the Highwaymen's route to stardom. I particularly enjoyed spiking Cliff's mineral water with something more alcoholic. He never did find out who it was until now. We didn't stick around to see much of the other acts, apart from the Shadows, particularly Hank Marvin, who was a regular kind of guy.

Reggie found us seasonal work in Great Yarmouth during the Summer Season of 1962. There we came across Shane Fenton & The Fentones. If you don't know who Shane Fenton went on to become, you were not paying attention to the music charts in the early to mid-Seventies or too young for Glam Rock. At this time, Shane (aka Alvin Stardust) was having minor hits scraping the lower reaches of the charts and had not discovered his magic glove, sideburns, stardust, and leather outfits. He was also blondish at that point for goodness sake!

One of the novelty things they used to perform when short of material, plain drunk or to get a reaction from the holidaymakers was to mime along to Alvin & The Chipmunks songs. I believe that's where Shane had the inspiration for the name change but the leather is probably from Suzi Quatro. Only Suzi can help us by confirming who was first, as Alvin Stardust died in 2014. Mike Sarne was also at Great Yarmouth - he of *Come Outside* with Wendy Richards. They used to get a man to sing her part just for a laugh from the audience. Also making an occasional showing was Joe Brown.

Pete left the band, citing musical differences (the difference being we didn't think he was any good and he did), which left us without a singer. I suggested my mate John, who was keen on joining the band and liked the idea because he was missing touring and had given his lady the heave-ho. The chance of getting to record, get famous and play to hundreds of screaming fans had nothing to do with it of course.

John fitted in with the rest of the band immediately and soon, he was pestering the rest of us about when we would cut our own record. Reggie kept putting it off and putting it off to the point that we were wondering if it was all talk. Then, just when we had given up hope he phoned me to say that we were to meet him in Muswell Hill the next day to discuss an overseas project he had in mind.

Magic Bus

Reggie had several contacts in Holland, and through one of these, he was offered the chance of some seasonal work in the Summer of 1963 for a band to play every night, entertaining the locals. When we met him the next day, we were half expecting that we might be about to record. We were all initially disappointed, but soon cheered up with the opportunity of performing overseas. However, we would have to decide there and then whether to go as the boat was due to leave the day after next.

It didn't take too much persuasion for four healthy young lads to decide on an adventure to Rotterdam. It wasn't the prospect of culture that we were thinking of! We all signed there and then without thinking of the consequences, and I had the somewhat awkward task of telling Mother of my departure. She was dead set against the idea, but as I explained, I was 20 and quite capable of looking after myself. She then suggested that if that was the case, I should move out, setting off another argument.

When I spoke to Reggie about Mum's concerns, he said it was nothing to worry about, and it had all been taken care of. He would talk to Mum and explain that travelling to Europe would be a great life experience for me and that there would be no time for me to get into any mischief. He would personally make sure that none of his boys would get into trouble with the local girls (and their boyfriends) and placed a ban on drinking. Mum said she didn't like Reggie and his attitude, but there wasn't much she could do other than warn me not to get into trouble while away.

Two days later, we met up in Muswell Hill on a Saturday morning, bundled our instruments into the back of George's white van, and drove down to Dover to catch the ferry to Calais. Why he didn't book us a Harwich to Hook of Holland crossing is beyond me, but it could be he was too tight-fisted to do that. Reggie had sorted out the necessary travel arrangements, and we drove through France and in the direction of Rotterdam.

The journey was an adventure in itself. 190 miles in a clapped-out old van, and we broke down soon into the journey. Reggie was a mechanic during the war, so he managed to get the van going again but it was touch and go that it would break down before arriving at our destination.

We arrived at Hotel Knaagdier late into the night and unloaded the van and prepared to crash out for the night but were given our first shock. We were due to perform downstairs in the Knaagdier Fosse Club in an hour to a rowdy bunch of revellers, and the second shock was that due to a miscommunication in booking rooms, we were all going to have to share one room. Five single rooms had somehow been mistranslated to a room for five. This did not go down too well within the band because we learned that Reggie had a room to himself on the other side of town before he headed home for a few weeks, leaving us to get on with things.

Left to our own devices in Rotterdam, the four of us got into all kinds of scrapes during our time at the Knaagdier Fosse. We were one of several bands playing overseas in the wake of the Beatles and their all too often told tale of Hamburg. It was in Rotterdam that I first met Billy Shears playing in a band he had named Billy Shears & The Londoners (so vain - nothing changes!) For a man of a relatively small amount of talent, he always seemed to land the best gigs, recording contracts, and even the best of the ladies.

He would perform at Carnegie Hall and The Royal Albert Hall in the Seventies, but at this point in his career, he was slumming it in the filthy and cramped conditions of the Knaagdier Fosse Club. Our first meeting didn't go well from the start because as I looked out to the audience one night, I saw Billy mimicking me near the front of what we laughably called *the stage*. He was probably standing on a stool, so I dedicated the next song to "the midget standing on a stool in the third row that looks like a poodle" and gesticulated at Billy. He jumped onto the stage in a fury, and I got in a couple of lucky blows. I soon learned that Billy was a boxer of some note who punched below the belt. Round 1 to Billy.

I decided there and then that we would be sworn enemies and went to extraordinary lengths to sabotage any event he was involved in. This included (but was not limited to) slashing his band's van tyres and tinkering with their instruments during showtime, sending his band pseudo gig details and defacing their posters around town.

The cruellest and funniest thing I ever did to Billy was let it be known that he had already collected a 'souvenir' from his time in Rotterdam from one of the floozies he hung out with. Unfortunately, the skin infection was quite contagious. I convinced his band that Billy's only remedy was to cut his hair off and rub in fungal cream, omitting to point out that the cream caused skin burns if applied too thickly. As for filling the drums with dynamite, that was an old trick before Keith Moon took it as far as he could go with explosives. The Highwaymen preferred a more subtle variant of this move - our toilet humour getting the better of us when Billy's band had a record executive checking them out. Unfortunately for Billy, he did not come up smelling of roses on that night.

It was hard work playing three evening shows six times a week to entertain the revellers: 8:30pm to 9:30pm, then 10:00pm until 11:00pm and finally, 11:30pm onwards before hitting the sack. Sleeping conditions were cramped but we were sharing two to a bed in two rooms now. Not an ideal situation and the money was poor, but there was free beer and if you were careful with the local skirt, you could have an enjoyable time.

Rotterdam was (and still is) a rather seedy port town with a rough & ready reputation and there were always plenty of girls available. We attracted quite a number to our shows who were more than willing to show their appreciation of our on-stage performances by throwing gifts at us, and by gifts, I am not just referring to teddy bears. Bras & knickers were fair game and who were we to complain?

We could tell how well we had played by the underwear littered over the stage. It became a challenge between us and our rivals, The Londoners, as to who could get the most. We just egged the audience on to see what they might chuck at us, but things got a little strange one night when a dildo was thrown (file under jealous boyfriend). I shouted, "Is that the worst you can do?", and was hit between the eyes by a ladies feminine product!

Many times, a band member was caught in a compromising position with a female audience member in the dressing room - sometimes even during the show. That was when our drummer Dapper Dave went into a ten-minute solo whilst John went AWOL in the middle of our set. He emerged with a massive grin and a blonde on each arm to an enthusiastic round of applause, whistles & catcalls from the men, and a *where the hell were you?* look on the rest of the band's faces as if we didn't know.

We had to be careful of jealous boyfriends, particularly after the gigs when they would wait at the stage door for the first sign of a musician coming out. You didn't know if they wanted an autograph for their girl or to administer a bunch of fives to the first person out the door. That's why I always let the guitarists go out first with their instruments. If there was no sign of an affray as they walked to the van, I would breeze out the door, but if so much as a scuffle could be heard, I was off and away out an alternative side entrance. Tip: always check entry and exit points, and that's not just me being a good fire warden. Sometimes it was even necessary to escape out of the toilet window rather than be beaten.

The Knaagdier Fosse Club seemed to like us and rebooked us for the rest of the year. The Londoners didn't stay much longer than three months and were deemed more trouble than they were worth. Our run ended one night when a large crowd gathered because it had been advertised that a famous musician would be playing that night. The local promoter had mistakenly confused my surname for that of an emerging US artist by the name of Robert Zimmerman. Quite what Bob would be doing touring in Holland is anyone's guess! But that was the situation we were in when 2000 fans arrived at the venue one evening to discover that the Bob Dylan they had bought tickets for would not be performing that night, and it would not be the tickets that would be *a changing*. Was this the work of Billy Shears? I wouldn't have put it past him. That night, I decided that there was only one Dylan in the music business, and it was not going to be me! It was time to start thinking of a new stage name.

The journey back to England was an interesting one. John and I travelled back together after settling some business in town, and in the process, we were late getting to the overnight ferry to Harwich and missed it by half an hour. We didn't have quite enough money for a stay at a B&B before getting the first ferry home the following day. We decided to find an all-night club where we could have a few drinks, waste time, and save ourselves some money.

All good so far, but not many places looked appealing to us. We plumped for a nightclub called The

Pink Pussycat, which should have been a warning straight off, but we were in a hurry as it was getting wet, and we wanted to get off the street and somewhere safe and warm. We had been drinking for ten minutes when John looked at me strangely and said something was quite odd about the place that he hadn't realised until now. It wasn't the fact that the only drinks for sale were cocktails and had I noticed the over-elaborate pink furnishings and room lights. Where were the women? He was right too, because either it was a male-only club, or we had stumbled across a gay bar.

Now, I don't want to go upsetting the modern-day gay community, but this was the Sixties and even though Holland was a little more relaxed about same-sex partnerships, we were not quite as liberally minded in those days. There were a couple of burly men sitting at the bar and glancing over and winking for us to come over, and I said to John that we had two choices: we either go back outside and walk around for six hours in the rain till we boarded the ferry, or stay where we were and held hands all night, and that was what we did into the early hours of the morning. We even took toilet breaks together. I told John that if he so much as ever told anyone about how we spent our time in the nightclub, I would kill him. He squeezed my hand and whispered, "no chance will I do that, sweetie."

Highway 61 Revisited

'The Ready Steady Go house lights went down, and Charlie Caine stepped onto the stage to momentarily take the applause of his adoring fans before the Dandy Highwaymen launched into their new single, The Colours Of Your Mind. Three years of continual success as the UK's biggest band had taken the Highwaymen to the peak of their careers and fuelled their super-sized egos. But they were still the same four cheeky chappies from London: except for an acquired taste for the high life, expensive penthouses, and cheap dates. Cathy McGowan applauded them off-stage and made an over-excited remark about how it was their best record yet.'

Record Mirror's article on the Dandy Highwaymen gushed over how popular the band had become in such a short space of time. It had caught everyone in the band unawares, but I placed the surge in our popularity to the moment I changed my stage name from Rob Dylan to Charlie Caine. I noted a connection between myself and Michael Caine because I had played at the 2i's Coffee Bar in Soho with the Toe Tappers early in my career and discovered that Michael occasionally frequented the bar. I adopted Charlie because it just fitted along with the surname. By a happy coincidence,

Tommy Steele had also made his name performing at the same venue.

The press we made from the riot in Rotterdam and the writ we received from that other Dylan chap in the States put our name on the map and brought us to the attention of the media and record companies. We arranged for some publicity shots of the band, and I would like to point out that Adam Ant stole the Dandy Highwaymen theme when he saw these early publicity shots of ours. The white line across the face hid burn marks from another accidental fire I had on the day of the shoot. He even stole our song titles as you will see.

We were quickly signed up by PMSL Records and dispatched to the recording studio to meet Roger Magneti our producer and record our first single *Stand & Deliver!* We had no experience with recording techniques but were quickly shown what was needed and knocked out a couple of songs that were provided by Reggie. Nobody was more surprised than us that our first single reached No 1 and I can clearly remember being in the offices of PMSL in Camden when word came through that we had topped the charts. We opened a bottle of fizz and began planning to head back into the recording studio for more of Reggie's compositions. And when these were just as successful, it was time to make our first LP. The songs we were provided with were not always great but hey, we were the name on everyone's lips and Reggie kept coming up with tunes for us to record.

Our second single *Hey Girl* was held off the top spot by The Beatles, but we would give them a good run for their money in the UK charts over the next year. We were in demand in the studio, on the television, and in the bedroom, but that's a story for the News of the

World to discuss, and not me. Life could not get too much better for a 21-year-old in 1963.

We spent most of our free time in the pub. Most of my bands liked a drink, and the first thing we would do after finishing a gig or recording was to head to the nearest pub, drink copious amounts of beer and then stagger off home, or if you were lucky, leave with female company. George Turpin our guitarist was the heavy drinker in the band, and we had to persuade him to go home some nights. I often wondered why he didn't become a landlord.

One evening while we were recording our *In Your Room* single, there was a power cut, and we all used the break to troop across the road and have a cheeky pint. Two hours later we had a call to come back as the power was back on, but George was in no fit state to return. No guitarist, what were we to do? As luck would have it a young lad was sitting in the foyer strumming a guitar. He could only have been 20. We asked him if he was waiting for anyone, and he said he had been helping out with a band in the other studio but they hadn't come back yet. We asked if he wanted to play with us while he waited for his friends to return and he said sure, why not? He said his name was Jimmy, but friends called him 'Lil' Jim P, but we called him Pea and it just stuck because we misheard him wrong after all the alcohol.

Jim started to play along with us and it quickly became clear that he was an exceptional guitarist. We asked him if he would mind if we recorded the track because George wasn't coming back any time soon and he agreed, just so long as he was paid a standard fee for his work. We never told George that he was not the guitarist on one of our biggest hits and of the day we met Jimmy Page.

Things were great, but there was one thing bothering John and me. We had noticed that whilst we had some money to cover our expenses, we still had to drive around from concert to concert in John's van. Touring was not as well organised as today with air-conditioned coaches and air travel, but surely we should have been able to afford something a little better? Where was the money we were making for PMSL Records, and when would it filter down to us? Reggie said not to worry about that because he was dealing with the matter as a priority, but we could not help but notice that he had traded in his car for something much flashier.

We decided to find where his newfound wealth was coming from, and what we discovered was that all these songs he was providing were coming from a Tin Pan Alley song writing friend of his who was also getting a cut of our royalties, and for the younger readers, Tin Pan Alley was located in Denmark Street in Soho where you could buy your instruments, look for the latest published songs available and even use one of the available recording studios. So clearly, we could see that if we wanted to make lots of money, we would have to start writing our own songs. That was our big failing, in that if we had written any Dylan/James compositions at that time, we would have had an even healthier bank balance.

John and I sat down for a brainstorming session and worked out what subjects triggered a reaction from the buying public. It didn't take long to see what the market was: Teenage girls and love songs. We threw everything into writing our first song. Five hours of graft later we came up with *Wouldn't It Be Good?* which, to be fair, was quite a decent attempt for a first try but has been somewhat eclipsed by the Beach Boys song of the same title. We stuck at the task and over a matter of months, we felt we were able to unveil our songs to the rest of the group. We had 10 songs that we considered to be good enough for inclusion on the second album but when we played a couple of them to the others, they burst out laughing because they were so bad and said there was no way we would ever be allowed to get them recorded if Reggie had anything to do with it.

We hatched a plan that once Reggie was away doing one of his business deals, we would trick Roger by substituting some of Reggie's contributions for ours but then we relented and told him our plan, saying that we would give him a cut of any royalties. It worked like a charm, so when it came to the unveiling of the second album *Rocking With The Highwaymen* to PMSL Records, we watched as Reggie's face turned from confusion to annoyance and then anger as he realised the substitution we had made behind his back. At first, he claimed that the songs were not up to the usual standard and when this didn't change the label's mind, he accused us of double-crossing him behind his back. A compromise was made and so we were given a Dylan/James credit for three songs on the LP with an understanding that there would be more on the next album if the LP sold well and the standard of our new songs was as good.

The Dandy Highwaymen fan club was set up and initially run part-time from PMSL offices by one of the secretaries, until it grew so big that a regular position was created. The vacancy was given to Joyce James, a former teacher who had grown tired of her job and was looking for a career change. She overheard her pupils talking about the band and realised even before PMSL Records that there was a gap in the market for a professionally organised fan club and approached them with a plan for reorganisation which included improving the membership enrolment scheme, organising newsletters, meet & greet opportunities for the fans and creating gift items with exclusive offers for members.

The club remained active throughout the time frame of the Dandy Highwaymen. During her time as a fan club organiser, Joyce was most proud of the number of fans who found love through meeting at club conventions. Joyce and I became very close as friends, but it never went further than that even though there were times when I felt a strong connection that I could not explain and we remain in contact to this day. I was 22 and she was 27 and more mature in many ways than me. I still contact her sometimes when I need to get things off my chest.

We were touring around the UK as part of the popular package tour thing that was all the rage in those days. The Beatles never wanted to be a part of our tours and that's probably for the best because we didn't want them cramping our style. Mick Jagger and his bunch of misfits were on the London leg of one of these tours and we blew them off the stage after playing around with their speakers and microphones to spoil an act that wouldn't change for the next 60 years! It was also our band who were responsible for the Kinks' sound because, despite what Dave Davies has said about slitting his speaker cone to get the desired effect on *You*

Really Got Me, it was because John and I had sneaked backstage at one of their shows in a drunken moment to nobble their gear. That's what bands used to do in those days to relieve the boredom of being on the road travelling from show to show. I remember at an awards ceremony at the London Palladium, one band got rather vexed that a naughty member of our band filled up their getaway van's fuel tank with a bottle of bleach to see how far they would get from the chasing fans before breaking down and being caught. The answer is Oxford Circus in case you are interested. Nobody was 'driving their car' for some time after that!

In the spring of 1965, we toured the States with Billy Shears' band The Londoners. Neither band was big in the States at the time, even though the Dandy Highwaymen had recorded three LPs and five singles in the UK by this point, but Reggie had discussed the arrangement with Billy's manager and they thought that we would work great together as a joint venture. But just to make sure that there was no trouble between me and Billy it was arranged for Roy B'Stard to accompany us and keep the bands out of trouble, and me and Billy apart. Roy was a 20-stone ex-wrestler, and whilst being an excellent asset to the tour, quite frankly he scared me shitless. He was part bouncer, tour manager and fixer.

Looking back on the tour now it was one of the most memorable times of my life, but at the time we appeared to be travelling by coach for most of the trip in cramped conditions. We had another vehicle carrying all the equipment between gigs but a couple of times it broke down so the band, roadies and equipment were squeezed into one uncomfortable confined space. The gigs were mostly on the East Coast in New York,

Boston, and Baltimore but we had some free time as well factored into the tour so were going to head to Memphis to record at Sun Studios to get an 'Elvis' feel to our next record and also take in Nashville.

I had not seen Billy for a few years but the hatred was still there. I'm not a man for a confrontation so I kept away from him most of the time but liked to play pranks which he could not blame on me such as when I got his amp to blow up when he took to the stage one night. Everyone knew I couldn't wire a plug so how could I have pulled off that stunt? The tour was for a month, and we fully enjoyed the first half of the tour until we started getting cancelled concerts the further west we ventured. It got to the last week and then we had nothing left booked. Roy said that we were going to spend the rest of the week on a working holiday and he had arranged for us to head to Nashville for a couple of days. We could spend time looking around and then do our recording sessions in Memphis and head home.

In Nashville one night we played an impromptu show to a meagre audience who were less than impressed with our songs and performance. We were booed off stage and quickly left, leaving the road crew to clear up our gear. We were followed by a young guitarist, Jimmy James, who was touring with The Isley Brothers' band. We got chatting and he was a quite friendly chap and, like us, had some free time on his hands. He was also left-handed and the two of us swapped stories of how difficult it was playing music in a right-handed world. In the end, he decided he would play right-handed guitars upside down, restring the guitar so that the strings were in their natural order (with the lowest tuned string being the highest in altitude and vice versa).

He had his guitar with him and I soon learned that he didn't go anywhere without it. He showed me some tricks he had picked up on the road, such as playing his guitar with his teeth and behind his back. He said he wanted to do his own thing and form a band. In a little more than three years, he would rewrite music history, but on that night he wowed us with his showmanship as we jammed for half an hour.

Jimmy was passing through the city on tour with the Isley Brothers, but in the early part of his career he had been based in Nashville. He knew the coolest bars and clubs to go to so that night we went out with him, drinking and playing music. At the last bar we visited, there was an awful scene when James' guitar started to smoke and caught fire, and for the second time in my life, I was trying to put a fire out on stage. Jimmy must have seen something he liked in that burning guitar because he incorporated it into his act in 1967 at Monterey, by which point he had changed his stage name to Jimi Hendrix.

I had a hare-brained dream that I was going to meet Elvis Presley and get invited to jam with him on guitar at his Graceland home. We all arrived in Memphis and checked into our motel for the night. The plan was to look around in the morning, but I was impatient and wanted to get to Graceland immediately. After saying goodnight to the band I headed to the room I was sharing with Dave but John was next door so he came over and we chatted for a while. I then told them of my plan for the night and how I would head to Graceland and see if I could blag my way in through the front gates. I was going to get a cab there and at the very least stand by the gates and hope that some of the Elvis magic would rub off on me. They said it sounded like a great idea and could they tag along? We told George where we were going, and he agreed to cover if Roy came by and tell him we were all having a quiet night getting some shut-eye.

Twenty minutes later we were on our way. Reception had called a cab for us and we asked to be taken to Graceland. Our driver was a young woman called Carla who told us it was her first month working for the taxi company, but this was the first time she had ever gone to Graceland for a night visit. So, what were we hoping to see?

We pulled up close to the gates and peered in. It looked as though we had picked the wrong night to visit as a queue was forming at the gates. A party or some sort of big event must have been taking place because two security men were checking people at the gate. My initial hopes of getting in were dashed but Carla was thinking. She said she had a playful idea of flirting with the guards so I could slip past with Dave and John, and she would come back in an hour and wait for us. I said hang on just a few minutes as this might be very quick as I was not confident of our chances of getting through.

"Looks like Elvis is at home," I said to the others. "I wonder if we can blag our way into this party?" Dave and John were unsure as they knew the stories of how I got thrown out of the cinema in my teens. Carla tried her flirting technique with the guards, but they were having nothing of it. Eventually, I sidled up to the shortest of the security men (just in case he got violent and I had a better chance in a fight) and engaged him in conversation.

"Okay, we've come a long way," I said, "and being musicians..."

"Oh, you're the band?" said the guard. "Why didn't you say so? Where are your instruments though?"

"They're inside!" said Dave. "We dropped them off this morning when we had our soundcheck."

"Which one of you is John?"

"That's me," said John.

"But there's only three of you."

"George couldn't make it." I countered, realising what was going on. "He's having his annual haircut."

"In you go, guys," said the guard.

We waved at Carla as we went through the gates and entered Graceland in a state of incredulity. I must tell you it was an amazing experience to have got this far as it was more than we had hoped for. I just wished we had a camera to record the occasion, though I did see a photographer mooching around taking pictures of the guests, so maybe they will show up one day on Instagram. Dave and John wanted to meet Elvis or, at the very least, pick up a souvenir of their visit, such as a guitar or some other item he may have touched. My needs were more clearly defined because I wanted to use the loo as I had been drinking all afternoon on the journey. I ventured up a winding staircase and immediately came to three doors. I took a chance and opened the first two, and they were bedrooms. The third door was a toilet. Sweet relief!

I made my way back downstairs and looked for my friends. They were in the reception area eating nibbles and chatting up a couple of dolly birds. "Stop fooling around!" I hissed. "We could be on the verge of the performance of our lives. We need to at least *look* like the Beatles so let's go and comb our hair down, adopt a Liverpudlian accent and hope nobody catches on to us. We also need to find some instruments and quick."

Dave told me to quit worrying as he had already located where the performance would be held, and the stage was already set up for us. One problem remained. What was going to happen when the Beatles arrived? This night seemed too good to be true. Meanwhile, at the front gate, George Harrison was being hauled off into a police car with his cohorts when he uttered the famous line, "do you know who we are?"

"They looked nothing like the Beatles", said the guard. "What a bunch of imposters."

We were ushered towards the performance area, which doubled as a home cinema. There was McCartney's Höfner bass he always used and two electric guitars and a set of drums. I took the bass, being a left-hander, because we had to stay as authentic as possible. It was 8:00pm, and everyone was making their way in for the main event. But where was Elvis? I looked to my right, and like the sea parting, Elvis made his entrance. He walked confidently to the stage, knowing all eyes were on him and over to us. He introduced himself (as if he needed to do that) and asked were we ready to entertain the guests?

"Uh hu... err I mean okay," said John. "What number are we going to start with?"

Luckily for us, we were well versed with Elvis and Beatles songs and went for *Blue Suede Shoes* to start with, followed by *She Loves You* from *our* back catalogue. We ran through half an hour's worth of tunes till Elvis stopped the show to introduce one of his friends and ask if he was enjoying his birthday party? We broke for something to eat and chatted more with the audience before continuing to play to Elvis and his friends until 9 o'Clock .

We chatted to Elvis about our music and our long hair and left shortly afterwards. He started talking about singing one of the new songs we had played him earlier in the day. We left in case our cover was blown, and as I went out the door, I heard one confused guest say, "which one is Mick Jagger?"

Elvis had arranged for us to be driven back to our motel and was surprised that we were not staying somewhere a little more luxurious, befitting our status. I nabbed McCartney's bass before I left as a souvenir. We congratulated ourselves on our good fortune and I said loudly, "You do realise nobody will ever believe us when we tell them this story?"

Elvis did meet the real Beatles later that year but was not impressed. "Imposters", he said. The bottom line is when I heard in 1977 that Elvis had died in the restroom, it made me wonder if we had that connection. Did I use the King's loo? It made for a good story.

The following day over breakfast, Roy asked us how we slept. If only he knew. We left for Sun Studios early because Roy could only get a morning slot as it had been solidly booked for the rest of the day. The studio looked much smaller than we had imagined, but size doesn't always matter - well, not according to Billy Shears.

We were coming to the end of our session when George suddenly stopped playing. I could tell something was wrong because he shot over to the door, blocking the entrance to whoever it was that had arrived. We could hear he was in deep conversation with whoever it was, and after about a minute he returned.

"Who was that, George?"

"Oh, nobody. Who do you think it was? It was Elvis!"

Elvis had come to the studio to meet the Dandy Highwaymen. He was due to record in the afternoon, heard voices, and was coming in to meet us. George said no, we were very busy and could not be disturbed. Could you imagine what would have happened if he had walked in and found us? But I had an idea. I told the band to adopt their Beatles poses, rushed to the door and called Elvis back to the studio. I told him that the Dandy Highwaymen had left the building early to head for their next show and so we had the studio to ourselves. Did he want to hang out in the studio with us for a while? Elvis called for Sam Phillips to come on over and with Elvis we knocked out three or four songs that morning before he had to leave. I don't know where the masters of that recording are now but someone, somewhere is sitting on a goldmine with the tapes.

Life was good with the Highwaymen. We breezed through the rest of the year, having hit singles and albums and travelling worldwide, experiencing new cultures and lifestyles. I did my own thing away from the band when I needed a break. I had been travelling through an airport in India when I discovered an old man playing the sitar. We chatted for a while, and he demonstrated how he played the instrument. I was so impressed I featured the sitar on one of our earlier LPs, giving George Harrison the courage to pitch the idea of using the instrument at The Beatles *Rubber Soul* sessions.

When George heard I had been taking lessons from Ravi Shankar he was mightily impressed and asked for his contact details. I think I set George on his way with his love affair for the instrument. I didn't tell him that I also taught Ravi a few guitar licks as well! The Beatles and their hangers-on made the journey to India in 1968 but by that time I was moving on.

With the release of 1966's *Let's Take A Trip (Far Away)* LP and its *The Colours Of Your Mind* single, we were expanding the group image, much to the annoyance of Reggie. He thought we should stick to the suits as a tried and trusted presentation formula. Why change it now when we were doing so well? Controversy was just around the corner when we pushed through the release of our *Linda in the Shop with Doughnuts* single, which was banned for its use of the phrase 'sugar coat you with my sticky drizzle.' It wasn't till a year later, when The Beatles unveiled *Lucy in the Sky with Diamonds* and its LSD-coded message that it was pointed out we had beaten them to that particular controversy.

We were becoming regular performers on *Top Of The Pops* with our appearances generating higher chart positions and sales of our 45's. These appearances went by in a blur, making it challenging to pick a favourite appearance. Very little footage of our performances remains, but it was my first and only live appearance on Juke Box Jury that I will forever hope to see one day on YouTube. Unfortunately, I doubt it will ever surface due to the BBC policy of wiping and reusing the tapes of the Sixties recordings and not bothering to keep any archive footage.

David Jacobs was the host on that eventful night where I got in a tangle with a couple of the judges when they failed to judge a new Highwayman song a hit. Four judges listened to six or so songs a show, and they had to vote each piece a HIT or a MISS. On the show, I encountered my nemesis Billy Shears who was also having success with the Londoners, along with one of his band mates. I thought I had the edge over him because I knew he was one of the judges, but I could not have expected that when he pronounced judgement on our song, he would have the nerve to have scrawled an offensive word on the card. Well, all hell broke loose as I lunged for Billy, and his mate (whose name I choose to forget) started grappling with Pete. I think it was either Lulu or Cilla on the show that week and whoever it was screamed loudly and ran off the stage.

I'll never forget the newspapers the following day. One read, 'JUKE BOX JURY FURY!!!' Reggie was delighted because he was getting maximum publicity for the band, and the record shot into the charts in the next couple of weeks. Shears' autobiography *Shear Delight* had an illuminating version of the build-up to this confrontation:

'We were asked if we wanted to go on Juke Box Jury, and Graham was all up for it. We asked what songs would be on the show, and when they said it would feature Caine's bunch of misfits, we agreed like a shot because of unfinished business with him. When we got to the studios, we headed straight to the BBC bar and were delighted that drinks were free so sunk a few and then headed back to the studio.

We sat through a few numbers and wondered when his record was coming on. We were quite drunk at this point because we had topped up our water with something a little stronger to get us through the show, and Jacobs was looking a little anxiously over at us because I guess he must have considered us to be quite boisterous. Anyway, The Colours Of Your Mind finally played. I'm looking over at Graham scribbling furiously and thought, shall I? And immediately scribbled an S in front of HIT.

I'm not going to say what Graham wrote on his card, but I like to think that by writing a harmless word on mine, the watching audience and the BBC were spared seeing his obscene message by the chaos that ensued.'

The aftermath of this episode is that Billy and I were banned from appearing on live BBC TV (more publicity), and it was not for many more years that this ban was lifted.

During the Summer of 1966, the whole country was gripped with World Cup fever as England held the tournament for the first and only time to date. To coincide with this event, the Highwaymen recorded a single with the England squad and hoped to give all proceeds from its sales to charity. Unfortunately, we had not been cautious with the subject matter of the song and were lampooning Scotland for not qualifying again. When the Scottish FA got wind of this, they threatened legal action should the song be released and the project was quietly shelved. It was featured on a compilation CD that was issued many years later. I listened to it the other day and it mentions haggis, bagpipes, kilts and Celtic FC in the most unflattering and stereotypical way.

It was one of the first attempts by a football team and a known artiste to create sweet music. Bobby Moore's singing voice will have to remain unheard for a while yet. As a result of the shelving of our song, England chose Lonnie Donegan's *World Cup Willie* as their anthem for the tournament, as inoffensive a song as there ever was.

As successful as we were, I was getting bored with how the band was being packaged. We had all grown tired of being dressed up in suits early on and had modified our dress style. I couldn't stay dressed as a Highwayman for the rest of my career. On one tour of the States, I remarked on how bright and fresh the clothing looked and even got myself kitted out one day and arrived at a concert to see what the others thought. They were horrified. I was also pressing for a change in direction with our music because, the way I saw it, we couldn't stay trapped in three-minute pop songs for the rest of our lives. We had to move with the times or we would get left behind as the next music wave came rushing to shore, and I wanted to be riding that wave. I even wrote some songs to give the band some idea of where I thought our music should be heading. We had released *The Colours Of Your Mind,* but only John was keen on the song.

Come 1967 I was still treading water in a band I was no longer interested in. I took an extended holiday, hoping a change of scenery would do me some good. The others knew I was going through the motions but assumed I would soon get over it, with our records still selling well and fans wanting to see us live.

I was at the BBC TV broadcasting of *All You Need Is Love,* dressed in my colourful finest with The Beatles who were riding high after releasing their *Sgt Pepper's Lonely Hearts Club Band* LP. That was what I wanted to be doing, creating and expanding the boundaries of music. It was a shame that all the available footage is black & white, though there remains a short colour footage of their performance on YouTube. I remember listening to *Sgt Pepper* for the first time, and aside from what I have already written about this musical masterpiece, there was one odd fact that had not gone unnoticed by many UK listeners: Billy Shears was namechecked in *With A Little Help From My Friends* and I heard that he was initially pleased but soon became furious about the part about singing out of tune. Were John and Paul having a sly joke at his expense by having the most unmelodic member of their band sing the song? I would like to think so. Concert audiences were shouting out for Billy to sing the song, and it all became a millstone around his neck. He would grow to resent the Beatles and all they stood for, an anger that culminated in his solo LP *Paul IS Dead*.

The Highwaymen were due to tour America again, but I was already making plans to leave. When would be the right time to drop the news? I told Joyce of my plans and she was devastated. She asked why I wanted to bring an end to the band when things were going so well. I asked her to keep the news a secret and told her that whatever happened, she would retain a job within PMSL Records - I would make sure of that. She agreed to keep silent but I could tell she had thought I had lost my mind and was going to walk away from a good thing.

In Joyce's Autobiography *In My Life - My Time With The Highwaymen*, she laid bare her feelings in no uncertain terms:

'Charlie called me one day and said he was considering quitting the music scene. When I asked him why, he said he had become stale and predictable and needed a new challenge in his life. He wanted to go off the grid. I asked him what he meant, and he said he wanted to get away from it all and start afresh. I told him he was mad. Actually, my choice of words were a lot stronger than that!'

I Still Haven't Found What I'm Looking For

It's true.

Working in customs is not a great deal of fun. Think about it: you're Mr Unpopular, always the killjoy searching for someone's contraband being smuggled in from Europe; you're the man who confiscated Auntie Nelly's bottles of rum hidden in luggage from Jamaica, and you are the man who stopped the entire entourage of the UK's No 1 band The Dandy Highwaymen as they returned home from a tour of the United States on a telephone tip-off to say they have a large amount of weed hidden on their persons. You searched every member of the band and their luggage and found nothing. Only one option left.

"Cavity search in sector 5."

At that precise moment, as I bent forward, touching my toes, I knew I had to give up life on the road and break from the madness of touring. I was living in a bubble of travelling, performing, sleeping, and so on. Musicians were such an easy target for searches because they stood out a mile as they trudged through the nothing to declare sector, usually zoned out from travelling but mostly from substance abuse. There had to be a better way of earning a living, but it had to still involve fan worship and a new chick in every town. A truck driver? That ticked one box, but I was not going to be able to give up the fan adoration just as quickly, but it was a start.

There was uproar when I spoke to the band and Reggie about my plans. How could I throw everything we had worked for away just like that? I told them that we had gone stale and that I needed a break from everything and everyone. I was tired of the constant pressures of life on the road and in the studio. I was stuck in a cage, going around & around a wheel and I wanted to get off. We were stuck writing music to a formula, and I was bored.

Reggie reminded me that I was under contract to provide the record label with another two LPs, and that if I did leave the band, I would not be in a position to record or play with anyone else for two more years. Why don't I go on holiday for a few weeks, recharge my batteries and come back refreshed and ready to knock out another album? Wouldn't it be much more convenient to see out my contract, keep everyone else happy and then make a decision to leave? I said that if I was a football player, would I be expected to play for a team if my heart wasn't in it anymore, to which he replied I was no Bobby Charlton, and I was expected to see out my contract with or without being in the team. He even started releasing titbits to the press, indicating that if I left the band, I would never set foot in a recording studio again. But it was a risk I was prepared to take. I told Reggie that the way I felt, I would leave the music business altogether. The complications from breaking my contract remained unresolved.

The band hated me, and the fans were calling my phone at all hours of the day to ask why I was leaving and what I would do next. I don't know how fans managed to get hold of my number because I've always been ex-directory. I was unsure what I would do but I counted how I was doing financially and knew it was time to cash in all my chips and see where my earnings took me. When I had decided on my plan of action and officially broke the news to the band, I called Joyce and visited Mum to let them know I would be away for a while but would be back in contact when I was settled. Three weeks later, I had made the break.

Randy Newman had once sung about Asia being crowded, Europe old, Africa far too hot and Canada too cold. He was right. The only place I wanted to go was to the USA. I sold the house and all its contents - funnily enough to a fan so I got top whack - and put most of my valuable items into storage until I was ready to have them shipped to my permanent address. The customs stories did not end there because on the way out of the country, going through the first-class departure lounge, I had another bad experience. I was pulling my suitcase behind me and had just gone past a couple of police officers and their dogs when Rover decided he liked the smell of my over-the-shoulder bag and started barking and pawing at it like crazy. He knocked me to the ground and growled over me till the police rushed to see what Rover had found. I opened my bag and took out a sandwich and a flask of coffee, doing my rock & roll credibility no good at all, but what was this? A small plastic container with an amount of white powder... "And what do we have here, Sir? Cocaine, Heroin?" It was powdered milk for the coffee flask, but you try explaining that away innocently with a dog barking like crazy.

I stayed for a while with friends and travelled most of the East Coast of America, sometimes meeting fans of the Highwaymen, but as we were not as famous as back home in England, I had a relatively hassle-free time of it. If I was going to get away from all the chaos and go under the radar, I would need to find another purpose in my life; another direction, another hobby.

The opportunity came along quicker than I thought because I was at radio station WNYC in New York one evening, interviewed by their resident DJ Ted Winkleman about my music career with The Highwaymen. I had shared everything I had to say on the music scene to date when he stood up to shake my hand and passed out on the floor. Having completed my St John's Ambulance badge when I was at school, I checked for his breathing while shouting for help, and when he was in recovery mode with station staff attending to his needs, I mentioned the dead air currently transmitting on WNYC.

"Unless you want to talk more, Charlie?" said the radio operator.

I selected several tracks to play and settled down to talk more about the current music scene, and while I only meant to stay for an hour or two, it was getting close to 10 pm before I was replaced for the graveyard shift. I left my details at the front desk to be informed of Ted's condition and returned to my friend's house.

He had heard the goings-on at the radio station that evening and said that the show was great and that I should consider doing some more radio work as I had a flair for it. I probably shrugged my shoulders and said I had better things to do, but secretly I had immensely enjoyed my time in front of the microphone and couldn't wait to get involved again.

A few days later, I received a call from the station manager to return to the radio station as they were interested in offering me some work. Ted was going to be away for a few months recuperating; he wanted to see how I was with interviewing guests. They started me off with a member of the local commune and said I was going to be in for a treat, judging by what was being written in an underground magazine that my guest was involved in.

Halluciano E. Genic sounded like a Spanish name, and despite getting to know him well over the coming year, he was never entirely comfortable when asked about his background. I assumed that his name was just a play on words and that his real name was David or something, but I called him Hal for short. He looked as though he had smoked one too many joints, and his words came out slow and measured; it was as if his mouth was at constant war with expressing the thoughts in his head. I nicknamed him a *medicated follower of fashion.* He described in a calm voice how narcotics opened his mind to all kinds of experiences and possibilities and how this affected musicians and what they were capable of creating. He also discussed a significant cosmic event that was happening right now. Call it the ramblings of a crazy pothead, but I was fascinated by this man and his demeanour.

The station was getting a lot of calls with the switchboard constantly lit up. People wanted to ask Hal questions about where he got this information from, his philosophy on life, and where they could get a big sack of what he was smoking! I had to jump in and explain that the station did not condone the taking of drugs, whilst fanning away the haze of smoke coming from the other side of the studio. Hal told me of his vision of a world where you could love your fellow man and be at one with nature and get high on music and substances, which I took as the drugs talking, and though it seemed like a beautiful world he was painting, could music really change the world?

Hal had escaped the draft by claiming to be a White Wizard and was classed as unfit for service. He had been trying to convince army recruitment officers that he was not soldier material and had produced a letter from his doctor that said his flat feet were a reasonable excuse to be signed off. It was not until Hal began talking about the spells and potions he could provide for the soldiers that he was classed as unfit for service. After that experience, he became interested in a commune. But didn't talk too much about this in the interview or the fact that he had joined a band of musicians who performed under the moniker Mike & The Magic Mushrooms for a joke. He was beginning to think the joke was worth taking seriously and planned to swap the commune members and the band members from time to time to keep them all on their toes and keep the ideas fresh. His plans to set the music world on fire did not become apparent until I joined the commune, and I promise I'll come to that in a while.

I got the radio job and for the next three months, I spoke to a wide range of people, from famous to not-so-famous. One of my most memorable interviews was with American psychologist and author Timothy Leary, known for his pro stance on psychedelic drugs. Leary coined the phrase '*turn on, tune in, drop out*,' which Hal took to quite literally. Hal insisted that I invite Leary to the studio, and the three of us spent an hour just fielding calls from worried parents that their children would turn into zombies if he had his way. The switchboard was jammed for days afterwards, with callers protesting our use of airtime to give a platform to Mr Leary.

I had to find a place of my own soon because I was getting later and later into the studio. One day my sound engineer had to fill time with a 20-minute album track that I had told him to play should I be late: *Revelation* by Love from their *De Capo* album. So you see, I inadvertently gave Love their big break when the reason for my untimeliness was the fact I was with Hal *potting his plants!* I soon found a house within a reasonable distance of the station.

When people talk about the Summer of Love they are broadly referring to the music, hallucinogenic drugs, anti-war, and free-love scene that encompassed much of the States and the UK. *A Whiter Shade of Pale* and *San Francisco (Be Sure To Wear Flowers In Your Hair)* were amongst the anthems of the times, but for me, the Summer of 1967 will only be remembered for catching Phthirus Pubis, or to put it another way, the dreaded crabs. While everyone else was on the love train, I was at home, regularly applying creams to my delicate areas. At one point, I shaved my head hair off till I was told that would not make the slightest difference. It would be a while before I boarded the love train again!

Then we come to the Billy Shears interview. I wouldn't like to say whose jaw dropped furthest out of the two of us when he walked into the studio one Winter morning in 1967, but I recovered my composure quickly enough to get in a few quick jibes about his previous 45 being a flop in the States and shouldn't his band concentrate more on the British market? That comment stirred something up between us. There was a period of verbal posturing until I poured him a glass of whisky from the station's drinks cabinet and asked him what he thought of the Fab Four's new 45. I was egging him on to say something controversial, and it took three double JDs for his tongue to loosen, but I could not have expected him to blurt out that his group was bigger than the Beatles and go on to trounce the good name of Liverpool's finest (if you exclude Ken Dodd of course).

That statement set the wheels in motion for a week-long series of protests outside the radio station to ban his band's records. I broke his single on-air and suggested that any unwanted albums and singles by Mr Shears could be brought down to WNYC where they would be trashed and then burned en masse. It gave me particular satisfaction to light the bonfire and bought even more publicity for the station. It was a shame that John Lennon had already claimed the Beatles were more significant than God. I would never have claimed the Highwaymen were bigger than God. Bigger than Rod Codpiece, perhaps.

My tenure with WNYC ended abruptly after I joined Hal's commune by accident when I completed one of their initiation ceremonies live on air, and the episode led to my sacking. In retrospect, it was not the wisest of decisions to kill a bat in the studio and drain its blood for inclusion in one of Hal's potions. I had given over fifteen minutes a week for him to come in and talk, and this particular occasion he discussed potions and their ingredients, which is when the bat was produced from a covered cage and mayhem ensued. Blood spurted everywhere as he cut its throat so I got in there about fifteen years before Ozzy Osbourne perfected his bat-biting antics. I stirred up a lot of hate from America's version of the RSPCA and their loony followers.

After the interview, I left the studio and made my way through Central Park. Two men were handing out things to passers-by. I grabbed a coffee from a stall and continued walking to clear my head of the crazy interview I'd just had. As I approached the men, they recognised me and, with a knowing wink, suggested I needed something to sweeten my coffee. They plopped a couple of sugar cubes in my coffee cup, and I continued towards a crowd of people gathering at a spot near a lake. I felt funny, but I could not explain why, though the walk was invigorating me and the hard surface I was walking on seemed to vibrate with my every step. I was going to head back to the studio and lie down, but I had enough sense to realise that I probably wouldn't make it back there now. I was stoned.

I sat down with my back to a tree and looked around. The music playing was the most beautiful and melodic I had ever heard. I felt that thousands of strangers had become my family. The music was coming from a makeshift stage, and I had the urge to go and listen and be a part of what was happening. Mike and his Magic Mushrooms were performing, and I thought they were coming out with the most melodic sounds I had ever heard. Afterwards, I was told it sounded like a cat was being castrated on stage. Women were baring their breasts, and I had the urge to feel the same freedom from my clothes. I stripped down to my Y-fronts and ran onto the stage.

Get Together

The next day WNYC sacked me for my misdemeanours. They took a dim view at my stripping naked on stage, trying to wrestle a microphone away from a startled compere and then doing cartwheels across the stage. The NYC police also took a dim view of my antics, and the press had a field day. Jim Morrison had nothing on me regarding exposure, but in Winter? HA!

I was offered a place to stay by Hal after I checked what I was letting myself in for with his commune. I first took a copy of their very handy guidebook (which was partly hand-written in what I can only assume was the chicken's blood) and began to read: -

What is a commune?

A commune is generally described as a pattern of healthy living, growing your foodstuff, farming, and meditating frequently.

But who was the commune leader? There had to be a leader within a group of people, or you would end up in anarchy! I heard that he never made himself known to the group and that he set the rules passed down through a chain of command until they got to the likes of Hal and then to the very bottom of the chain, which was me, being the newest recruit. Not many people got to meet him, but he was said to be either a wise old man in a white robe and flowing beard or a badly disfigured man who could not face the world. So, it was either Gandalf or the Elephant Man. I could not decide.

I was already familiar with the initiation ceremony (p30) but was unaware that this entitled me to a choice of partner within the commune (p35), as well as a chicken providing as many eggs as I could eat (p7). Hal told me I was invited to the next Mike & The Magic Mushrooms session and my joining of the band was a formality, but I had to go through a customary joining ceremony. He also had an ulterior motive; he wanted to gauge what I thought of some of the material they had been writing and practising for the past few months.

This was the night he revealed his plans to take the music world by storm with his peace and love philosophy and I was going to help him achieve that dream. My initiation requirement was a simple one because it required me to create on the spot a piece of music or lyrics to show my competence. This was relatively simple because I had three songs that I had written and were fully formed in my head for if I returned to the music business.

I decided that friend or no friend, I would be brutally honest with my opinion of the sounds that Mike & his Mushrooms were making. To be frank, it was an utter mess of chanting, banging of bongs & gongs, and a variety of guttural sounds that I don't even want to describe. Hal wanted me to lead the group to success, having heard what I had achieved with the Highwaymen, so I told him my mind wasn't made up and that I would have to think about it. But as the evening progressed and I drank a little more and smoked a little more, it sounded better and better. Could I make them stars? Of course I could! Were they going to be successful? No doubt. Did being rich and famous go against their beliefs? Well of course it did, but screw that, Mike & The Magic Mushrooms were on their way!

I woke up in the dark, and I was not alone. A pretty brunette was asking me if I was okay. This must be one of the partners I was promised I thought to myself, but it wasn't. It was a woman who was bringing me something to eat & drink. Her name was Gail and she told me that I had collapsed in a drunken stupor the previous night, been loaded into the camper van, and was currently in a location not far from Woodstock. I had slept through to the following evening. Gail knew of my time with the Highwaymen and was fascinated as I told her of being in a band and the scrapes we got into. Over the next few days, we spent a lot of time together and got to know each other.

I liked Gail, but she was a little forgetful. She told me that she was only with the commune because she was a fan of mine and had heard Hal and me talking of the commune on the radio the other day. She had also gone through the initiation ceremony, but they had not used chicken blood on that occasion. Tomato puree was the substitute ingredient.

I was welcomed into the commune and began to accept their ways of living. We were sometimes hassled by the local community, who thought of us as strange. I concluded that this was a community with a more liberal stance than your regular communes, and though drinking and substance abuse was frowned upon, it was tolerated to some degree which was fine by me.

I spent the first few weeks in the commune observing others and how they behaved. There must have been about thirty or so of us, ranging from young children to middle-aged men and women. It was like an episode of the Seventies BBC TV show *The Good Life*, with everyone growing crops and sharing what extra they had with their neighbours or selling any surplus to the broader community. I tagged along with Hal, working out in the fields with the crops. He was quite a green-fingered fellow and would have put Alan Titchmarsh to shame. Previously, my only gardening experience had been watering the plants for Mum or growing tomatoes in the garden.

Hal gave me lots of gardening tips. Very soon, I was helping to cultivate an acre of land roughly the size of a football pitch with lettuce, peas, radishes, turnips, runner beans, potatoes, onions, tomatoes and spinach. At the very end of our land was a huge greenhouse where we were trying to grow the more exotic items and Hal's pride and joy were enclosed within, hidden right amongst the densest of undergrowth where he had his pot plants nurturing away. He kept the greenhouse locked at all times and was even more protective of it than the beer he was brewing elsewhere on the property.

The commune had been running for about a year before I arrived. They were into their second spring and had learned what should be planted and when. Me? I had absolutely no idea about gardening, so I left decisions to the more experienced in the commune. I understand how things grow, but my only interest in food is when it arrives cooked on the table. The same went for farming. I love meat but could not bear to watch the slaughter of an animal and have been known to pass out at the sight of blood (but not the blood of chickens, as discussed earlier).

My talent lies in music, where I was of greatest use within the community. I identified those who had some musical ability and those who were tone-deaf. We bartered for instruments in town and returned with tambourines, bells, whistles, a guitar and bongos, and even a piano that was badly out of tune and had seen better days. Those who could not sing were playing free-form tambourine, and a couple of other girls were assigned singing duties. I was on acoustic guitar, trying to make sense of what we were playing. We were improvising with sound collages ahead of what Frank Zappa was playing with The Mothers of Invention.

Two or three evenings a week after we had our evening meal, we had band practice out under the stars, though I preferred to think of practice as just entertaining the commune because I could see that it was going to take something or someone extraordinary to make this bunch stand out from the crowd. Hal was too stoned in the evening to care, so it was up to me to call the shots musically. I could see that we were not going to shake up the music world, which was a relief in a way after coming out of the wild ride I had been on with the Highwaymen. I wondered how they were getting on without me and if Reggie and the boys had forgiven me for the way I upped and left a year ago.

We were still short of money, and whilst we were never going to starve, we were short of tools and heavy machinery. We had built a shed for a carpenter to make items to sell at the local market. The only problem was we did not have enough money for tools. I suggested that if the commune were okay with it, I would be willing to do some session work in New York for a week or two to earn enough money for the items needed. This was readily agreed, and for a few weeks, I was off gardening duties and recording on some of the biggest records that year, but under an assumed name so that PMSL Records would not know.

And then Apple joined the commune.

I'd Like To Teach The World To Sing

Apple Blossom is the Cher to my Sonny, Courtney Love to my Kurt Cobain, and Yoko to my John. She joined the commune in 1968 and we were immediately attracted to each other. She was a twenty-one-year-old from California and had travelled the world as her father's job took her family from continent to continent, soaking up new cultures and new experiences like a sponge. Apple was an avid journal writer, took a keen interest in the arts, loved astrology and studied history. Joining the commune was another experience for her to absorb. I have never met another woman like her since and never will. We became very close friends, much to the annoyance of Superfan Gail, who wanted exclusive friendship rights to my time.

Another of Apple's talents was that she could sing like an angel. This was obvious when she joined band practice and blew everyone away with her pure voice. She was a natural beauty with sparkling blue eyes and short blonde hair. She mostly wore skirts or long dresses and exuded an aura of confidence and a complete lack of self-consciousness. She was constantly dyeing her clothes, adding pins, studs, beading, patches, and embroidery or whatever it took to improve her outfits, be it a scarf or some cheap jewellery she bartered for within the community. She was Stevie Nicks nearly ten years before Stevie discovered she could twirl a shawl around to good effect, and she was a hippy chick in every sense of the term. She truly believed she could change the world into one that valued love over materialism through psychedelics and music. Music practice became a pleasurable experience for a change, and the caterwauling days of The Mushrooms were over.

Hal was happy too. He teamed up with Gail, who always tried to make a big thing about how lovey-dovey they were whenever I was around. It was as if she was trying to make me jealous but not realising I didn't care too much either way. Hal was also pleased that his dream of fame and fortune was starting to look like a reality, with Apple front and centre. He had seen what the likes of Jefferson Airplane were doing with Grace Slick as a crucial part of their band and thought Apple could have that same charismatic presence. I decided that singing traditional songs around the campfire was one thing, but we ought to be creating our own and seeing how they sounded. I began writing again and used the songs I had used to audition for the band and my new experiences as a foundation.

Cause you were mine for the Summer
Now we know it's nearly over
Feels like Summer sunshine
But I always will remember
You were my Summer love
You always will be my Summer love

Apple came up with the melody, and we thought we had a winning song. Everyone learned their part and had it down in a few days. Through me providing the lyrics and Apple supplying the tunes, we had about eight excellent tunes in the bag and were eager to get them out to a broader audience. This happened sooner than we expected when a roving camera crew was in Central Park looking for a good story. The Mushrooms were brave enough to show their face after my rather embarrassing performance. This time I kept my clothes on and avoided the free sugar cubes to get an enthusiastic round of applause from the crowd. It went so well that from there, we were invited onto a regional TV show to perform our songs and to dance and amuse people. I had already thought about the possibility that this may happen, so I donned a costume to avoid being recognised by Reggie Cramwell. I wasn't sure that the aggrieved Highwaymen would be ready to forgive my desertion, though it was doubtful they would have been watching in New York at that precise time.

I dressed up in a mushroom costume, and it has been said that this appearance of mine influenced the Banana Splits' outfits in 1968 and was a few years ahead of Peter Gabriel's antics in the Seventies. It also scared many children who happened to be watching at the time. It was not the last time I was parading around in a silly outfit. The costume got so hot and heavy during performances over the coming months that I took to slipping into it naked and modified it to allow me a full range of movement on stage. However, I did become a cropper one night in Orono, Maine, when I accidentally trod on my leading leg and once again revealed my bottom half to a shocked audience, I got away with it because it could not be proved who was in the costume at the time and there was hardly going to be an identity parade of penises was there? The most that could be done was to ban us from Maine because we quickly packed and were out of town before anyone could object. However, I felt uneasy about returning to the music world so soon.

I had envisaged a year or so break from the hectic scheduling and touring, and though this was never going to be quite as intensive with the Mushrooms, I felt that Hal's need for stardom was pushing me too quickly into a position I did not want to be in. But with Apple around, it always seemed more bearable. She was already teaching me how to relax and meditate, which I have kept practising to this day.

That was the year I tried and failed with vegetarianism. Apple said it would help my health if I cut back on things such as meat, fish and eggs, sugar-based items and alcohol because she was concerned that when I went back to the outside world, my boozy lifestyle would be the death of me. She suggested that I try it for a couple of months to see how I fared, though I insisted that if I did try, I would at least be allowed milk products because there was no way I would give up my morning tea and my cheese sandwiches. I gave it a good go, and for the first two weeks, I was as good as my word and stuck to the regime. Little by little it became a chore to stick to such a regimented and boring lifestyle of eating what was a fruit and cheese diet with some 'rabbit food' as I called it of lettuce, carrots and such. The downside was that it affected my digestive system and gave me bad wind.

I didn't know how long I would be able to keep it up and one afternoon I snapped and went straight to the nearest Mcdonald's and ordered the greasiest, fattest item that I could find and devoured it plus another one for good measure. I was cross with myself but felt so much better. I decided it would be better not to mention it to Apple because she had been so proud of my initial success, and I wouldn't repeat the episode, or quite as often. She was so happy with my perceived results that she was hell-bent on converting the rest of the commune to my new lifestyle. The men were horrified and said I had to do something, or we would all become malnourished skeletal beings before the end of the month. I don't know how Apple found out I was visiting Mcdonald's every other week for a big blowout of burgers, but I feel one of the men must have squealed on me.

I spent most of 1968 within the commune and as part of The Mushrooms, apart from the occasional foray into session work that didn't feel too much like hard work. Still, I needed a proper break from it all. One day I just upped and left with Apple to travel to Miami in May, hitchhiking all the way, and attended what has become known as the Miami Pop Festival. However, it had the slightly less exciting name of the '1968 Pop and Underground Festival' at the time. There we met Michael Lang, who had partly organised the festival. There were about 25,000 in attendance. He was a NY resident who was a friend of a friend, and I met him occasionally when he was in New York. He hoped I could perform in Miami, but with my contractual problems with the Highwaymen, it was a no. However, I told him that he had a talent for organisation and that he ought to do something closer to home. He should rent out a field somewhere and invite the most prominent bands to attend, and I would try and find a way of playing with my band. A site near Woodstock perhaps?

Back in New York, I went to see a new musical that everyone was raving about called *Hair*. It had opened on Broadway to a storm of controversy due to its profanity, advocation of the use of illegal drugs, sexual overtones and nude scenes. It was hilarious! That's where I met Marvin Lee Aday, aka Meatloaf. I told him of my escapades, performing naked on stage, and he persuaded me to audition for a small part in the show, and when I write a small part, I'm not referring to the nude scene you understand. Marvin's involvement in the show made the difference, and I was offered a role singing with the cast, but it only lasted a week because word got around about an ex-British pop star in the show, even though I was still trying to keep my identity a secret.

When I returned to the commune, they were all very unhappy with me for going away unannounced. Gail, in particular, was highly agitated that not only had I gone, but with Apple and not invited her along too. Hal was also aggrieved that he had been left to handle band practice.

Woodstock, And All That

Everyone knows about Woodstock. Peace, love and music and all that, right? For me, it was being stuck on the road to the festival and then in a field with a bunch of religious freaks and planning an escape. The community I joined had turned sour for me, and I needed to get away from everything again. The initiation ceremony I was made to participate in had long since stopped being the familiar passage into the community. Anyone could join now, and there was no vetting of new members. The commune had become all that I was trying to escape from in the first place. Harmonious living was a thing of the past, and there were now disagreements at every turn ranging from who was supposed to be cooking to what we were to do with any surplus money. They were less interested in helping than sitting around smoking and having a good time and were little more than hangers-on who wanted the benefits of the community without the effort. I retreated from group gatherings rather than have to listen to the bickering and cursing that was going on.

I heard that Michael had made good on my suggestion of a concert on the East Coast and had turned it into a massive weekend of music and arts taking place near the city. I wanted to be a part of it and envisaged playing music to a large audience though I could not have imagined there would be 400,000 or so other people who shared my enthusiasm! I wanted to be in a band again and missed playing to audiences night after night, missed the travelling, and most of all, wanted my music to be taken seriously, not just three-minute pop songs as I had sung in the past. The music world had changed since I had been away, and the Beatles and their peers had moved on from *Yeah, Yeah, Yeah* to *Strawberry Fields Forever*.

At this point, I was introduced to Cynthia Plaster Caster, and if you've never heard of her before, she was an American visual artist and self-described 'recovering groupie' who gained fame and notoriety for creating plaster casts of male musicians and their erect penises. This was the Sixties, and anything goes, right? I had heard of her work and found it to be amusing in a smutty sort of way. I was put in touch with her through Jimi Hendrix (the first rock star she moulded) and met her in 1969 for a casting.

At this point I have to say with no feeling of embarrassment that my appendage was nicknamed *Charlie's Cracker* after one particularly satisfied conquest. When I asked her why she said it was because all the girls would want to pull it and it always ends with a bang. Since then I've always been nicknamed *Cracker*.

Cynthia explained that after I was prepared for the casting, she would plunge my erect quivering member into a bucket full of slimy white goo called alginate, then yank it out the moment it got soft (instantly, it was cold!) and then pour a mixture of plaster into the gaping hole, and leave it there until it got hard.

I put myself in her capable hands! I don't know who has ownership of my plaster cast after Cynthia died in 2022, but I would like to think that in many years to come, someone is looking at my member in a museum for dead rock stars and their artefacts and being mightily impressed. I asked if there had been any disappointing participants, and she said some were embarrassed or intimidated size-wise.

"Have you ever met Billy Shears?" I asked.

When the commune heard of the plans for Woodstock, they were just as excited. They thought the Mushrooms would be able to play on the opening night, but I knew we weren't good enough, and I told them so. However, I was determined to be there in one form or another, even though nobody would know who I was (unless there were any Brits in the audience) and a seed was sown to either find a way of making sure I was on the guest list or to buy myself a ticket and disappear for a few days. Things got out of hand when the Mushroom members decided that they would get a camper van and make their way there the day before the event and that I was to go with them. I protested that I wasn't keen on wearing the mushroom costume again in the height of Summer but was talked around to their way of thinking. We were going to make the short trip to Woodstock!

Getting to Woodstock should have been a straightforward journey from New York City. Just head north in the same direction as the Hudson River for 100 miles on Highway 87. Easy peasy, or so it would seem. Camper vans usually carry four people, but with some modification, a three-person rear bench seat could be fitted out to take six. We considered going in two vans, but in the end, ten of us (the ten who were going to perform, or so we thought) squeezed into our own beat up camper van and headed north.

We thought it would be a simple case of arriving on-site, pitching a couple of tents under the stars, and preparing ourselves for an attempt to get on the stage that evening. It was late afternoon on Thursday 14th August 1969, and little did we know it, but already a crowd of 80,000 were on site, and the numbers were growing. We thought we had allowed for everything: food, alcohol, drugs and such, but there was one item we needed more than everything else. Petrol. I knew we shouldn't have left it down to Hal to ensure we had a tank of gas to get us to Bethel, NY where the festival was taking place. He protested that he *had* filled up just before we left, but on the way there, we had been leaking gas, and this had slicked up the freeway and made for treacherous conditions for those following. Whilst the sheer number of vehicles all heading to Woodstock led to a massive traffic jam, Hal's gas spillage did not help those trailing in our wake. At least till that point, it had not rained. That would come later on Friday evening.

We spluttered to a halt 10 miles from Woodstock around midday, and already the traffic was growing and we considered our options, of which there was only one. Like everyone else we were stuck where we were, so to kill some time and while waiting for the traffic to move, I got out my acoustic guitar and was idly playing a couple of tunes when a voice from the van started singing along with me. It was Apple. We had written this protest song the week before, and here we were, the two of us singing it to a captive audience. Well, they couldn't run away, so the passengers in the other vehicles started singing along:

I'm going down to Woodstock, gonna play a little song,
about dodging the draft,
I'll sing it all night long.

The following day, Friday, we woke and there was no movement ahead of traffic. A decision had to be made as to what we would do. Were we going to entertain the crowds there for the next few days, or should we attempt to walk all the way? Many people were already doing that and abandoning their cars, so we all had a discussion and the men and Apple wanted to walk, whilst the other women in the group decided they would stay put. The men split up and made their own way, whilst Apple and I struck out together and hit upon a plan of her attempting to hitch a ride on a motorbike and then when she had flagged a ride, I would appear. She would persuade the rider to let us ride pillion part of the way. This plan worked to a degree and it was slow and uncomfortable progress, but we did manage to slowly weave our way between the vehicles and get a little nearer the site. When we arrived, we saw that it was possible to walk through what flimsy attempt there was of security because it had been declared a free concert by then.

Finding shelter for the night was easier than we thought because many spectators welcomed strangers and were more than happy to share what they had. We fell in with a group of what we now call Jesus Freaks who were willing to share what they had as long as you listened to their ramblings for a while. There were four of them, three young males and a female. I had no problem with this though Apple had doubts about their motives, and were we not going to be trying to get on stage that night? Looking at the enormity of the crowd, I reasoned that this would not be possible, so best to hunker down for the night and see what we could do tomorrow.

Their food wasn't great, though. It tasted like a right mouthful of depression. I didn't get to the top of the food chain to eat rabbit food. My body craved meat, but instead, the female handed me a green paste, potato-based food in a bowl from a cooking pot. 'There's more food left' she kept saying. 'Who wants the last lot?' To be honest I didn't want the first lot but I didn't want to appear rude. They were strange bedfellows, getting out of the tent every other hour, going into a weird chanting thing, and then coming back to the tent. Apple thought that they were having a rain dance or something like that. How funny was that after what happened over the next few days?

One of the men tried what is now known as self-other merging, that is, staring into each other's eyes. I wasn't too comfortable doing this for long but was told it was good for telepathic communication and bonding. I knew this to be a load of cock & bull because if he had been aware of what I was thinking, he wouldn't have been so happy to have known!

I went to sleep with a banging headache, and when I woke in the morning, I felt wretched, but I dragged myself out of my makeshift bed and looked out of the tent. Same as last night, with folks as far as the eye can see, though I couldn't see Apple anywhere. She must have gone to look at some of the needlework & craft stalls that had popped up. I can't see the fascination with it myself. It's like accepting that you are a spinster and have nothing better to do with all your spare time.

I was mooching around to see what other people were doing when one of the men appeared by my side. He encouraged me to come back with him for a light breakfast consisting of more dreary food, nuts, berries, turgid green paste, and a funny-tasting raspberry drink. My headache continued throughout the morning, and still, with no sign of Apple I was reluctant to move off. My plans for a stage performance were put on hold as I battled with how I felt. If only I could clear my head, I would move off and try to find Apple. I was growing tired of listening to the incoherent ramblings of my hosts and was connecting my headaches and nausea to what I was being given to eat. I had to get away, but I could tell I was being watched. What did they want from me? Did they know who I was, or was I someone they thought could be manipulated to their will?

At the same time all this was happening, Apple had escaped and made her way to the information desk where she was able to get a message read out by announcer Edward 'Chip' Monckto for me to come to the information booth and meet her there. He had been warning the audience to beware of brown acid doing the rounds, but he should also have been warning of the disgusting green potato paste I had been eating for a day. Even the thought of it still makes me want to hurl. Apple had hooked up with Advent, an up-and-coming British band who were out of place playing Prog music to a psychedelic crowd. Their performance at Woodstock has gone unrecognized like so many others who played but never got mentioned because of the great acts that went on after them.

I heard my name mentioned over the tannoy and knew I had to get away from my captors. It was into this situation that Gail stumbled. My super-obsessed fan had decided to walk to Woodstock after all, rather than let Apple and I go on alone. She barged her way over to the group as we sat around whilst another of the bores droned on about the coming of the Super one with hopefully better culinary talents and a cookbook. This wasn't quite how they had expected it to be as Gail unintentionally created a diversionary scene, and I was able to gather what strength I had and exit stage left, treading and falling over someone's sleeping tent and knocking cooked food, beer, and other sundries over. I was well rid of that scene, and I hoped Gail wouldn't hang around too long either.

It took a long time to make my way to the information booth because of the sheer number of people and also because I was so disorientated and needed to stop often and think about what direction I was heading in and try to walk off the sleepiness, but it was in the direction of the stage and over to the left. It was now afternoon, and I had not come good on my intentions of playing at Woodstock. I had lost contact with the Mushrooms, but at least I knew where Apple was.

I was soaked to the skin when I made it to the information booth and relieved to find Apple there waiting for me. Being the talented and resourceful lady she was, she had managed to get friendly with the stagehands and could get me backstage. There she introduced me to Advent, who I took to immediately, not just because they were English and all from

London. I didn't have much time to chat or get to know their names because they were due on stage in ten minutes, and then they surprised me: would I like to join them on stage? I quickly explained that due to contractual obligations, I was not allowed to do this, and they explained that it wouldn't be a problem because my contract was probably a recording one and not a performing one, and wouldn't it be great to take a chance and be on stage in front of the largest crowd ever assembled at a music concert? They were down in numbers because their multi-talented singer had not been able to get into the States on a passport technicality. If I could improvise around the quiet sections, that would cover his absence.

We hit the stage early on Monday morning, squeezed between Creedence Clearwater Revival and The Who. You won't find any mention of our performance at Woodstock because, just like Ten Years After, the recording equipment failed. Advent could have been one of the well-remembered acts of the event if the loss of power had not rendered their performance unrecordable, and with only an audio recording of us being there, it is easy to forget our performance ever happened.

Reggie Cramwell sat at his desk and sipped his coffee. His secretary rang through with an international call from the States. He hardly spoke as the caller passed on a message. He thanked the caller and put the receiver down and smiled. So, Charlie's in the States, he thought to himself. How interesting. How very interesting.

The Boys In The Band

In my opinion, the birth of Rock Music came in 1967, when British A-list bands such as The Stones, Beatles, Who, and The Kinks were abandoning the singles format and reaching out to a broader audience. They wanted their music to be taken seriously, appeal to a more adult audience, grow up with their fans, and gain a harder edge. At the same time in the States, the Psychedelic scene was flourishing and the counterculture was emerging.

I'm not here to give a music history lesson, but that's just the way music was in the late Sixties. Progressive Rock was becoming known for pushing the boundaries of rock beyond the traditional instrumentation of guitar, bass, and drums. Whether they used a flute, a mellotron (an early synthesizer based on tape reels), a Moog (an early electronic keyboard), wind instruments or actual orchestral instruments, many progressive bands were seeking a broader palette to play with, plus the musicians wanted to show off their musical chops. A curious aspect about Prog was that in its early days, it was played by white middle-class, educated types with names such as Peter, Phil, Tony, Mike and Steve, and that's just Genesis for starters.

This was the world I had barged my way into by accident. After appearing at Woodstock, there was no way back and I needed to engineer a way into the music scene. If this meant going to Reggie Cramwell and apologising for the error of my ways then so be it. Maybe he would let me back into the fold and allow me to see out my contract as a solo artist. But fate, as ever, was already lending me a hand.

Two weeks after Woodstock, I received a telegram at the commune asking me to collect a couple of tickets at JFK Airport and head back to London for a meeting with PMSL executives. Word must have got around about my Woodstock performance (which I have to say was excellent). Even Ravi Shankar applauded me as I came off stage after using the sitar in one of Advent's tunes. All that practice we had together paid off handsomely, and I am surprised that of all instruments, the sitar has never made its way into the Prog virtuoso's bag of tricks. At the end of our performance, the band said thanks, and I asked them if they could keep it quiet that I was ever there. It seems they were unable to fulfil that promise. I assumed that the other ticket was for Apple to accompany me back to the UK, which she was more than happy to do as she hadn't been to London since her teens.

I explained to the commune that I was heading back to London. They were still peeved that of all of us who travelled to Woodstock, I was the only one who made good and got to perform that night. Hal in particular, was put out by this and thought he ought to be the one accompanying me. My apologies Hal if you are reading this. I don't think London was ready for Mike and the Magic Mushrooms, not then and not ever!

We had an enjoyable first-class flight back to Heathrow Airport, as it had been recently named. A limo picked us up at the entrance and we were whisked into Central London to Mayfair. Quite obviously, PMSL Records had made enough money to move offices away from Camden to somewhere classy. It occurred to me that whatever was on the agenda for the meeting, they were keen to talk to us or else they would not have been making so much effort in making the journey as pleasurable as possible.

I had made full use of the free alcohol in flight, and by the time we were whisked up to the 30th floor, I was high as a kite. At this point, Apple was asked to wait in an adjoining room as I was ushered into an oak-panelled office for the meeting. The room contained a long table with ten people seated on each side, and at the very end was Reggie Cramwell. Dear Reggie. Since I had last seen him, he had put on weight and now must have weighed in at almost the size of a sumo wrestler. He was quite obviously enjoying the wealth that I had earned for him. He had also worked his way up the company ladder and was now Chairman of PMSL, though I would not have put it past him to have greased a few palms and scratched a few backs on his way up.

The rest of the seats were taken up by executives and assorted bods of PMSL, mostly puffing on cigars. Around the outer edge of the room were members of Advent. This I had not expected. I recognised Dave, Greg, Brian and Keith but one seat was vacant. I sat at the end of the long table opposite Reggie, and the meeting began. We exchanged pleasantries, and there was no outward sign of any bad feeling towards me, which I found surprising. I had expected Reggie to go for the jugular, metaphorically speaking, and threaten me with all kinds of bodily harm & accusations, but all he did was smile (was that a knowing smile?) and motion for the Chief Executive to begin speaking. At first, he was talking about company financial details and it hadn't been too bad a year by the sound of things. Singles and LP sales were up and the label had three or four bands on their roster that were selling exceptionally well. I think this was to impress on me that they didn't necessarily need me, but I let him continue regardless. The conversation then moved on to those in the room.

Advent were introduced as a band of seasoned professionals just signed by the label, playing a kind of music that was becoming increasingly popular with a more discerning audience. Each band member was an expert on their chosen instrument, having been in bands before and now teaming up to form one of the earliest versions of a Supergroup. They were a late addition to the Woodstock bill and were quite the wild card, not having recorded up to that point. They were added after being recommended by Jimi Hendrix.

Greg Jones - Guitar God.
Brian Blessing – Bass.
Dave Sermon – Drums.
Keith Howells – Keyboards.
Frankie D'Lane - piano/Keyboards/Flute/Vocals.

It was Frankie whom I had yet to meet because he was unable to attend Woodstock. I thought Advent was purely an instrumental group, but it made sense to have a vocalist, and a flute was a good touch too. Something different for the audience to get into. Frankie was running late, which was something he was prone to do.

We continued the meeting, and the conversation turned to Woodstock. I was thanked for my help in the performance, though it was pointed out that this put me in breach of contract. Of course, there was one way to get around this problem, and Reggie put it to me thus: Advent and the label had discussed the matter, and if I were to join the band and sign a new contract keeping me tied to the label for another four years then PMSL was prepared to let the matter drop. This caught me by surprise because I had not even realised Advent were looking to expand its numbers. I wondered if Reggie would sound me out about returning to the Highwaymen. They were doing alright, so they probably were better off without me.

Reggie continued, explaining I would be expected to provide rhythm guitar and backup vocals for Frankie. I was more used to being lead guitarist on stage, so I had to think long and hard about whether I was prepared to be second string to anyone.

I wasn't keen on working again with Reggie, but he was not as hands-on with the artists as he once was. His role had been taken on by Roy B'Stard, who I knew from touring the States in 1965. He now managed Advent and had decided that if he could look after bands with threats of violence, he could look after their contractual needs with threats against suits trying to screw them over. He could be as sweet as pie one moment and then living up to his name the next. He perfected the art of hanging a hapless promoter out of a window 20 floors up by his feet to punish the victim for shafting his band out of their takings. A man to keep on your side in a fight!

B'Stard had been recommended to Advent by word of mouth, and they were delighted that he had signed them to a very good contract and probably knocked a few heads together just for the fun of it. Reggie was only unhappy with the arrangement because he knew B'Stard's capabilities and was decidedly nervous about contractual negotiations with the man.

I asked to speak with the band before I decided anything, and all assembled agreed to resume the meeting in two hours. The band, Apple and I all trouped out of the building and decided on a liquid lunch. Within some bands, the drug of choice is cocaine, but in Advent, it was alcohol. I could tell we would get on well together as I ordered the first round of beer but stuck to something a little less demanding because I was still a little hungover from drinking on the flight.

We demolished a tray of nibbles which were put on company expenses, and I asked about the band name and where it came from and asked did it have a Christmas theme? Keith said they picked a book at random and then a word from the book randomly. It just so happened that the book they picked was The Bible, and Advent was the random word. Right before that, they had picked out the word 'crucifixion', which was turned down as probably offensive (to date there have been seven bands by that name), and then Genesis was refused. I wonder what would have happened had they picked that name? So finally, they chose Advent as it was the least offensive choice they could find.

Greg their guitarist hailed from Wales and was the comedian of the group. On that first afternoon he had me in stitches as he recounted tales of life on the road with his former group the Lardbirds. Their drummer Paul Thrasher was even more destructive than Keith Moon, and one day he decided he did not like the decor of his hotel room in Glasgow and set about throwing it all out of the top floor of the hotel. First though, he arranged for six taxis to block roads leading to the square because, being the thoughtful man he was, he didn't want to hit any passing vehicles or pedestrians. Task completed: He phoned the local council to come and clear the streets of broken bits and pieces of furniture before realising that he had nothing to sleep on that night, so he swapped rooms with a crew member.

Paul also liked to eat Smarties before a show but disliked the red ones. A naughty person had once dropped some uppers in amongst his Smarties before a show, resulting in Paul embarking on a thirty-minute drum solo that only ended when he was carried off the stage, still thrashing about with his drumsticks. After that, he made it a condition that all red Smarties must be removed from the tubes before being given to him, but even that didn't solve the problem because the green ones were being tampered with.

Now Paul only likes to eat wine gums before a show.

Greg had us in fits of laughter when he told us about meeting a young lad called Phil Collins (or Spill Collins as he liked to call him) at the Marquee Club on Wardour Street when Phil was hanging out watching a new band called Yes. Apparently, Phil couldn't hold his pint, or to put it another way, he was always dropping the pints on the floor when it was his turn to go and get a round. "He wouldn't be any good on a night out with Advent because he would constantly be out with a mop and bucket!" roared Greg.

Brian & Dave told me they had been in various bands and then decided to form a duo when the Beach Boys became popular. They were riding on a crest of a wave in the early Sixties with surfing music, and one hot Summer's Day, their management team decided it would make for a great photo opportunity if they hired the local lido and arranged for some scantily clad ladies to come along and pose with their surfboards. All this was fine, but after a couple of drinks to loosen everyone up, the ladies decided to jump in the pool and everyone else joined in, including Brian, who couldn't swim. He didn't realise everyone was at the deep end. He nearly drowned, but from that unfortunate incident he came up with their No 30 smash hit, *Splashing Around The Pool.*

After that watery episode, they had a short spell as The Rocking Vicars. They had the surnames to pull off something like that, and for their first gig, they dressed up in full cassock attire but, in an almost unbelievable fluke, arrived at the wrong venue and instead of being at a church hall to play to a private function, they had set up their instruments next door. Dave said he knew something was wrong because he had never seen such a miserable-looking audience. They were expecting a couple of acoustic guitars to play some soothing music. Dave said he should have been alerted to their location error by the choice of songs they had been asked to play ("anyone would think this was a funeral!"). It was when Brian asked, "is everyone here having a good time?" to try and gee up the audience, and the looks of displeasure and grief that greeted this remark that decided it. They packed up quickly and left.

Keith was the electronics/keyboard genius. He hailed from Cambridge and drank in all the bars around town. He met entrepreneur and inventor Clive Sinclair and they quickly became friends - Keith taught Clive all he knew about designing homemade instruments and demonstrated this with a prototype that took in keyboard, flute and guitar elements. Sinclair turned down an option of financially backing Keith's work, and the project fell through when Clive discovered that the keyboard that Keith was describing was not computer related. Clive then had an idea to produce a build-your-own mellotron kit which you could make over 20 weeks of instalments, but that project never became popular as he hadn't thought through shipping & postage costs. Keith used this setback to design a foot pedal that he used throughout time with Advent to fire off a special effect from his keyboard.

It's a little-known fact that Keith had a side musical project with Clive while Advent was in their infancy. They formed an electronic duo called ZX71 with Clive the deadpan and silent type in the background on keyboards, inspiring the likes of Ron Mael from Sparks and a host of Eighties British electronic bands such as Pet Shop Boys, Yazoo, Depeche Mode, Soft Cell and OMD in the process. Demo recordings of their time together were published after Sinclair's death in 2021.

Nobody knew much about Frankie, but he always said his brother was a proper arsehole. He was a bit of a loner, but he had a fabulous stage presence and would have been better suited to be a drummer, what with all that pent-up frustration when he couldn't put his musical ideas across. And like all top-notch Prog bands worth their salt, he was their flautist. That's my definition of what Prog is. Of course, a mellotron is also high up on that list as well.

After that, we had a quick stop at the Greasy Cafe, down a dingy backstreet and after two and a half hours, we had all decided that I was going to be in the band come hell or high water. We made our way back to the meeting and there was a look of displeasure on Reggie's face as we walked in, a little too merry for his liking. I don't think he'd forgiven me for the vodka and school fire incident ten or so years before. He asked what we had decided, and Greg piped up "yes Reg, you're a tosser!" which made the room burst into stifled laughter but incensed Reggie.

Once things had sufficiently calmed down, he asked if I was prepared to sign a contract to commit myself to Argent for the next four years. He said there was to be no repeat of the fiasco bought on by my leaving The Highwaymen, and that if I were to leave Advent out of contract, there would be consequences. Then I played my trump card. I informed him that I had put the matter in the hands of my lawyers and that the contract that I had signed with him and The Highwaymen was null and void because when they had looked at the documentation and the small print, he had not signed one of the photocopied pieces of paper in the contract, and so I was a free agent. Reggie didn't believe me, so I called my lawyer from the office, and in full earshot of everyone, my lawyer made mincemeat of Reggie's claim of a broken contract. Reggie was furious, but what could he do? Despite all this, I was ready to sign but asked where the last member of the band was.

Reggie motioned towards the door and loudly called for Frankie D'Lane to come in. It was my brother.

He Ain't Heavy, He's My Stepbrother

Frankie D'Lane, aka Frankie Dylan, was the only child of Meg D'Lane and my father, Raymond. They were together for two years as a family before Dad met Mum. When Meg died during WW2, Dad found he couldn't cope with a child, so Frankie stayed with family and friends who would look after him for a month at a time. Mum felt so sorry for Frankie's plight and insisted he stay with her to be looked after, and it was not long after he arrived in the household as a three-year-old that Raymond met his unfortunate end. So, Mum had a small child from her lover's previous relationship and one of her own on the way. She did not have the heart to put Frankie up for adoption and decided to bring the two of us up together. It was never going to be easy.

It was quite some time before Mum told me the true story of Frankie's past. All I needed to know was that he was my big brother, and we got up to all kinds of scrapes together. He was blond, blue-eyed and more athletic than me, never seeming to have to put in too much effort at anything and had a natural flair for whatever he put his mind to. As he grew up a confident man, he attracted ladies from miles around and what amused him most was seeing me as the opposite of him. I had to put in a lot of effort to get where I am today, and I became jealous of his talent and resentful of my clumsy efforts to emulate or even keep up with his achievements.

What used to gall me the most was his musical prowess. Frankie was self-taught and could memorise a tune by hearing it once and repeating it back faultlessly. Mum let him listen to her classical records, and in turn, he became interested in the wind instruments such as the flute, which was a relief for me because two guitarists in the house would not work. When I got my harmonica, he also wanted one of his own. I eventually gave up on this because he was good at playing that too.

Mum took Frankie to classical performances, which would also make me jealous because this made him closer to Mum in interests than I was. We were in the same school but not the same year, and he would hang out with the more boisterous boys who were there to fool around. Frankie could misbehave but knew how to knuckle down and study when needed. He achieved excellent qualifications, and Mum had high hopes that he would take up a job in the city with all the fine recommendations he achieved, but he threw it all away (according to Mum) by choosing a career in music. One night in 1960, he announced he was moving in with friends, and they would form a band and be bigger than The Shadows. Once she had stopped laughing and he had stormed out of the house in a huff, she broke down in tears. I hated Frankie for the way he had upped and left Mum without so much as a goodbye, and the only way he kept in contact was to send the occasional newspaper cutting to show Mum what he was doing and how well his music career was progressing.

The letters became fewer and fewer and we were just wondering what had happened to Frankie when Mum came across a sighting of him on television. It must have been a recorded concert on the BBC at the end of 1965 and there he was, playing the flute for the London Symphony Orchestra in some televised world tour from New York. Mum was so proud of him yet so angry that Frankie had not told her of his current success and travels. She thought he would have wanted to let her know of his joining such a well-renowned orchestra and was also deeply hurt. So, what made Frankie give up his position in the LSO? He had become bored of doing something he knew he could do for the rest of his life. Playing in an orchestra wasn't enough of a challenge, and he had kept his eye on the music scene. Unknown to me he had been following my career with the Highwaymen and felt that the time was right to get back in touch with the family. When he was approached by Reggie about the possibility of joining Advent, he was sure this was the right way to get back in my good books, and for Reggie, it was an excellent way to rile me when I got to hear he had hired my brother.

This was the first time I had met Frankie in 10 years, and I was consumed with many emotions, mostly anger. I amazed everyone present by vaulting over the table and grabbing Frankie by the throat with both hands, throttling him before anyone reacted. It was the first and only time I had completely lost it, and immediately I felt regret but only because I should have kicked him in the bollocks in the ensuing melee. No way, no bloody way was I going to ever join a band with *him*.

I stormed out of the office as best I could after consuming copious pints of beer, closely followed by the band and Frankie. I headed straight to the bar for more liquid refreshment, got myself a drink and sat down to think. Frankie must have known that I would be offered a slot in the band and had a jolly good laugh at my expense. And Reggie - this must be his revenge for how I left the Highwaymen. But was I just as bad for walking out on them when they needed me?

I got myself another drink and considered my options. Reggie must have wanted me back in the fold; he would not have flown me from New York to play a joke on me. On the other hand, was he trying to play me off against my brother and what would be the point of that? You would have thought he would want to keep tensions within the band to a minimum. My beer was doing the trick of relaxing me as I observed the two-pint rule. Anybody who drinks regularly will understand the subtle effects of alcohol on the mood and it goes something like this:

Pint 1: The first pint's function is to take the edge off any problems or concerns you currently have. The drink does not solve these concerns but smoothes over rough edges and relaxes your mind and body.

Pint 2: You are now chilled. You order another packet of peanuts and have a smile on your face.

Pint 3: Deep into your third pint, you reach your alcoholic Nirvana, a Zen-like state of mind where calm oozes from every pore of your body. In this state you know you will find a solution to all that is troubling you, and have the makings of a pleasant beer buzz

Pint 4: At this point, the time factor kicks in. What seems like twenty minutes flashes by in ten, and an-hour flashes by in what seems like half an hour. This is particularly noticeable in company. It's not a bad thing in itself, but if you are due to meet someone or, God forbid, you have a partner or wife to meet later, then it will create a problem.

Pint 5: By now, your bladder starts to remind you of your bodily function duties unless you are a master of the sponge game, in which case this is where you begin to collect your winnings. Not to be confused with the biscuit game. You order food.

Pint 6: When you get to this stage, time accelerates further and what you think was an hour of drinking time has flashed by in twenty minutes, and you are beginning to think of excuses for your failure for not being home/at the concert/meeting the in-laws/at the restaurant.

Pint 7: Time to phone the wife/partner to beg forgiveness...

I could go on, but I think you get a general idea.

As I began the third pint of this particular session (remember that I had been drinking on the plane and briefly with the band) Frankie found me, propping up the bar, and I was telling any passer-by who would listen what an absolute tosser my brother was "and here he is!" I shouted as he approached. But he then did something completely unexpected: He hugged me and told me that he had been to see Mum that morning, and she had told him that she wanted us to patch things up. She said to mention the tale of my going home sick from school one lunchtime and asked if I remembered the story.

I told Frankie that yes, it was a family gathering at our house when I was twelve, with all our neighbours and friends invited though I don't remember the occasion. The night before, Mum had bought lots of bottles back to the house in preparation for the event and had left them in the drinks cabinet for the next day. There was a great selection of whiskies, brandy, vodka and gin, as well as Watney's beer and Mackeson for the men. When Mum left for work each morning I followed her out shortly after and shut the door behind me, but on this particular day, I waited till she left the house and was walking up the path and then I thought of the alcohol. I tried a couple of the bottles to see if they were open and found that the brandy top was already loose. I knew where to get a glass and also a mixer to go with it. I liked the taste and so quickly gulped down two fingers worth and then thought I would try some of the gin because that's what Mum liked the best. This was followed by a bottle of stout.

I looked at my watch and knew I had to head off to school. I was already at a comparable Spirit 4 level and weaved my way through the school gates, narrowly missing a couple of teachers smoking at the entrance. I ran to my classroom and rested my head on the desk. I must have been in this position for 5 minutes before my teacher approached and prodded a few times to see if I was okay. As it happened, I wasn't feeling great and made a hasty dash from the classroom to the toilets, where I heaved up copious times before heading back to the classroom.

I was too afraid to say I felt ill in case the nurse smelt alcohol on my breath, but by midday, it was evident that something was wrong. The school called Mum at work, and she called one of my neighbours to come and collect me. As we were walking the short distance home, I was violently sick down an alleyway, and he immediately recognised the symptoms. With a knowing laugh, he asked what I had drunk and promised me he would gently tell Mum the real reason for my illness. Since that day, I have had a better relationship with alcohol. I know my limits, and I know when I need to stop and when I need to drink to get over something.

The band were in fits of laughter over this revelation. I asked Frankie about his change of name. He said it was based on Mum's favourite singer Frankie Lane, and he just added a D' to make his name sound Greek and exotic. I wanted to know why he had quit the LSO. They were a world-renowned orchestra, so although it's a different kind of fame, why had he given up orchestra stardom for rock? Frankie explained there were two reasons: his time with the LSO came to an end when Andre Preview joined as principal conductor. Andre didn't like long hair, and they had an inevitable personality clash. Boredom was setting in for Frankie, and he longed to play something a little more contemporary. He sometimes switched the scores set up before practice, so sections of the orchestra played the wrong tunes. As Frankie explained afterwards, "they were playing the right notes, but not necessarily in the right order."

Frankie had been with the LSO for nearly six years and hadn't made a lot of money but had played with many talented musicians and mastered the cello, recorder and trumpet to go with his flute. He looked on his time with the LSO as a musical education and was now looking to get into the contemporary music scene, which he had longed for all along, having been side-tracked when his first band broke up soon after he left home to seek fame and fortune. The other reason was more straightforward: groupies. Just as Frank Zappa & The Mothers of Invention had their GTOs (Girls

Together, Outrageously), the LSO had their own female admirers: old-age groupies who followed them everywhere they went. At a concert hall, they tended to hang out at the merchandise stall to get the latest souvenirs and interact with the sellers, who sometimes had performers at their booth and swapped knitting patterns. They hung around in packs outside the venue after the show for a chance to engage with the musicians.

One night as he retired to his room after a particularly demanding concert in Vienna, he turned on the light to find a particularly old wrinkly named Ethel Crabtree posing seductively on his bed. Groupies can be so crafty, you see. This particular lady had promised sexual favours (or similar) to a variety of staff till she finally got access to Frankie's room, though what 'favours' an 80-year-old granny can offer is open to debate. She probably agreed to do the doorman's dirty washing and something similar for the bellboy. Then she got to bribe a maid before finally getting to his room and making herself comfortable. Groupies getting his washing done certainly cut down on bills, but as for sexual satisfaction, this is not what they are usually after and anyway, Ethel never stuck to her side of the deal, and a room full of laundry was found afterwards. Most old-age groupies only want a cup of cocoa and a cuddle from the object of their desire, but this more senior groupie wanted more than just tea & biscuits. Frankie wanted to get away from the Ethel Crabtree's of this world.

Unfortunately, Ethel Crabtree was not going to give up so easily.

Star Maker Machinery

In July 1972, Advent appeared on BBC TV's Premier music show *Top Of The Pops*. A large crowd of over-enthusiastic teenagers were waiting as we prepared to lip-sync our new surprise smash hit single *There She Goes*. Simon Crisp's excited introduction faded as the camera panned away from him and focused on Dave Sermon's cheesy grin as he sat at the front of the stage. It was his first time on TV, and he was making the most of it. I had been on the show quite a few times with The Highwaymen, plus that memorable Juke Box Jury appearance, and to me, it was just another day at the office. I never understood why drummers were predominantly placed at the front of the stage when the traditional place for a live performance was on a high riser at the back of the stage.

These were the days when it was still possible for a group with serious music credentials to appear on *Top Of The Pops* with a hit single and not have it affect their street cred. In any given week, you could have Black Sabbath on the bill with Tom Jones and David Cassidy fighting it out for the most spacious dressing room, though after what I endured in Rotterdam, I could put up with most things. I was on the show to see the lovely

Babs Lord, and, as luck would have it, she and Ruth Pearson were complementing our performance by prancing around in their hotpants behind us. It was deemed by the BBC director that our stage performance would not be exciting enough for the average teenage viewer, so the two ladies were there to provide a pleasant onscreen distraction. I tried bravely to converse with Babs, but she had to run off and prepare for the group dance that week. All this whilst under the watchful eye of Apple, who had supplied backing vocals. I think this is the reason why our single was selling so well. She didn't want a regular place in the band but was happy to provide backup when we needed it. She was more into tarot cards and tea reading so she was always on hand to offer a handy cuppa and a reading when required.

We were watching *Top Of The Pops* that week to see just how cheesy our performance was. The viewing public liked what they saw because the song went into the top 10. Little were we to know it, but that was the band's last performance on the show and my last chance to get Bab's telephone number.

We had met the flamboyant Elton Johnson the previous week, and though he liked our music, he said we ought to liven up our stage presence. We went with him to his flashy abode and he showed us some of his stage gear which, to be fair, was rather impressive. He showed us the largest pair of glasses I had ever seen and suggested I ought to wear something like that for the show to make me stand out from the crowd. I went for a pair of red satin trousers and a T-shirt, while the others wore similar clothing. Advent were not the prettiest band for sure, but we were more concerned with our music than with participating in the glitter contest held between Simon Crisp and his radio colleague Noel Tidy-Beard.

Crisp is still to be heard on BBC radio doing retro charts and looking at his reaction to our single, you can guess that it would never get played when he featured a July 1972 chart. Well, that's okay because I don't particularly like his *Jazz On Sunday* shows on BBC Radio London, and I told him so on social media, resulting in my being blocked on Twitter. Badge of honour!

Simon was the pin-up boy of the BBC in the Seventies and had his own style of presenting breakfast radio. He had become a regular presenter of *Top Of The Pops* because he never said or did anything controversial to sully the show's reputation.

Simon and I had a little history because after I left the Highwaymen, I spent a few weeks working with him on pirate radio, broadcasting on Radio Caroline. Those were the days when there was no dedicated radio station catering for the current music scene, and the pirate station overseers had filled a hole in the market and had been broadcasting since 1964, financed by advertising. From a highwayman to a pirate... you couldn't make it up!

Before sea sickness got the better of me, it's a little-known fact that I also made jingles for the broadcasting stations at the time. For instance, the one advertising *Bubby Soap for bubbly people* was me. I regretted not turning that particular tune into a hit single. I particularly enjoyed scratching Billy Shears & The Londoners latest 45s and used to throw them overboard for a laugh. The pirate stations glory days were to end when the Marine Broadcasting Offences

Act came into legislation on 14th August 1967 and I had jumped ship (another pun) well before that.

David Bowie, Hawkwind, Alice Cooper and Don McLean were riding high in the charts in the week of our *Top Of The Pops* appearance. Bowie would always be massive, and dear Alice has always been such a gentleman. His band & mine were great drinkers when we met up on our tours. I was glad that Don was doing well with his follow-up to American Pie. Still, I was a little peeved because a year earlier, I had written what I thought was a wonderful song encapsulating British music's history to date. I would have called it *Bye, Bye, Apple Pie* or something similar. Then I heard *American Pie* and knew I was beaten. *Apple Pie* would finally be released on a compilation of unused tracks from this period of my time with Advent, whilst *American Pie* will forever be regarded as an all-time classic.

I had already recorded with Advent on two mega LPs and was finally making enough money to buy myself a nice little place of my own in Highgate Village, a quiet leafy little place in North London with lots of quaint pubs where I could go about my business and not be disturbed.

My first LP with Advent was *Arrival*, which arrived (ahem) in 1970 on the back of a wave of publicity by PMSL. No expense was spared in positioning us at the top of the rock table at a time when Progressive Rock was not known as a genre, making good use of our appearance at Woodstock and the IOW festival, where we supplied Bob Dylan with a variety of harmonicas to use when he forgot to bring his own. Frankie came to the rescue on that occasion and joked with Dylan about my ill-fated concert in Rotterdam. Dylan did not know of this, so I put this all down to Reggie, stirring up the press on the adage that all publicity is good publicity.

One of the first things I did when I returned to the fold of PMSL Records and joined Advent was to search for Joyce James. Was she still around? She had handed over the reins of the Dandy Highwaymen fan club to a dedicated fan and found a job within the music industry as a publicist for the PMI label, dealing with press releases for their stable of artists, fixing up press and television interviews and maintaining a media presence for their artistes. I asked her if she would represent Advent at PMSL for the right salary, and she said she couldn't wait to get away from PMI because most of their artists were older men and always trying it on with her. I said I couldn't promise it would be any better at PMSL, but I would make sure to match or even better PMI's wages. She accepted my offer on the spot. With Joyce now as our publicist, I could relax because Roy B'Stard could leave all that side of things to her.

We were reluctant to release any singles from *Arrival* after hearing Led Zeppelin speaking disparagingly about editing their masterpieces down to a radio-friendly three minutes. *Arrival* featured seven songs of varying lengths and the best of these *Listen To Me* was our choice to be released as a 45 until we complained to B'Stard about the label going against our wishes and issuing a heavily edited version of *The Final Word*. We were using this complaint as a way of testing how good a manager he was going to be for us, and he came through with flying colours, though I could never get to the bottom of how he managed to persuade Reggie to back down and withdraw the single. Copies of *The Final Word* are scarce and sell on Ebay for £100.

Our next album *The Coming Of Advent* (released in 1971) sold a million copies by the time we made our *Top Of The Pops There She Goes* performance, and I was still celebrating after a surprise 30th birthday held by the PMSL label and my bandmates at a local pub. We had bowed to pressure and released the single on the proviso that it wasn't edited but faded out and continued on the B-Side. B'Stard had also told me of the label's intentions of releasing a Greatest Hits LP, which would also please me financially. Then he indicated that he wanted to tell me something much more personal.

We went to the toilets (as you do) where he revealed to me that he knew Reggie was screwing the band over with our current record sales royalties and that if we were to cut ties with PMSL records he would negotiate a record deal that far outstripped what we were currently on. He would be able to get a sweet signing-on deal as well. I was tempted but said that I had only recently patched things up with PMSL Records and this would create more bad blood between me and the label.

I needed evidence of how badly we were being screwed over and I would have to chat with the band and agree to this together or not at all. B'Stard pointed outside to the car park and said, "firstly, look at his car. That's what you bought him on the back of your royalties that he is keeping from you, and secondly, this is your 30th birthday party, and he hired out a pub? How cheapskate is that? He could have had this at a nightclub and invited all your showbiz friends. By all means, chat with the band and when you have decided, come back to me, and I'll get the ball rolling. You won't have to confront him because I'll personally see to all those arrangements."

I chatted with the band over the next few days. At first, they were hesitant, but I slowly won them over and we then met with B'Stard who came up with some numbers that we all agreed with. If we were to sign with ARSEA he could get us a 4-year deal with the label only requiring 4 albums in that time. He suggested we go out on the road for the summer and leave him to conclude the deal when he sat down and thrashed something out with Reggie. *Hopefully not his brains,* I thought to myself. We were kept busy with our concert schedule.

The European tour of 1972 kept us on the road for four solid months, and our records were starting to get noticed in the States too. We had some fun when I complained in the NME that Cliff Richard's new single sounded remarkably like our *There She Goes* hit, and that drummed up some more publicity for us and kept the name of Advent in the public eye. There was even talk that Cliff would invite us onto his TV show to sweeten us up and persuade us to drop the accusation, but that would have done our street cred no good. Of course, it would have helped if his offending song had sold in the millions, but that wasn't likely to happen.

As a footnote to all this nonsense, we put a little backwards message on one of our latter LP's inner grooves, and if you are too young to remember LPs, I'm referring to the playout groove of the record once the music ended. It was us singing Cliff's first failed Eurovision Song Contest song *Congratulations.* The other side had the other failed entry *Power To All Our Friends.* News came through that Roy B'Stard had indeed thrashed something out with PMSL. Reggie's face turned a whiter shade of pale and he had immediately agreed to match anything that ARSEA offered us. We took Roy's better offer and were on a new contract with a better percentage of record sales, and Roy was also rewarded for his sterling efforts.

Dave came up with the idea for the 4LP concept set, *The Centipede & The Slug* to accompany our North American tour and we recorded quickly to get it released in time. Roger Magneti was producing this one after I insisted we use him. Jethro Tull had released their magnificent *Thick As A Brick* LP and Dave thought he could come up with something similar, if not better. You may think we had a prolific work rate to come up with something so elaborate so fast, but we were just making it up as we went along. Frankie and I wrote most of the work, but there was still space for Dave to get a quirky little song of his in there a la Ringo Starr, whilst Keith set himself the task of a whole side of keyboard and mellotron improvisations. His work with Clive Sinclair and ZX71 opened his mind to sound collages, and he let rip, particularly with the twenty-minute *There's A Frog In My Garden Bed.* Set in a garden in Kent, this mammoth LP set followed the unlikely friendships that formed between members of the insect world and their constant battle for survival against their amphibian enemies.

It's the story of centipede finds slug, centipede loves slug, centipede loses slug and finally centipede eats slug. Songs such as *Slug Dance*, *Don't Eat the Pondlife, The Pond of Dead Snails, Grub Wars* and *Toad Party* were to become firm favourites with our fans. Frankie decided he would go full centipede when we performed the LP in its three-hour entirety at The Royal Albert Hall. He crawled about on his belly for the whole forty minutes of the 3rd LP, looking for slugs to eat, while Dave completed his drum solo of The *Ants From No.22* in full ant gear. It hadn't gone unnoticed that Adam Ant lifted highwaymen, pirates and ants based on my first two bands, and good luck to him!

Prognosis designed the cover art, stretched over a double gatefold sleeve so we could fit all the LPs into the package. Its cover was crammed with general garden insects and creepy crawlies inching across a food tray. Grotesque and yet very sleek in its way. Fans were delighted with the new LP; the music press was confused and record shops were furious. After all, it took up so much space on their shelves - not that it stayed on the shelves for long because it was selling quickly. They had to have a separate section for Advent albums.

We finished 1972, having outsold our previous two albums, and things were on the up. Joyce James went to town with its promotion, and there were soon life-size cardboard cut-outs of the band outside most well-known record shops. This frightened the children, with creepy crawlies all over our clothes. That was the photo shoot to end all photo shoots. Funnily enough, I had no problem with bugs and the like crawling over me. Dave was put off Liquorice Allsorts for life when one was offered from a box of sweets and he nearly bit it in half before realising it was a slug. Poor Dave!

At the end of 1972 I met Judee Sill. She was in the UK playing a few dates, appearing on TV and promoting her newish self-titled debut album. Judee was appearing on BBC TV's *Old Grey Whistle Test* at the start of the year and I happened to be on the show talking to Bob Harris about *The Coming Of Advent* LP. I did not know of her but was intrigued when told she was better than Joni Mitchell which was high praise indeed. Dave came along as well and it would not be an underestimation to say we were mesmerised by Judee's performance and I had to meet her after the show and tell her how much I enjoyed her performance. She once described her music as *occult-holy-western-baroque-gospel* and I wouldn't argue with that.

I introduced myself and was surprised she had heard of the Dandy Highwaymen. We hit it off immediately and backstage that night we played together for the first time. She told me she was playing a few gigs in the UK and I asked if she would play with Advent. "I don't play with no snotty rock bands," she laughed, "but we could do a few acoustic sets if you are free during the week."

When she came back to the UK to promote her second album *Heart Food,* we met up in London. She was appearing on The *Old Grey Whistle Test* again and I had a word with Bob Harris who sneaked me in to watch her perform two songs that day. Judee was destined for great things at that point but was prone to be outspoken. She alienated herself with some controversial comments about Asylum record label David Geffen and how he was favouring other label artists such as Joni Mitchell over her, and from that point her career spiralled out of control. She did not release another album in her lifetime and died in 1979 of a drug overdose.

There is very little footage of her available, and all I have found are the two songs I saw her perform on her second *Old Grey Whistle Test* visit and some grainy black & white footage of her in an open-air concert. The BBC recorded over lots of recorded shows they had in the late Sixties to early Seventies and what little they had of her work, but her fans live in hope that someday more may be found, safe in the BBC vaults.

Wanted Dead or Alive

In 1973 we took our *The Centipede & The Slug* concept album on the road to North America. We had to compromise and play the album in condensed form as it was deemed to be too long for the average American's attention span, but it had the same level of popularity as in the UK and Europe. The Americans took things one step further and started dressing up for the shows. At one point, slugs, beetles, ants, frogs, and even a cockroach were sitting in the front row at our Boston gig. Every audience was trying to outdo the previous one. I concluded that we should have based the LP on Playboy models, which would have led to a better front-row view, but it was too late for that now. Frankie had stopped crawling around on his stomach after an unfortunate episode when dirt was thrown onto the stage. It was said to be dirt, but Frankie knew better.

The American music press didn't know what to make of us. In scenes similar to the Beatles' 1964 NYC press conference, they fired a variety of questions at us that confused more than enlightened them:

Q: "In Chicago, they're handing out car stickers saying, 'Stamp Out Advent.'"

GREG: “Yeah, well... first of all, we’re bringing a Stamp Out Chicago campaign.”

Q: ”A psychiatrist recently said you’re nothing but a bunch of British Cliff Richard’s.”

KEITH: (shaking like Cliff) “It’s not true!! It’s not true!!”

DAVE: (dances like Cliff)

Q: ”Will you be having a shave?”

GREG: ”I had one yesterday.”

Gail and Hal met me in New York. The commune was now history, but they were still together. Hal had given up on his dreams of being a global superstar and was now a pharmacist in Brooklyn, working under the name of Drugstore Dave, or Dr Robert, supplying to the rock elite. They wanted to know the meaning behind the slug’s relationship with the centipede. What was I trying to say with the lyrics? What was the more profound meaning? I had learned from Carly Simon to make my lyrics as vague as possible and allude to something without actually naming names or events. The listener would have to make their own judgements. I told them it was all meant as a joke and not to take things too seriously, but they wouldn’t accept that. They had been listening closely to the lyrics and wondered if the slug was JFK and the Centipede was Charles Manson.

The pair came on the road with us for a while so we could catch up on our lives since the commune. Apple was going to join us halfway through the tour, so there were no awkward moments between the ladies. At first, this arrangement worked well, but Apple was phoning daily because she heard all kinds of saucy details from the press about what was happening after the shows.

I'm not saying I was an angel by any means because within the bubble I lived in, it wasn't possible to shut myself away from what was happening backstage.

The dressing rooms and after-party gigs were filled with young women eager to get to know us and take it further, given the opportunity or encouragement. Some things were too knowledgeable to be just the work of any old crank taking guesses at behind-the-scenes shenanigans. It had to be our new guests, so I told Gail and Hal they were off the tour. They protested and said that the stories were not coming from them, but I couldn't take the chance of antagonising Apple when the evidence was so strong.

It was about this time that Joyce told me the fan club were receiving threatening letters warning of the dangers of disrespecting the garden creatures by imitating them on stage and on vinyl. B'Stard showed us some of the letters she had forwarded, and we had a right laugh because they were from the Invertebrate Protection Society. We assumed it was probably just a bunch of cranks from the States getting hot under the collar about nothing. Then the letters went from being written in red ink to what looked like blood, which is when things took a sinister twist. Rivers of blood and all that. B'Stard beefed up the security, which worked for a while until one night after a concert, we trooped back to our dressing room to be confronted by a pig's head on a spike. We laid down an ultimatum to B'Stard that he had to find the culprit (or culprits) as a top priority or else nobody would feel safe on the tour.

We had grown tired of travelling from city to city on the freeways. The initial excitement of being on the tour bus had worn off, and we now had full-on travel fatigue.

We complained to B'Stard that this was affecting our performances and that he either found an alternative mode of transport or stopped the punishing schedule by inserting more breaks between shows.

He quickly came back to us with an agreeable solution. We hired Led Zeppelin's Starship for most of the tour. If you are unaware, this was the plane that Zeppelin kitted out to their required taste to avoid the inconvenience of hotel stays and using standard air travel. What they got up to on their plane has gone down in rock folklore. The aircraft (an ex-United Airlines Boeing 720) had a seating capacity of forty, with a bar, seats and tables; a thirty-foot-long couch along one side of the plane; revolving armchairs; opposite the bar, a TV and a video cassette player with a well-stocked library and an electronic organ and piano. There was also a working fireplace. At the craft's rear were two back rooms, one with a low couch and pillows on the floor and the other - furnished as a bedroom, complete with a white fur bedspread and shower room. They hired the plane out to their friends when it was not being used, so the likes of The Rolling Stones and their *Need For Greed* tour, Deep Purple, Elton Johnson, Peter Frampton and Alice Cooper took to the air. The first time The Allman Brothers boarded, they were greeted with 'Welcome Allman Brothers' rendered in lines of cocaine on the bar.

All we got was a plate of sandwiches and a crate of beer. The band made good use of the facilities and being single lads, they invited an occasional friend or two that they hooked up with at the show to come along for a ride on the Starship. Just as long as they didn't mind hitchhiking back.

We enjoyed touring New York, Boston, Chicago and Pittsburgh. There was a curiosity for our music, but when we got to the Southern States, there was a different mood, not as open and receptive to what we were playing. The venues were smaller, and we could hear everything said between numbers. Road stops were not as fun either because it invariably meant a disagreement between the locals over who looked the more effeminate in the band, but we made Roy enter the bar after us to challenge anyone bold enough to want to pick a fight.

There was a bar room brawl in Dallas when a member of our crew took a dislike at being served biscuits 'n' gravy, a breakfast commonly served in the South which consists of tender dough biscuits covered in a thick gravy, usually made from the drippings of pork sausages, flour, and milk. The second dish he was offered was Grits, and this was even more unpalatable because he had asked for porridge and was told it was a similar-tasting meal. Roy knocked out a couple of Hells Angels, and by the time it came to the evening's concert, we were looking out into a sea of Hells Angels surrounding the stage and outside the venue, which resulted in the National Guard being called in to quell the disturbance and us being escorted out of town by the police with orders never to return. It wasn't quite Altamont but it was close!

Frankie's Old Age Groupies were now following us in more significant numbers. His fan club was a great source of fun for all of us (except Frankie of course). They were still hanging around outside the gigs into the early morning hours when they should have been at home in their slippers and sipping cocoa. They were led by Ethel Crabtree, and she had not given up on getting to grips with Frankie and persisted in sending him love letters, roses and knitted jumpers at every opportunity. She was said to be an eccentric wealthy widow whose late husband had been a conductor for a famous orchestra though I could never discover if this was just a part of the fantasy she lived from day to day or the truth. She could indulge herself in whatever way she chose and believed that money could buy anything or anyone. She thought she could purchase Frankie in this way.

He kept her at arm's length as best he could and bluntly told her one day that he could not envisage a time he would share his toothbrush with her false teeth. You would have thought that this would put Ethel off, but it only inspired her to redouble her efforts, though she never again managed to breach hotel security. Still, on several occasions, we did sneak her back to his room and listened in on the resulting commotion as he came out of the shower to find her in his bed.

At the end of the tour, we were reliably informed that the culprit of the threatening letters had been found. It was none other than Ethel Crabtree. This was a shock to us as we could not understand how such a sweet old octogenarian could write such vile letters. We were told Ethel had escaped from a mental institution in Chicago two years before and was on the run from the authorities. This sweet little old lady was a killer who the authorities felt would be better off in a mental institution than behind bars. She was only caught when she applied for a passport to travel to Europe. Should we contact the police and get her arrested, or would someone discretely speak with her to stay away from the shows and never contact Frankie again? Fate had other ideas as we heard she had been put into a mental institution after trying to take a machete through Dallas airport on the way to one of our shows.

Before we flew home, we were invited to have our pictures taken for the cover of Rolling Stone. It was a big honour, but to me, it was no different to being on the cover of New Musical Express or Melody Maker. We had a day set aside for an interview and were asked what we thought of Lester Bangs, who had come away from one of our concerts with a very negative opinion of our latest LP, offering the opinion that we were: *"soulless sellouts", participating in "the insidious befoulment of all that was pure in rock."*

We chuckled about that and took the insult as a badge of honour. After that, we attended a baseball match in Chicago with the band pitching balls simultaneously, which created some mirth when I took out a kid's soda & popcorn. I had caught my arm against Keith in the process of pitching. I gave the lad a T-shirt, but that didn't appease the poor lad.

Advent and baseball are synonymous due to an event in Chicago in the summer of 1979 when local shock DJ Steve Dahl decided that enough was enough and he would arrange a Prog and Disco Demolition event at nearby Comisky Park, the home of Chicago White Sox, the event sponsored by his station WLUP. Admission to the double-header was discounted to a dollar as long as you brought a record along that would be ceremonially blown up in a controlled explosion in the break between games. The average attendance for the White Sox that season was 20,000, and the club hoped to put another 5,000 on the gate. Instead, 50,000 came that night, and thousands more broke in after the gates were closed. A drunken crowd situation worsened after the records were destroyed in an explosion with fire littering the playing field, and any records that had not been collected were used as frisbees. A pitch riot ensued, and the second game was abandoned.

Behind the scenes, there was much talk about making *The Centipede & The Slug* into a Broadway show or, at the very least, turning it into a blockbuster film. But who would be auditioning for the lead role of the Centipede?

A Song for Europe

One night while watching TV, I got a call from Greg. He sounded very excited and told me to switch to BBC1 and watch *Top of the Pops.* I wouldn't normally do this unless there was something good in the charts, and this being 1973, there was an awful amount of dross, what with the Osmonds, Jackson 5 and the glitter bands currently dominating radio and TV. Greg insisted there was something at the top of the charts that I really ought to see. I switched over from ITV and yawned through the usual teeny bop dross till right at the end of the show, an act came on looking ridiculous in a glitter outfit that Gary Glitter would have turned down as over the top.

I looked closer at the singer and looked again. It was Billy Shears, but not as I knew him. He and his band had shiny outfits that caught the rotating lights of the studio in a dazzling display. I picked up the newspaper, turned to the TV listings, and discovered this was Terry & the Tinsels, Billy being Terry of course. They had a No 1 song called *Do The Tinsel* and were predicted to be top of the charts for quite a while. I had not heard much from Billy Shears since 1967 and assumed he had quit the music business, but here he was under a new guise and doing very well for himself. Damn!

Over the coming months to the end of 1973, Terry's Tinsels continued to dominate the UK media. I could not turn for seeing his cheesy face on advertising boards, magazines, buses and newspapers. The final straw came when he brought Central London to a standstill when thousands of his screaming fans caused a bottleneck in Trafalgar Square, causing traffic chaos. I had been heading to an important business meeting that afternoon and was delayed for an hour by his screaming fans. "Will no one rid me of this turbulent pop tart!" I yelled, but no knights were within earshot.

I decided I would have to do the dastardly deed myself. My competitive side resurfaced as I decided to check what he had been doing in the intervening years. These days it is easy to do an internet search, but back in the Seventies, it was a case of looking through music magazines for the facts. I wouldn't find out much in the rock newspapers so I turned to the teen magazines such as Jackie or Melanie for my information. I read that he had come out of semi-retirement and jumped on the Glitter bandwagon with great success.

So, who was the most successful of the two of us? Artistically me, no doubt about it, but financially it could well prove to be Mr Tinsel if this band of his continued their current level of success. One thing for sure was that I would not be dumbing down my music in the hopes of fame and success. No platform boots, sequined clothes, glittery, sparkly bits on my face, or writing the word YOB on my guitar (okay, the last one was very nearly me a few years later). It looked like an adult had put glue on their face and then tipped a whole load of nursery glitter on their temple. One of Billy's dubious quotes was:

"Should it ever come to pass that the biologically produced waste matter of our species become prized highly from a financial standpoint, those members of our society who are hereditarily underprivileged would henceforth come into the world devoid of the necessary means of production."

He stole that from a Rubettes fan club letter. Don't ask how I know!

I decided I would have to be sneaky and look through my mementoes of Rotterdam to find something for the press. I told Joyce about my plans and she said she wanted in on the action because the pint-sized terror (her words) had tried to corner her one night after a show she had attended. She wanted to get even with the little squirt (more of her words) and when I found pictures of Billy in Nazi gear with a hot blonde sitting on his lap, she made sure they were anonymously released to the daily papers and their sleazy Sunday rivals for publication. Of course, there would be no chance of Billy knowing for sure who had released them, but he would have a shrewd guess.

The pictures were published as expected and the newspaper had record issue sales that day, so much so that the paper asked if I had any more around the house. I did, but this was getting out of hand because I intended to discredit the man and not make him any more popular. Realising I was beaten, I scooped up all my pictures and worked a deal with Joyce to issue them in book form, conveniently to be released in time for the Christmas market. We made a fortune over the festive season, and I was able to put a few baubles on the tree with what I made.

The book was so successful we followed it up with a batch of T-Shirts, keyrings and the like. I hate Billy Shears was a popular mug though I am sure there are still a few more available in the garden shed (£2.99 if anyone is interested). *Top Of The Pops* Christmas was a white-knuckle ride that year, with Terry's band, Simon Crisp, and Noel Tidy-Beard again decked out in glitter. The only good spot was Babs Lord and Pans People flouncing around to a Gilbert O'Sullivan tune.

1974 was the year of my first involvement with the Eurovision Song Contest. Joyce told me I had been asked by the BBC if I wanted to go on a judging panel for the show. In those days, it wasn't the bore-fest that it was to become because only 17 countries were competing, and none of the current semi-finals/finals that we have now and the French had pulled out for political reasons (it was the day of their president's funeral).

I was contacted at short notice because one of the ten judges had called off sick because he had overdone things in the free bar the day before the show and was in no condition to judge what he heard. Or maybe that was the correct way to approach the show? At that point, each country issued points based on the judgements of 10 high-profile media folk. They whisked me down to Brighton, where I would be casting my vote and meeting the lovely Katie Boyle. One small problem, though - there was to be a little skit in the middle of the show when some top-quality local entertainment was being organised, and I was asked if I wanted to do something pre-recorded for that slot. Sure I could! I agreed to play something and the BBC man said not to worry, go in that room and get changed.

Puzzled, I went into the room I was pointed towards a Wombles outfit and told to quickly put it on.

In 1974 The Wombles, like Terry Tinsel, were everywhere. They had an animated tea-time slot on the BBC aimed at promoting keeping Britain tidy by picking up rubbish on Wimbledon Common. They got popular very quickly and soon they were churning out pop tunes written by Mike Batt and selling by the bucket load. The only problem was how to present them in the flesh for *Top Of The Pops* performances and this was quickly solved by finding five or so volunteers to don a hairy costume, and dance around a bit for the cameras.

For the rest of the day, I was driven around Brighton dressed up and waving to children, put in a high-powered speedboat to surf the waves near Brighton Pier and then sent back to get ready for the show. When it came to voting on the songs it wasn't drinking that caused me to feel ill, but the seasickness from being ridden round and around in circles. I can't remember whom I cast my vote for, but an oddity of the United Kingdom's vote was that the winners from Sweden that year were ABBA and they received nil points from our jury. How odd! One fact from the contest that year that gets overlooked is that when the Portuguese entry sung by Paulo de Carvalho "E Depois de Adeus" was played on Emissores Associados de Lisboa Radio Station on April 2nd, it was a signal to captains and soldiers that a coup that became known as the Carnation Revolution was beginning.

The Wombles were involved in one of the more remarkable music events of the decade when they appeared at Mallory Park in 1975 as part of a BBC-organised fun day out which also featured Slade and the Bay City Rollers, who were hugely popular at the time. The Rollers had set up camp on one of the small islands in the middle of a vast lake within the racetrack, and young girls were dashing across the track and evading security by attempting to wade across the lake to where their heroes were waving from an observation platform.

The BBC Sub-Aqua club were also acting as security for the day and were catching the girls as they crossed the waters, aided by members of the Wombles and taking them back to the bank, whilst Tony Blackburn was hurtling backwards and forwards in a speedboat, waving to the crowds, in a speedboat driven by a Womble.

Afterwards, DJ John Peel expressed the opinion that if he lived to be 200 he would never experience anything like it ever again. ,Despite all the speeding cars, water and mayhem there were no serious injuries but 35 were treated for minor injuries on site.

The following year the Wombles and the Goodies were among the top-selling British artists of the year, and both were products of the BBC. I will leave the dear reader to ponder on that titbit of information. We played some shows in Europe and began writing our new LP, which we were trying to get released for the Christmas market. We wanted to move away from the concept album approach as we felt that the Lester Bangs criticism was unjustified. The next album was going back to Prog basics and would be a purely instrumental affair. We had recorded most of the album by the time I set off for Africa for a change of scenery and to recharge my batteries, if you will - and to take in a boxing match between the two greatest fighters of the day. It would be a while before we got to complete the rest of the album.

Welcome To The Jungle

In the first week of November 1974, Lord Lucan vanished from the face of the earth after allegedly bludgeoning his children's nanny, Sandra Rivett, to death in the family home's kitchen. He managed to leave the UK, and there were numerous sightings of him in France, India and as far away as Australia. To date, he has never been found. He was declared legally dead in October 1999, and it was not until 2016 that a death certificate was issued.

At the same time, MP John Stonehouse faked his own death. Waterhouse had been suspected of being a Czechoslovakian spy since the 1960's. In financial trouble, Stonehouse faked his death by leaving his clothes on a beach in Miami and making his escape under an assumed name to Australia. He was on the run for a month before finally feeling the long arm of the law on Christmas Eve 1974 in Melbourne. His arrest came with a very odd request to drop his trousers to identify he was not Lord Lucan, who had a six-inch scar on the inside of his right thigh.

There was a third disappearance and that was yours truly, though this was by accident. I was in Zaire to watch Muhammad Ali beat George Foreman to reclaim the world heavyweight boxing title in Kinshasa, the capital and largest city of the Democratic Republic of the Congo. The charismatic Ali christened the boxing bout 'The Rumble In The Jungle'.

I'm not a huge boxing fan but I was invited to the event by PMSL executives who had tickets, so I flew out a few days in advance to top up my tan ahead of the bout. After a long and arduous journey, we landed at N'djili Airport (named after the river, apparently). I got tired of sitting around the pool and, being the adventurous type I am, asked if there were any guided tours because I wanted to see some of Congo in the wild. I was offered a visit to the Congo River to see some crocodiles and, as my guides put it, "play around with snakes.".

I was collected from my hotel in a jeep the following day by Percy and his companion Scott (a man reassuringly named after the Artic explorer of the early Twentieth Century, he told me), and we drove North-East for a couple of hours along dirt roads until the terrain became less firm and sure. Abandoning the jeep in a safe, secluded clearing, I followed my guides through the dense jungle until we reached a path of sorts and had a short break.

We had brought plenty of food and water and were ready for anything. Percy told me he loved scaring the tourists by rushing ahead down the path and then doubling back and scaring the shit out of them from behind. I was all for turning back, but he laughed and said he would never do that to me. Ten minutes later, I was alone, wandering as lost as possible. I had taken a tumble over a root, and when I had gathered my wits and stood up quickly, they were both out of sight. I shouted out, but nobody returned my call. I began to run fast, and this haste caused me to fall over again, and this time I fell heavily and hit my head on a large rock, rendering me unconscious.

I only have a vague recollection of what happened next. I do not know how long I had been prone on the ground but I felt my body being lifted into a vehicle and felt the movement one would feel when being jostled and jolted in a car or on a London bus. I was experiencing the unconscious version of the five-pint rule where time was speeding past quicker than it seemed. Water was splashed on my face and in my mouth and I could hear the concerned voices of four or maybe five men talking in a language I did not understand. The journey I was on seemed to go on forever, drifting in and out of reality and my dreams until we finally came to a halt. I was lifted gently and carried for a short while, brushing against vegetation and the like, and more voices were heard. After that, I was unaware of anything until I felt I was being lowered onto a soft surface. Here I slept for a while.

I was in darkness when I came to. I could not immediately see anything, but I knew I was not alone. It was hot, and I was perspiring. A smell of stale sweat filled the air. In a solid Aussie accent, a male voice asked how I was. I wondered if I was dreaming because I had not expected to be able to communicate with my captors if that's what they were. I replied that apart from a massive headache, I was okay. He introduced himself as Mick Oz and said I had been found lying prone in the jungle when he and his friends passed through on their way back from the city.

At first, I was thought to be dead, but upon inspection, I started groaning about Highwaymen and Christmas holidays. Maybe I was delerious? Mick had medical experience, so checked me over for injuries and my pockets and backpack for any ID. My passport and ID were safely locked up at the hotel reception, so I had none. He decided it would be best to try and get me back with his friends to their community which was a three-hour drive north-eastwards. He told me I was now with the Umbooko, a peaceful community living a life away from civilisation but embracing the traditions of their country with no interference from the outside world.

Mick was helping with a music project. I asked him what the project was, and he said he was an ethnomusicologist, field recording the sounds of the Umbooko for The International Library of African Music (ILAM). Like a modern-day Hugh Tracey, who recorded traditional African music, Mick was fascinated by its complexity of rhythms and flair for storytelling. He had been sent with what we now consider relatively primitive equipment in the shape of a Phillips tape recorder and told to integrate himself with the people and record whatever happened. Armed with only the recorder and an astonishing number of batteries, he was introduced to the Umbooko through contacts, and had been living and recording there for a year. Every few months he would take his recordings back to the city to be shipped back to the States and then pick up fresh cassettes and batteries.

I was intrigued to see him at work, so after a couple of days of rest I was introduced one evening to the four men who had also saved me. Afterwards, he set up his tape recorder & microphone whilst dinner was being cooked. My hosts entertained me but it was not like the Western World's misconception of African music. Instead, it was a type of traditional African dance. Many tribes have a role solely to pass on their tribe's dance traditions, dances passed down through the centuries, often unchanged, with little to no room for improvisation. I was fascinated.

And meanwhile, what of my band back home? When I failed to return to the hotel that night and my fight tickets remained unclaimed, there were worried faces at PMSL. Where had Charlie gone? When I failed to return after three days, the story broke in the UK and I made the front page of all the newspapers, sharing my face alongside that of Lord Lucan and John Whitehouse. Some of the seedier tabloids thought there was more to the timing of my disappearance than met the eye. Could there be a connection between the three of us? Meanwhile, Billy Shears was up to mischief by using my disappearance to stir trouble, as he wrote in his biography:

"When I heard Caine was missing, I did a dance of glee. Now I could have some fun. I was being interviewed about his disappearance by the music press and happened to mention in an off-the-cuff manner how he and his bird were always arguing and jokingly pointed out how odd it was that Stonehouse and Lucan had gone at the same time. Maybe they were friends? I mused. They say there's no smoke without fire, and within days my quote was in the national newspapers, minus my name as a source of course."

The details of my trek to the Congo River were revealed, and both Percy and Scott, my guides, had concocted a fake story with the aid of certain elements of the gutter press to say that I was up to no good and had probably run off to bury my rucksack which looked as though it contained something heavy that rattled. I was described as a shifty character, and they claimed that the moment their backs were turned, I was off and away before you could say Jack the Ripper. Joyce was trying to smooth over the cracks and give a more positive spin to the story but what could she say without knowing the full facts? For all she knew, the rumours could have been true and I was a murderer.

Mick said he would send a message back to Apple when he travelled to Kinshasa to drop off the next batch of recordings, but the next drop was not due for three months. I pleaded that I needed to get back and tell my family and band what had happened to me, and I also had an album that I needed to complete, though by now we had missed the Christmas market so I was clutching at straws to get back home. Mick said it wouldn't work as the whole idea of what he was doing was that he was to be isolated and immersed with his people, and if he was to take me back to the nearest town it would be valuable time lost. What could I do?

I had no option but to stick around for three months and then return to Kinshasa and get home. In the meantime, I would help Mick any way I could because I owed him and the Umbooko people a big debt. Between recordings, I helped produce the major crops grown locally, including cereals (rice, maize), tubers, cash crops (coffee, cocoa) and sugarcane. In my spare time I began writing songs for the LP but I could not guess when they would be recorded or if I was ever going to get back home. What would the music press make of our current effort? The meaner papers were now describing our last recording as *The Slug & Lettuce* LP.

Living with the Umbooko was not too unlike living in the commune in the Sixties. In fact, I would go as far as to say it was more enjoyable, apart from the fact that it was so hot! Five young couples were in the community, along with Mick and I but I don't recall seeing that many children. We had fresh water from a stream nearby, so we would not die of thirst. The men were able to provide a supply of fresh meat, but I never wanted to know what I was eating because some things are best left unknown. I gave up on any attempt at shaving after the first few weeks and quickly grew stubble.

I was introduced to Lotoko, or as the locals know it, 'pétrole'. Lotoko is a home-distilled alcoholic drink made from maize. Heads of corn were cut up and boiled into a mash, fermented and distilled using improvised stills made from cut-down oil drums. It came with a very high alcohol content (over 50%), and on one particular night, I consumed just a little too much for my own good, so I went to bed early. As I dozed off, I swore I heard a very familiar song. It was a tribal version of Simon & Garfunkel's *Cecilia* - a song they played to excited tourists if they travelled into the city in small groups. I put this down to just a little teasing from the Umbooko and a lot down to Mick.

As Christmas drew near, I wondered what the folks back home were doing. I wanted to visit Mum, and Frankie and I were going on Christmas Day to see her. It was a ritual we had been doing since Frankie was reunited with the family. But I knew that, as hard as the Umbooko tried, it would not be quite the same for me without having my Christmas dinner and then collapsing into a chair and sleeping it off for the rest of the afternoon.

On Christmas Eve, we all sat for a traditional meal consisting of rice and yam paste (called fufu) with stew or okra soup, porridge and meat. Fufu is a thick paste usually made by boiling starchy root vegetables in water and pounding them with a mortar or pestle. For Christmas dinner, we all sat outdoors to share rice, beef and biscuits.

The three months of waiting came to an end and it was time to head back to the city with Mick to get fresh supplies. I headed to the hotel and collected my things, and had a lot of explaining to do. High-ranking law officials were interested in where I had been, and the hotel told me there were hundreds of messages for me to collect, mainly from PMSL and the media who were interested in my story. I asked if they could contact PMSL and let them know I was okay and would be heading home when I had sorted out a lot of loose ends to do with overstaying my welcome and discussing the hotel bill that I thought had been paid for me but was in fact my responsibility. I could only get my passport back once I made arrangements to settle the bill.

I did not know what kind of reception I was in for when I returned home but I felt I had used my time productively and the rhythms I had absorbed during my stay were going to inspire me to write the next Advent LP. I just hoped the band was ready for what I had recorded in my spare time with the help of Mick. Looking back, it was ten years ahead of its time, before

Paul Simon hit on the idea of *Graceland* but fitted in with how Joni Mitchell was experimenting with her Burundi drummers on her current recording *The Hissing of Summer Lawns.*

The flight home was the worst I had ever experienced. An electrical storm meant we had to make an emergency landing in Malta. After such a fraught journey, we all trooped off the plane in various degrees of shakiness. My passport came under scrutiny, and so did my visa papers which were not stamped correctly or something. I was close to using the tried and tested "do you know who I am?" but when I thought about it even I didn't know who I was because, looking in the mirror I looked scruffy and dishevelled, needing a good shave and a bath. I also needed a holiday. I contacted PMSL and said I needed to be sent some more money as I was stuck in Malta and would be there for a week or so. They readily accepted this, so I booked myself into a decent hotel and for the next week, I bought myself a new set of clothes and prepared for the journey home.

Unleashed In The East

As soon as I stepped off the plane at Heathrow Airport, I was met by plainclothes police officers, escorted to a side room, and asked to remove my trousers.

"Well, that's a funny welcome home," I said, dropping my trousers and revealing my brand-new pair of navy-blue boxers for inspection. If they thought I was Lord Lucan, they were very much mistaken. I certainly didn't have a six-inch scar on the inside of my right thigh, but they had a good look at my passport to make sure.

I made my way through Customs and out to the front of the airport. There were 'Welcome Back Charlie!!!' placards everywhere, and I thought there was going to be a media scrum with the press clamouring for interviews, but I soon discovered that it was the Rolling Stones coming into town on their endless *Need For Greed* World Tour. There was nobody to meet me, despite having sent messages informing all of my arrival details. Crestfallen, I hailed a cab back to Highgate through the evening traffic and had the surprise of my life when I opened the front door to find all my friends waiting to start a welcome home party. It was a lovely gesture, but I wasn't in the mood for it. I downed a couple of beers and ate a plate of food, but I just wanted to crawl into bed and sleep for a week. I also had a lot of explaining to do to Apple and everyone at PMSL Records, but that would have to wait until the morning.

I was nervous about how my reception with PMSL and the band would go. Had I been replaced in my absence? I arrived early for the meeting at the swanky PMSL offices and had a quick drink in the pub opposite to calm my nerves. I felt as if I was auditioning to join the band again.

The reaction was mixed. Joyce said that while everyone was glad I was back safe and sound, in my absence, the forthcoming tour to Japan had been put on ice because the band felt they could not do it without me. I was glad to report I was fit and well, so the Summer dates were confirmed and the tour finalised. They were also waiting on me to see if I had come up with any new material while I had been away to complete the LP (and boy, were they in for a shock there). The other news was that *The Centipede & The Slug* film was going into production very soon. Lots of names were being bandied around for the title role, but who did I think would be best suited to play the centipede or the slug? I had no idea and cared very little.

I told everyone that I had come up with some remarkable material and I wasn't exaggerating because I felt that what I had recorded in the Congo was going to form the foundations for another knockout album after we finished the current one. All would be revealed at the next recording session, so we agreed to meet in a few days and run through what we had. We also needed to discuss how we would fit the rescheduled tour to

Japan in with the recording sessions. Over the next couple of days, I played Apple some of the tapes and even she was asking if this was the direction the band were ready to be heading in. How would I label this music: 'Prog Beat?' I said "sure it may be a little rough around the edges but give me time to work on it, and I'll come up with something palatable for the band", but she remained unconvinced.

We met up at PMSL's recording studios in Camden. Despite the financial success of the label since I signed my first contract with them in 1964, they had yet to upgrade their studio facilities. I was amazed at times that they had moved on from mono. It was my ambition to own a recording studio of my own that I could rent out when off touring and have a hands-on approach to bands who I wanted to record when I was free. But for now, I was happy to use the label's facilities until I could afford a place of my own and not have to pay the astronomical rental fees. I had got Roger Magneti on board again with instructions to capture the magic that was about to unfold.

We needed to complete a couple more tracks and have enough material to choose from. PMSL Records could have released what had been recorded up to that point, but the band insisted we would finish the LP as a team, and we all had to be happy with what would be released in our name.

Keith started the ball rolling by unveiling a complex piece he had written on the piano that he thought would suit an opening number. He was rather pleased with himself, and with good reason. Everyone nodded approvingly, and Roger suggested we record it and see where the mood of the piece took us. He was hoping that we would come up with a suggestion for a guitar here or a bass line there to fill in the sound. Keith was okay with that because one thing he was not keen on at concerts was playing a solo. He was already thinking in terms of performing it live. Good. Greg suggested he follow it up with something he had been working on and proceeded to play a restrained, beautiful guitar solo.

We all nodded along to that and Roger suggested that Brian follow and add a little bass to see how that sounded. By and by, Roger was coaxing a great sound from the band with some complex chord change suggestions and long improvisational pieces. Then he asked Dave if he would like to add something light on the drums, which was the moment I had been waiting for. I went to my coat pocket for my cassette recorder as the others looked on in interest. I hit the record button by accident, and everybody laughed. Oh, dear! Their laughter soon turned to confusion when the sounds of the Umbooko filled the studio. They listened for about a minute till I turned it off. There was stunned silence, then Dave piped up, "so you're going to replace me with *that*?" and they all started laughing again.

I could see that I was not going to win them over the first time, so I let it go, but every so often over the next week in the studio, I pointed out how good it would sound if there was a different beat to the song. It's Prog, after all, but with different instrumentation, I kept saying.

Roger took me aside one morning and said that the boys were not really into the new sound I was presenting to them. Wouldn't it be better to channel some of my newly-found rhythms towards a solo project when the time was right? I felt crushed that they could not hear the music as I did but I could see that I would not bring anyone around to my point of view any time soon. I was so annoyed that I went away and wrote an angry, defiant piece that they should have identified as being about their pig-headedness, but I cloaked it with so many vague references that they just thought it was about Billy Shears. The fact that Shears thought it was about him as well cheered me up no end.

I bit my tongue and let it go. If my band did not believe in my overtures for a new direction, then so be it. I wouldn't be leaving just for the sake of it, and I had learned nothing from previous experiences if I were to jack it in at the first sign of conflict.

I usually had a few beers with Greg after everyone had left our late-night recording sessions, popping over the road to the pub where Jackie the landlady had given me a spare set of keys and said that if I was ever stuck overnight in the recording studio, I could let myself in and sleep at her place. I never quite got to the stage with Jackie where I fully took advantage of the offer that she was suggesting but after a few weeks of the temptation of after-hours drinking I slipped in for one with Greg and set off the intruder alarm. Jackie came down with a cricket bat in a blaze of fury till she saw Greg and me and we sat down and discussed music and our plans for the coming year. By that point, the Japan tour was back on, and I was thinking about what we could do to make the tour a memorable one. "You could wear a Kimono. That would be hilarious!" she suggested. It was a start.

The new album was called *LOST* and was a double LP. I wasn't so enthused about its content after my new recordings were turned down, but kept my thoughts to myself. I went along with the pun of a title and we had photos taken in a mock jungle setting with me on the run from, yes you guessed it, a tribe consisting of the rest of the band plus assorted dolly birds hell-bent on putting me in their pot. The PC Brigade would have a field day if anyone tried coming up with that as the concept for an album cover these days, and copies of that original cover art sell well on eBay. Nowadays, the artwork is just me being chased by the dolly birds. I wouldn't have minded that scenario in the first place. We could have hired Constanze-Karoli and Eveline Grunwald, the semi-clad ladies on the cover of Roxy Music's *Country Life* album cover, set in a jungle no less.

I dreamt one night that Genesis were auditioning a bunch of singers to take over vocals from Peter Gabriel. He was going to leave the band due to creative differences. Tony Banks started with his mellotron, with the beginning notes from *Watcher of the Skies* as the first trial vocalist got ready behind the scenes. It came right to the point where the vocals began, and it was then he made his dramatic entrance: it was Billy Shears, and he had decided that he was going to break from the pre-arranged song and try out his own material because he wanted to impress on the band that he could write great songs too. The song came to a crashing end as Tony Banks couldn't stop laughing, and Billy left with his tail between his legs.

The tour to Japan and the Far East was fast approaching. It would run from July 1975 through to October with a couple of breaks to recuperate. Roy B'Stard said that he had lined up a great support act for us which I would find amusing, announcing with glee it was the Highwaymen, my old band. On tour, it got shortened even more to The Highways.

Since I left in 1967, they had dropped the Dandy motif, and as they approached the Seventies there had been a change of style as they had done what I suggested three years before and changed their band image and adopted a harder musical edge, much in the same visual style as Status Quo but without as much success. Sure, they were selling out concerts but they were booking much smaller venues. The hits had dried up to the point where they hardly ventured into the top twenty any more but they were still selling well in Japan, due to their management flooding that market with heavy advertising and even naming their latest album *Japan*. I knew a lot of this information because I had got back in contact with John James when I joined Advent. Even though he was mad at me for leaving when I did, he still followed my career as I did his. It would be interesting to be on tour with him as well as George Turpin and Dapper Dave.

Roy B'Stard was our tour manager keeping watch to ensure that neither band stepped out of line. It was going to be like the old days, and even though Roy could have hired somebody else to keep tabs on us all, secretly, I think he enjoyed the travelling and the challenges we threw at him on the road. We were going to start in Tokyo before heading to Nagoya, Kobe, Okayama, Shizuoka and then Yokohama. That would do for starters. We were still looking forward to performing *Centipede & The Slug* compositions but were going to unveil some of our new compositions to road-test them for worthiness. After a break in the tour, we were to head to Australia and take in concerts at Perth, Adelaide, Sydney, Melbourne and Brisbane.

The tour started well with the Starship being hired once again. It was the first time the Highways had been on board and they ran around with glee, looking into every corner and checking out the facilities. We landed at Tokyo to a huge crowd of fans and curious onlookers, eager to see the Highways in the flesh. Out came the denim-clad foursome, followed by the Advents with a smaller but keen band of followers making their voices heard. On the plane, we had all been discussing how the tour would work because it was clear that Highways were more popular in Japan because of the sheer weight of pre-publicity they had on their side. Advent were okay to go on first for about an hour and then hand over the stage for the rest of the show, coming back for joint band applause at the end. Greg, being a showman, always came back out wearing a traditional Japanese kimono dress (but without the full make up I hasten to add). Tokyo loved the show we gave, so we added a couple of dates to the tour.

We didn't see much of Roy at the start of the tour. He was working in the background, making sure everyone was doing their job; to be fair, we couldn't fault him for that. However, we could tell he had taken a liking to Saki, a fermented rice beverage popular in Japan, and although it isn't as potent a drink as whisky for instance, drunk in large quantities, it can floor even the most experienced drinker. We mentioned to him a few times that he ought to be careful with how much he was consuming, but Roy wasn't the kind of man to take advice and we didn't know that his marriage was on the rocks so he was seeking comfort any way he could. He would only come alive after midday on the day of a concert when we arrived in town and he began putting the road crew through their paces, making sure everything was just so for the show.

After the concert in Tokyo, he was arrested for causing a nuisance in an Izakaya opposite the Budokan where he sat drinking after hours, refusing to leave after the owners had begged him to go home. I got the feeling that the real reason Roy had volunteered for the tour manager position was so that he could get far away from his troubles at home, but it was all to come to a head in the last week of the tour when his wife arrived unannounced in Australia and that is when the shit hit the fan because far from being a reconciliation it turned into a fully-fledged bust up of epic proportions, resulting in fist fighting and bruises - all on Roy.

His wife Sheila was one tough cookie, being an ex-wrestler as well. Funnily enough, she stayed on for the rest of the week as a personal bodyguard in the absence of Roy, who we carted off to the hospital to have his wounds looked at. Sheila was needed almost immediately when Gail returned after being away for two years. She had split from Hal and his chemist's empire shortly after I booted them both off the 1973 US tour when I mistakenly assumed sordid gossip coming from the dressing rooms and reaching the music papers to be coming from them. It was in fact from Ethel the old age groupie, but I didn't tell that to Gail because at the actual moment of our meeting, she had a long-bladed knife in her right hand and that kind of look in her eyes that a woman gives you when you have done something wrong but she is going to make you guess what it may be. Game over. She ran at me with the knife but straight into Sheila's fist.

"shutō-uchi", said Sheila.

One night we were due to play at a small theatre conveniently situated in the grounds of a hotel. I was going down in the lift from the 30th floor to the theatre with my guitar when it came to a sudden halt. I smiled at the occupants who were also on the way to the theatre and had not expected to meet the evening's entertainment on the way down. The lights were on so at least we could see each other and chat. As we were going nowhere fast and there were signs of nervousness among the ladies, I decided to lighten the mood and sing and play for them.

I spoke of how I had been stuck in a lift with Billy Shears one night when our bands stayed at the same hotel after a show. Not the greatest of nights. I also spoke of funny episodes on the road mentioned previously and we were stuck for an hour before the lift began moving again. There had been a minor earthquake which had shut down the electricity supply. The positive reaction from this small gathering gave me the idea of incorporating it into my act and many years later, I would use it as the basis for a one-man show of music and conversation.

Other than Ray and the bust up, and Gail and her knife it had been a successful tour for all and there were hardly any disagreements between the bands, other than what we would choose as a closing group number. We would be going at it for a minute trying to figure out what to play and then someone off stage would shout out "Stand & Deliver!" We would all play the first record that John and I ever recorded. After the tour, John and I agreed to meet on a more regular basis and that is how my life took its next twist.

Gob On You

Advent's demise had started with the Umbooko recordings rebuff. I began holding back some of my best material with an eye on a first solo album, so the follow-up to *LOST* was light on numbers from me. It was a single album with its shortcomings dressed up in a futuristic fancy gatefold sleeve. Released at the end of 1975 it had moderate sales of a couple of million and was not on as pleasing on the ear as our previous efforts. We called it *Earth,* but I had another less subtle name for it. I had already decided I would not tour with the band anymore, and it had nothing to do with the music or any personality clashes.

Ever since the flight back from Africa and the electrical storm, I had been suffering from a fear of flying and it was getting worse. I had to take a lot of Valium to even get on a plane, and though this calmed me down, I was becoming increasingly aware of how much I needed to reach the state where I just didn't care. I required a stiff drink before boarding the Starship to send me to sleep and would have to be carried on and off the plane. The Japanese leg of the tour had been simpler for me because I travelled on the highly efficient Bullet Train (or 'Shinkansen'), and whilst this meant I sometimes had to negotiate excitable fans and hold impromptu autograph signing sessions at my seat, at least I was able to get from gig to gig without a fear of dying or being hit by lightning. It was also quite an experience to race like a demon from station to station.

I had broached the subject of quitting the band and explained how the travelling made me feel, but there was a distinct lack of sympathy because I had gone missing and they had waited for my return before continuing. Now I was ready to give up? It was suggested that I undertake hypnotherapy to see if I could work around this anxiousness, and I did try a couple of sessions but found it to be of little use because it became too much of a challenge *not* to go under and subject myself to who knows what. I didn't want to be in a group hypnosis session and wake up to be told of all the ridiculous things I had been made to do. I didn't want to be part of a circus act.

Reggie Cramwell called me over to PMSL Records HQ one morning. He wanted to know my intentions concerning Advent and whether I would join the band on the upcoming US tour in 1976. Now was the time to crack that market fully because even though we had not been happy with the sales of *Earth* we had Europe lapping up everything we did; likewise, Japan. He wanted reassurance that I would be committed to the tour but I couldn't do that. He brought out a printed document from his desk drawer and pointed out that I had signed to PMSL Records till the start of 1978.

Roy B'Stard was sitting in on the conversation and as Reggie pushed the papers over to me, Roy put a hand over the contract. "I don't think we need to discuss that right now Reggie," he said. "You have more important problems to contend with." I didn't know at the time what hold Roy had over Reggie, but I could tell Reggie was being told to back down. Later I learned of Reggie's marital problems, but Roy had also warned Reggie not to screw over his clients because that was *his* prerogative.

I never officially left Advent. We all took a long break and went off to do solo work and intended to get back together at the end of 76, by which time I meant to have resolved my fear of flying. But the way the music scene shifted that year, I think we dodged a bullet.

The musical landscape changed in 1976 as Punk Rock reared its ugly head. I would have been on the outside looking in and shaking my head like most of the old guard if it had not been for a rainy night in Manchester and needing to find somewhere for a quick toilet break. I had previously explained to John how Advent were as good as finished, which was the premise for the meet-up in Manchester where he now lived. He said the Highways were coming apart at the seams, and he was on the point of quitting. John and I had been drinking in the town centre all day and we filled up with fish & chips before heading back to his digs for the night. It started pouring down, and we stumbled across the Sex Pistols in full flow at the Lesser Free Trade Hall.

I met John the morning after our Saliva gig and at the B&B buffet, over burnt sausages and inedible bacon

& eggs we pondered what we had witnessed the night before. Was it fashionable not play your instruments in tune any more? I picked up a copy of Melody Maker and flicked through its pages. Nothing but the latest on Led Zeppelin, Deep Purple and Jethro Tull as far as I could see.

Who were these Sex Pistols and if they were already known in London and Manchester, maybe we should check them out again? They had a manager Malcolm Mclaren, and later that year he managed to get the Sex Pistols on the *Today* show which was only broadcast on ITV in the London area on weekdays. They were a late replacement for Queen, who had called off their studio visit when Freddie Mercury had to have emergency dental work. Bill Grundy, the presenter of the show, was goading the Pistols to say something outrageous throughout their interview but bit off more than he could chew when all four band members turned the live show blue with their profanities. A clip from the show became one of the most requested clips in the ITV canon and features highly on YouTube views.

After watching this train-wreck of an interview and reading the front-page newspapers screaming out THE FILTH AND THE FURY I was sure it would get them banned for life, but the notoriety fuelled interest in the group, and they became the flag bearers for the punk movement. Of course, all that was in the future but in the present moment, I was contacting John with a brilliant idea.

The week after Saliva made their debut, we met up again at the PMSL Camden recording studios. John didn't recognise me because I had cut off most of my hair, and the beard was gone. I wouldn't be needing that for a while. I now sported a spiky haircut which I thought would shock him and get me in the mood for what I was about to suggest. We were going to make what became known as the first Punk single, and I had been sounding John out as to what I thought would be both catchy and controversial but not controversial enough to get banned before it made an impact on the radio waves. A radio-friendly punk hit was what I was looking for, so I was coming up with all kinds of song titles that would grab the listeners' attention. *Gob On You, Spit In Your Eye, You Make Me Puke...* nothing too fancy at this point. The tune didn't seem to matter as long as it was something you could hang a few choice words around.

We were short of a drummer so I asked Phil Jones the teenage tea boy to sit in on the recording and play with the sticks, but he was quite good at that, and I was too good a guitarist to play badly, so as a last resort I suggested that Phil switch to guitar and I take on the drums. Phil protested that he couldn't play the guitar but I insisted that was the perfect qualification for the role. He strapped on my guitar, and I showed him a chord, then another and finally a third.

"Okay, let's form a band!"

We stuck with the name Saliva because that was the first thing I had come up with when put on the spot in Manchester. We needed to think of individual names and put our thinking caps on and crack open a beer. The Summer of 1976 was the hottest I can remember, and we were all glad for a break and sent someone to go find us all ice lollies. Phil immediately came up with Phil Phlegm, John was Johnny Jerk and I was Choleric Charlie, but that was something we could work on later.

By now a few beers and ices had been consumed and we were bouncing ideas off each other. I was wondering when was the last time I had so much fun in the studio apart from when Apple was fooling around with me.

A thought occurred and I said it aloud: "Wouldn't it be fun if Apple was our singer instead?" It sounded like a great idea and would give the two of us a great excuse to spend more time together on a joint project. Apple had cut my hair and wondered if I was going through a mid-life crisis. *Gob On You* was the more coherent of the songs we played that day, and we recorded it in one take, with an instrumental version for the B-side featuring fake gob sounds in the background to a wall of noise. Put that one as your record of the week, Simon Crisp!

When I approached Apple and explained what John and I were up to she thought it was hysterical and committed herself to the band there and then. She was going to become the centrepiece of the group and wanted her image to be just so and explained it was an excellent excuse to go out and buy some new clothes, not understanding the punks' attitude to dress. Purposely ripped clothes held together by safety pins and tape. Black bin liners as well as rubber, leather and vinyl clothing. She saved her new outfits for another day but wholeheartedly embraced the Mohican wigs and stark make-up. Her only concession to joining the band was that she would not adopt a stage name. She was Apple or nothing.

We got her into the recording studio to add her vocals to our recording and explained we were not looking for a perfect performance. We wanted her to get angry and shout the lyrics if need be. We listened to the playback afterwards and knew we had something good.

Patti Smith, Poly Styrene and Debbie Harry were early examples of females fronting punk bands and it worked for a reason. I couldn't see many ladies following the Sex Pistols or The Clash because they fancied Johnny Rotten or Joe Strummer, but Apple was going to attract male admirers in their droves. With the record in the bag, we tried to manufacture a way of getting it released by PMSL Records. Would it be possible to play what we had to Roy B'Stard and talk about this great band we had discovered and recorded? We could get it released as a joke and play along as everyone at the record company tried to trace them down if it became a hit.

At that point, we never expected *Gob On You* to sell more than ten copies which goes to prove my judgement with hit records. John and I took Roy out for a few beers. We discussed his marital affairs, and he was open about how he and Sheila were going through a trial separation after the Australian escapades. We stopped drinking and asked him to come to the studio and listen to something we had been recording. I knew that Roy didn't pay much attention to my work with Advent so played him a few of the later tracks we had recorded, which he nodded along to in the agreement and then I pulled the masterstroke. I put on the Saliva track and his eyes lit up. "Who is that?" he asked. I feigned a nonchalant opinion of the song and he asked me again more earnestly to tell him who it was.

I explained it was a punk band who had come into the studio and over a few drinks, we had recorded the song. He asked if I knew the band and I said no, but I was sure I could find out who they were. I told him that

John and I had written the song and his eyes lit up as cash symbols. When I played the completed 45 to Joyce she immediately sent promotional copies of the single to all the music papers and radio stations with no further details other than writing 'Who Are Saliva?' and leaving it to the press to wonder who was behind the music.

To get around the problem of not providing the real identities of those on the record we hired a couple of musicians to audition the song to the record company. Apple was able to deliver the vocals again because she came in full punk regalia and nobody recognised her. I wish I could have filmed the reaction of the record label executives who were drooling over her and not listening to the fact that the song they were listening to bore no relationship to the master tape. Our plan worked like a dream. In a month, the record was due to be released and John, Apple, Phil and I were laughing when we saw the music paper ads for *Gob On You* alongside Advent advertising. If only they knew. Joyce arranged publicity interviews, which were also amusing because we still had to keep up the pretence of not being the artists. We stuck with hiring the same musicians to speak on our behalf with some pre-rehearsed lines.

Then came the day when *Gob On You* was reviewed in the daily papers. They hated the song with a passion and dismissed us as no-hit wonders. The music press were fairer, pointing out it was the first punk single, and older generations would detest it: something your parents would hate. This last sentence must have ignited the readers' curiosity because the very next week, we heard it had entered the lower regions of the chart at no 37. This was mostly by word of mouth because until that point, I'm sure it wasn't getting played on BBC Radio. It wasn't high enough to be played on the chart rundown on Sunday, which only featured the top 20. It was high enough to startle the Radio 1 DJs who were unsure if they were allowed to play it or if it was to be banned to discourage spitting. There was a high-level meeting where it was decided the song could be played but only after an 8:00pm watershed on BBC stations. Meanwhile, *Walk On The Wild Side,* with its sexual overtones, continued to be played at all times of the day.

The first DJ to play our song was John Peel, who described it as the best song he had ever heard. Or was it *Teenage Kicks* by The Undertones, or something by The Buzzcocks? Never mind - we were off to a good start by getting an approving nod from Radio 1's most esteemed DJ. The following week we were in the top 20, which posed a potential problem for the BBC. Were they going to play our record on The Official Top 20 countdown that Sunday? Yes, they were, and it just got better because we were also invited to appear on *Top Of The Pops.*

I don't know why the BBC had a change of heart and allowed *Gob On You* to grace the airwaves and I wonder whether it was because they saw us as a novelty record and thought no harm could come from a bit of fun. How wrong they were. In the space of a year, the Sex Pistols, The Clash and assorted three-chord wonders would kick down the doors of decency and come crashing through, turning the music world on its head whilst everyone figured out just what had happened to popular music. The Sex Pistols had written the unofficial soundtrack to the Queen's Silver Jubilee, and the music establishment and the elderly general public were up in arms as youth culture swept the country. The Sex Pistols were once quoted as saying that Prog Rock was boring, but Johnny Rotten admitted he had two Alvin Stardust albums. Work that one out.

My last appearance on *Top Of The Pops* had been in 1972 when I was hoping to catch the eye of Babs Lord, but since then she had left the show, much to my disappointment. On the show that week were Terry & the Tinsels, so another chance for Billy and I to lock horns. Billy and his band had not fared so well since the glory days of Glitter. It had proved to be a fad and hadn't lasted much longer than last year's Christmas decorations. By the end of 1974, Glitter Rock was well and truly over and Terry & the Tinsels were scrambling around trying to hang on to the coat tails of the next passing trend. They became disco kids and were appearing more because of Billy's fame than the strength of the record.

This was to be the unveiling of the actual members of Saliva, and John & I were chuckling at what a stir it would cause. Up to the point of the rehearsals we had not revealed our identities and were using stand-ins, but come to the show recording we had ensconced ourselves in the dressing rooms, put on our Mohican wigs & rubber fetish gear and were ready for action. As luck would have it, the Tinsels were on immediately before us. Simon Crisp absolutely loved their song and said it was bouncing around as a potential chart breaker next week, which is industry-speak for just scraped into the top 40 by the skin of its teeth. He then grimaced and introduced us through clenched teeth as he must have thought we sounded disgusting and looked absolutely horrified as he caught sight of me. Our eyes locked as he remembered me but could not place where he had seen my face before.

He looked from me to Apple in her fishnet tights and back again to me in leather as we ripped through our song in precisely 2 minutes and 30 seconds.

All the time we got to the chorus of "spit on you, spit on you, all I wanna do is spit on you." I was gesturing over to the other stage at Billy as he watched on in amazement. He eventually stomped off to his dressing room, but was to be in for a shock when he got there and saw all the graffiti over the mirrors and walls. There was a shriek, and just as we finished our song, Billy jumped onto the stage and swung out at anything that moved.

Billy wrote in his biography: *"My dressing room was covered in filthy graffiti, and I knew who had done it. Bloody Caine again. He had even nicked all my stash! I didn't wait for him to return to his dressing room, and was on him as he made his way back off the stage. My height worked to my advantage as I got in quite a few below-the-belt blows on him. I was sure he would get booted off the joke of a record label he was on at the time, but far from being sacked, they applauded him for all the extra free publicity he stirred up."*

Gob Save The Queen

Saliva were called into PMSL HQ the day after the *Top Of The Pops* episode was shown. The BBC had contacted PMSL to say there had been a disturbance at the recording of the show and to expect the Metropolitan Police to be in contact regarding criminal damage to BBC property. We protested our innocence because we were too busy preparing for our performance to mess around in another band's dressing room. The police had interviewed everyone backstage and confirmed we had been nowhere near the Tinsel's dressing room. We were also the innocent party regarding the violence after our performance. Apple had run off stage to escape the melee as Billy had thrown punches at everything and everyone, hitting a camera operator and knocking over a stage set. Ruby Flipper, the dance troupe, were legs akimbo as they fell over each other, and dear old Simon Crisp was wailing about allowing yobs into the studio.

There was also discussion regarding the band and its members. Why had we gone to so much trouble to keep our identities a secret? We were treating it all as a joke and explained that we thought it would create a bit of a stir when our identities were revealed on the show, but we never expected anything like what had occurred. Joyce said she could not have planned it better, and the media saturation after the event would keep our names in the press for weeks. The Metropolitan Police had been in contact to say there were to be no charges against Saliva, apart from one of crimes against music (a little constabulary humour there). The mystery of who had defiled the changing room went unsolved for many years until recently, when an ex-manager of Billy Shears owned up to wrecking the dressing room after a business deal with Billy went wrong.

The question being asked of Saliva now was, where do you go from here? I still believed that the Saliva project had a short shelf life, but we would pump it for all it was worth. Punk was going to be a charm that would only be broken when people sat up, took notice of what they were listening to, and realised that it was only a case of style over substance. We set about thinking of ideas for our next single, which would be timed for the Christmas market. While doing this, we filmed a very basic video to accompany the single but were careful not to make it too vulgar in case it was not shown on *Top Of The Pops*. The BBC were a little nervous about us returning to the show until the fuss from our first performance had died down, so a video would be a great alternative. The director had a thing for Apple and crammed as many provocative shots into the two-and-a-half minutes as possible.

(Let's Have A) Glue Sniffing Christmas was the tentative title for our second single. I was trying to get a title with tinsel in there as a wind-up to Billy Shears, but it wasn't forthcoming. We recorded the song in one take just for authenticity and threw in a few jingle bells to get the

listener in the Christmas mood. For the B-side, we followed the previous pattern of an instrumental version with various unsavoury gobbing sounds.

We were all gathered around the radio when the following week's chart was announced. It was up to No 9 and creating quite a stir, with NME and Melody Maker all looking to have an exclusive interview with us. We weren't ready for this, so Joyce sent out a press release with our bios for a laugh:

Apple - Vocals
Likes: Ponies
Dislikes: Simon Crisp
Favourite Pastime: Singing in the bath

Johnny Jerk - Bass
Likes: Gobbing
Dislikes: Prog Rock
Favourite Pastime: Unprintable

Choleric Charlie - Drums
Likes: Sniffing Glue
Dislikes: Johnny Jerk
Favourite Pastime: Gobbing

Phil Phlegm - Guitar
Likes: Tea
Dislikes: Led Zeppelin
Favourite Pastime: Annoying Johnny Jerk

In June 1977, the UK held a big party in honour of The Queen's Silver Jubilee. Whole streets closed down and tables were laden with food and drink as communities came together and made a great day of it.

Punk was the soundtrack to the Jubilee, with the Sex Pistols being denied the No 1 spot with *God Save The Queen* when everyone knew the charts had been rigged not to offend HRH. I've never been a Royalist and had no qualms about offending her or even officialdom.

We bit off more than we could chew with the release of *Churchill Is A Punk Rocker.* The band had been out drinking one night with the music press to chat about the single, which was a spoof of the Ramones song *Sheena Is A Punk Rocker.* We were all walking near the Houses Of Parliament when John, aka Phil Phlegm shinned up Churchill's statue and stuck his punk hairpiece on at a jaunty angle, cheered on by all and sundry, including the same press lads who had been plying us with drinks. It was all a setup and we should have known better. The four of us felt the long arm of the law and were taken to the police station, where our wrists were slapped and were verbally warned about repeating our actions or else we would not get away so lightly. It was all over the front pages of the gutter press in later editions of the morning papers and went nicely with news about the new single being released. So, I ask, who was using who?

Questions were raised in Parliament the next day. Prime Minister James Callaghan was all for bringing back National Service and had installed us as public enemy No 1. I explained to the press that I was too old to be up for National Service. I had managed to avoid it the first time and was not about to start afresh at 34. Not to be outdone by the Pistols hiring a boat on the Thames to take a drunken ride from Westminster to Tower Bridge, Joyce hired a red top bus and we were driven around Central London, playing to tourists who would stop us and ask to board the bus for photos. We even made a tenner in fares. This helped promote an image that Saliva were the good boys of punk, an idea that we were happy to promote when we were in trouble with the law. We weren't arrested but had a big cake fight at the end so the press could get their photographs.

Brian and Keith got back in touch with me in 1977 and asked when I would be returning to make a new record with Advent. I hadn't given much thought to recording with them again because Saliva had given me a more youthful approach to music, and I couldn't go back to a recording process when everything had to be just so and perfect, mostly all recorded on 16 track as it was at the time. I liked a more direct approach to music where the band could play mostly together and not worry about a perfect result. Prog was on life support, if not actually dead according to Punks, and with Punk in 1976 being a year zero for music where nothing before it was of consequence, I couldn't have a foot in both camps. I told Brian and Keith they ought to release a 'best of' compilation to keep things ticking over because I was too busy making Saliva's first LP.

We were at the vanguard of Punk novelty, cornering the market before punk was fully established as a musical trend. We couldn't have it all to ourselves for long because of acts like the Rezillos, Toy Dolls, Splodgenessabounds, Jilted John and then Kenny Everett with his magnificent Gizzard Puke punk caricature. We could either quit before we ran out of ideas or go out in a blaze of glory with the mother of all stunts.

I always liked to check out the opposition and went into my local record shop looking for the Buzzcocks' latest LP. It was called *Love Bites,* and I asked the rather attractive-looking young woman at the till if she knew where I could get love bites. She gave me a cheeky smile and said it wasn't in stock, but if I was free later after 6, we could head to the back room when things had quietened down in the shop and have a good old rummage around in the Punk section, and that's exactly what we did.

Saliva now had three hit singles and were currently working on the rest of the album that was due to be released on the Queen's birthday. We had plans to invite her to its launch outside Buckingham Palace in June. Reggie and PMSL Records did not have a problem with my work with Saliva, and as long as I was making music that was selling well, they were content to leave things as they were. Besides, Advent could continue without me as they were multi-talented and no one-man band.

Roy wanted to discuss *The Centipede & The Slug* and bring me up to date with the plans to make it into a musical. The script had been written and rewritten so many times and in so many ways by so many people that the project had been temporarily shelved in 1974 as unworkable. Andrew Lloyd Webber now wanted to revive the story by bringing it up to date with a more contemporary feel and making the slug an angry young punky slug and the centipede his love interest was going to win his heart and tame him. We were also in the running to record a soundtrack to the film *Punk Panther*, but Peter Sellers was against the idea, so that project was quietly set aside.

We completed the album, *Gobbed On You* at the same time as the Winston Churchill incident but were unable to invite Lizzie to a party outside Buckingham Palace. The release date was for August so we kept ourselves busy giving controversial interviews and stirring up other musicians by saying our songs said more for today's youth than theirs ever could. The first week of sales was steady but not spectacular, and so Roy B'Stard arranged at short notice for us to appear at *Pebble Mill at One* on the 17th August.

Pebble Mill was a BBC show that aired every weekday, and on this particular day, I believe it was Jan Leeming who was interviewing us in our full regalia. Roy had said to try and drum up more controversy, but could not have imagined the furore that our interview was about to cause worldwide.

News broke the day before that Elvis Presley had died, and we were asked to give a soundbite on the man and his career. I've never hidden that I liked Elvis since the Fifties, despite what I have already written about Punk and Year Zero. Before I could say my piece, Phil Phlegm jumped into the conversation and made an off-the-cuff remark along the lines of Elvis being way past his sell-by date and a fat washed-up loser, and how were they ever able to stuff him into his jumpsuit? When Jan reminded him that she was asking him about Elvis' contribution to music and not an opinion on his appearance, Phil requested someone order a large burger, fries and a fat Coke for after the interview to toast the 'huge' legend with his favourite food. I explained to Jan that Phil was of a younger generation that had not grown up in the Rock n' Roll years, but the damage had been done.

The next day his quotes were all over the newspapers, clips of the show were being shown across the globe and listeners were phoning radio shows to register their disgust at the insensitive comments. Hot on the heels of the Winston Churchill incident, this was just fanning the fire of controversy and the last thing we needed. Talk about saturation coverage.

Record shops were having to deal with angry customers wanting to remove and damage our records. They took to buying them so they could burn them publicly in the parks and on the streets. It was claimed that we had stirred up the controversy in time for the launch of the new LP but that was far from the truth. Then it emerged what I had done in the late Sixties when I gate-crashed Graceland with the Highwaymen. It had been hushed up because nobody had heard of Charlie Caine at that time but now the story was all over the tabloids.

PMSL Records were not laughing about the extra publicity. There were threatening letters by the sackful from people saying how disgusted they were about our criticism of a music legend who could not defend himself, and how they were going to come down and sort us out and called for the band to be booted off the label. *The Elvis Mafia* (a group of Elvis Presley's friends, associates, employees and cousins) had seen the footage and were outraged at how we had sullied the name of Elvis and, more sinisterly, there were death threats from fans.

Teddy Boys and Punks were fighting on the streets outside the label's offices with their contrasting views and Reggie had his Rolls Royce damaged as he attempted to drive through the hordes on his way to the underground car park. Even my home in Highgate was no refuge from the madness. My address had been leaked by a mischievous press member, and the police were called on a few occasions to disperse the crowd. Reggie suggested that the four of us needed to get away for a few weeks until it all blew over - to a remote Scottish island, for instance - but I knew where I needed to go. Back to Mum.

Ghost In The Machine

I hadn't seen Mum for a while, what with the touring and all that. Even though I lived in the UK, I did not get back to Edmonton to see her half as much as I should have. We spoke on the phone often but there's nothing quite as good as a face-to-face conversation. She was in her late fifties and still did things that made me laugh.

Her latest laugh-out-loud story resulted from my buying her a microwave oven. They were becoming commercially available in the late Seventies, so I convinced her how easy it would make her life in the future as microwavable meals became readily available. For now, she could cook a jacket potato and heat things like soup rather than use a conventional stove. She liked that idea and so one day, she thought she would make a rice pudding. She had overestimated how long this would take and took it out of the microwave, and found the result resembled a solid brick of rice. There was no way it was fit for human consumption, so she left it out in the garden to cool down while she decided how to prise the rice out of the bowl without smashing it.

She forgot about it overnight and when she looked in the garden the next day, the birds had been having a go at it and had made a little headway with their beaks. She left them at it, but afterwards had guilty thoughts that in future the birds of Edmonton may be hereditarily challenged, with wonky beaks after their forefathers' (or forefeathers') battle of the bowl of rice.

When I arrived at her home, I was pleased to see Frankie was already there. He was filling Mum in with all the juicy details of my life so there wasn't much I could add. Even though Frankie and I had not been recording with Advent for over a year, we had remained in contact and he was my unofficial Advent connection with news on the band. He still wanted us all to get back to recording and had been filling in his spare time in the studio, recording several local bands. We sat down and discussed my current problem with Elvis and were thinking of how we could defuse the situation. I could give a non-apology where I said something like, "I'm sorry that you felt that way about what my band member said about Elvis" but that wouldn't sound sincere. Mum suggested running an apology in the music papers but that was too obvious. It had to be an apology with a difference to show we regretted Phil's off-the-cuff remark.

As I drove home, I considered what we needed to do for some good publicity. What could Jenny and I do to defuse this situation? It had to be extremely clever. It had to be something that apologised to everyone, not just to the Elvis fans. A tribute to Elvis that said we did care and appreciate his work? Now I was on to something. How about a record... a charity record? A record with all funds going to a charity that Elvis would have chosen? I pulled the car over and started writing a couple of lines down and when I had sufficient notes, I began humming a tune as I drove home.

I arrived back late and the crazy demonstrators had gone home for the night but they would be back the next morning. I called up Apple, Phil, John and Jenny in turn and discussed what I had in mind and they thought it was a great idea. With the approval of PMSL Records we went back to the recording studios and laid down *We're Sorry, Elvis* which I had written as our apology and tribute to the King of Rock n' Roll. We even made a video to accompany the song with all of us dressed in a different era of Elvis. I had the Fifties version, Phil had the Hollywood version, Apple took the 1968 leather-clad Elvis, whilst John claimed his *Aloha From Hawaii* rhinestone jumpsuit.

I was looking for an excuse to make a video for one of our songs because although Queen and *Bohemian Rhapsody* was not the first video ever made, I could see what a visual representation of a song could do for sales and popularity. A decent video could turn a bad song into a popular one. (I'm thinking of most of Billy Shear's back catalogue as I write this.) On the other side of the coin, it could turn a poor song into a terrible one

For the video, we split the screen into four quarters and had each of us representing Elvis simultaneously as we sang the song. We were going to sing it Punk style but decided to have a retro Fifties Rock n' Roll feel to it. Later that day we recorded a Punk version for the B side when we couldn't think of anything else at short notice. When we watched the finished video, we were pleased with the result and waited to see how the public would react to the song when it was released.

We didn't want to go on *Top Of The Pops* to play the song so sent the video to be shown and sat around a television at PMSL Headquarters Thursday night to gauge the audience's reaction. We were pleasantly surprised there was little booing when our video was introduced. There was so much controversy to do with the group that the BBC decided to play our song even before it charted; a feature of the show in the early Seventies. The test of its popularity would come the following week when the record hit the shops.

It had been decided to ask Elvis and his contacts where he would have wanted the song profits to be sent, but he could have sent them to the RSPCA for all it mattered because right then we were only interested in some good news for us and a positive outcome to the sorry affair. The signs were good. Not everybody was buying the record to burn it. We had asked for the record sleeve to carry a message saying we were donating all money raised to charity to drive home the point that we would not benefit in any way.

The following week the song charted, and within a month, it had reached the top spot. More interviews followed and we made sure to Sellotape Phil's mouth for these, following on from the amusing front cover of the single. We then played a concert at Finsbury Park as part of a Punk festival. We only intended to play a couple of numbers but were on stage for half an hour and ran through some of the new LP, which got a decent reception. Roy B'Stard met me offstage after the show and said that audience feedback had been good and the punks were on our side.

I told everyone I needed a holiday to recharge my batteries for a few months. We all did. I had done some research and concluded that I could build a recording studio and save a lot of time and money by using my own facilities. I found a tiny location in Crouch End that was previously a place of worship and had been tastefully rebuilt to function as a recording studio. It also doubled as a small resting place for me to stay overnight if the work finished late and the artists or I did not want to travel. I named it Caine Studios.

I wholly gutted the previous recording facilities and installed 24-Track recording (the best available at the time), which meant we could record on 2" tape. I still had all the tapes from the Congo that I wanted to use for a solo project and was going to get them backed up at the recording studio and see how I could utilise them for what I had in mind. The drums could be used as the beat to a new type of music. I could hear what I wanted but was unsure how to put it into words to get musicians to play it back to me. It was the sound of two drummers playing at once. Bow, Wow, Wow beat me to it by releasing *C30, C60, C90 Go!*, but using their sound as a guide, I began searching for musicians who could play in the style I wanted.

I found just what I was looking for when I went to the West Country for a week. Between Cornish cream teas and pasties, I saw Morris Dancers performing in a pub. Here is a misunderstood type of music and performance if ever there was one. A Fifteenth Century form of entertainment that creates bafflement even in Cornwall where it is said to have originated. They went dancing into the pub and out again, causing merriment to all who watched. As I listened, I thought of what it would take to bring this type of music up to date-and relevant. Add some acoustic guitar and it was Steeleye

Span - no, that was a bit too obvious. How about a backing track of my recordings from the Umbooko people? After explaining who I was and what I had in mind, I took some contact details, more in hope than expectation, and said I would be in contact during the week. I did some recordings on my cassette player to take home with me and see how these types of music could fit together because even I had doubts at this point.

Roger Magneti asked to come over to see how the studio was progressing and I told him he was welcome any time he chose. I was counting on Roger to show me how to use this new toy because I had taken a back-seat view of the recording process and needed a more hands-on approach. Now was the time to learn. I played to him all I had recorded of the Umbooko people and he remembered the reaction when I had played the cassettes to the band. I asked if we could at least get them onto audio tape because I was afraid I would lose these recordings one day, mangled up in the cassette player which was a regular risk with cassettes. I had ten tapes of varying quality and length and Roger picked out about an hour's worth of decent recordings from them, though it was quite a laborious process going through them all. We stuck this on two 30-minute reels.

I asked him what he thought of the Morris Dancing idea and he thought I was nuts, but he said that if I wanted to record something entirely out of my comfort zone, why not listen to a tape he had of pan and flute music from Peru that he had in his car. When we put the two together, it was a perfect match. It would never sell by the bucket load but it would show I would never be pigeon-holed. I asked Roger if he knew where we could find some decent musicians so we could record the Peruvian music to a higher standard. In the next few days, he assembled three men in the studio. I asked if they could play a standard composition so we could get the recording levels correctly aligned. They played the opening number from *The Centipede & The Slug*, which I assumed was a joke by Roger but was in fact a best-selling single in Peru in 1972. Who knew? When Roger aligned the drum beat from the Umbooko it sounded like it was meant to be. Over the next few weeks, we recorded enough for an LP.

Apple came into Caine Studios the night of its official opening. Roger was there and the rest of Saliva and a few close friends. In all, a round dozen. She had brought a bag of Tetley's with her, which I thought was for a brew up, but she explained that she was now into tea leaves and I ought to make her a cuppa and then scatter the leaves onto a tissue so she could read them. After looking at the results, she explained that it was unsafe to ever enter the recording studio again. I asked her what she meant. Apple explained that it wasn't the tea leaves she was referring to. A male spirit in the room wanted us out of the building.

"Do you think I still haven't been forgiven for the Elvis Presley slur? Is he a fan? Or is it the music I'm recording?"

"We need to go now," said Apple. "Immediately. And please don't make any jokes about Elvis."

"He wants me out?"

"He does. He says it's unsafe for us to be here." Apple sounded highly nervous.

"Don't be ridiculous. There's no such thing as ghosts or spirits or the supernatural."

The lights went out at that precise point.

Pause.

"Err.. hello? Would you mind so much turning the lights back on? I'm all shook up"

The lights immediately came back on.

I asked Apple how she had sensed the presence in the room. Why hadn't she told me about it on her previous visits to hear how my work was progressing? She said she had noticed a slight temperature change on her last visit but tonight it had been more pronounced and whoever the spirit was had been keen to be noticed by her and had a lot to say about the work I was creating. I was intrigued by this and asked her for an opinion by our spirit.

"Oh yes, he thinks you could do much better if you put your mind to it. He thinks you should scrap the Peruvian nonsense and record a solo album from your Congo tapes or utilise them for another project. I'm no expert though."

"Well, that was pretty good for a start. Did he say that?"

"No - it was written down in the dust on your desk. Don't you ever clean the office?"

"What did he write?"

"Your music sucks, try again," said Apple, "I just filled in the blanks from that!"

Everyone was listening to the conversation and asking Apple how they could learn more from the presence. Apple explained that the only way to find out who was in the studio with us was to hold a séance, and she was not an expert on this but knew a medium who would jump at the chance of contacting the spirit world. Would everyone in the room be able to come back tomorrow? It would be best if everyone there was in on the séance because the spirit would probably be more receptive to the same crowd. We all agreed - a little nervously but with a lot of curiosity as to what we were dealing with.

The next evening, we all assembled in the studio for an 8:00pm start. Apple introduced her friend Gregory, our medium for the night who would host the séance, and he ran through how he worked and what to expect. Firstly, he preferred to work by candlelight, which created a mood to encourage the spirit world to communicate. We lit twelve candles and placed them around the studio, providing a lovely glow to the surroundings. Music worked best for him in the background and being in a recording studio, this was perfect. He would explain that more as the evening progressed.

"Should we hold hands?" someone suggested.

"Not unless you're a steaming Jessie" Gregory responded.

Everyone laughed at this and the mood relaxed. Gregory explained that audience participation for now was minimal. Once he had made contact with the spirit, we could then ask questions and whoever we were in contact with could respond through him. "So, I hope you have lots of questions written down. You won't have to bring me out of the possession because the spirit will know when it is tired of talking and will go. Apple has seen me at work before so follow her lead. She's worked with me for a while and knows all the cues and how to get the best results. Are you all ready?"

He produced a tape recorder which he switched to play. A light soothing whispering and chanting of voices and piano could be heard over the background hum of the building. He closed his eyes and took a deep breath and slowly exhaled. For a minute, there was complete silence in the studio and then the candles flickered and two went out. I went to relight them but Apple stopped me. Gregory was muttering to himself and then sat bolt upright and stared into the distance.

Apple asked, "Who are you and what is your name?"

"Ande," replied the spirit through Gregory.

"How long have you been here?"

"Since the electrocution," was the response.

Searching High And Low

Ande communicated with us for the rest of the evening and from what we learned and from subsequent library research, Ande was a record producer who worked with many prominent artists of the Sixties but decided he wanted a recording studio of his own so he could tinker with whatever took his fancy. He only had a 4 track but used this to its fullest extent, recording local artists and even himself at times for his own amusement, but Ande was talented without realising quite how talented he was. One day he was rewiring plugs in the studio when he accidentally electrocuted himself and went into cardiac arrest. His lifeless body was found the next day by a cleaner. That was why he wanted everyone to leave because he still regarded the studio as unsafe. The press cutting said that his parents died when he was young and he was survived by a sister.

On a second evening with just Apple, Gregory and I, Ande revealed there was a cupboard in the studio containing some of his recordings. I had not seen anything like a cupboard when the studio was being refurbished but Ande insisted it existed and described its precise location. Unfortunately, all I could see was a smooth wall in its place, which we hadn't felt needed repainting, but I rubbed my hands over the section and found nothing.

The following evening, when I was alone in the studio, I took to tapping the wall to see if there was a difference in sound. After covering a 10 ft square area, I struck gold. There was a hollow sound, so I pencilled in where the sound was most prominent and then scraped with a penknife to see if I could find a crack or a gap. I was on the point of taking a break when I found an indent, worked my penknife in some more, and worked the incision for 8 inches to a point where the indent headed upwards. There must be a drawer flush against the wall. Why would anyone paint it over like that? Knowing the rough shape of the drawer, I got a chisel and a hammer and began working at the gap in earnest. There was a splintering sound as part of the drawer broke and I could make out books and writing material plus what looked like recording tapes. I coughed from the dust created and continued working away with the chisel until I could get at the contents. I somehow managed to pull the drawer out; it looked as though it had not been opened in years.

I picked out a folder stuffed with papers, blew away more dust, and sneezed. I could make out written on a folder *'Words And Music By Ande Krick'.* Inside, meticulously written songs were enclosed. I could not read music and would get Roger to look at these folders later. Also in the drawer were some day-to-page diaries with recording details, personal thoughts, and such. A bunch of phone numbers were filled in at the back, and

I noted all had ladies' names. Was Ande a ladies' man? I laughed.

There were about 15-20 tapes of mostly good quality that I could listen to there and then. I imagined it was something he must have recorded for someone and was keeping them locked away and were forgotten. I picked one up and cued it up to be played. The tapes looked as good as new as if they had been used once and were fit to play. The first one I heard was introduced as Take seven by Ande. It was a simple song with acoustic guitar, piano, and orchestration and played quite beautifully, and at the end, it occurred to me that it was Ande who was the creator of the work. I played some of the others and they were of the same quality. Why had Ande not tried to get these released? Even in this demo form, his work was of a high standard.

There was so much to look at that I took the drawer and contents home to examine overnight. I also phoned Roger, told him what I had found, and suggested he meet me at the studio the next day if he was not working elsewhere. I looked at a 1965 diary and began to read. Ande certainly was the ladies man I had imagined him to be, with details of his dates and conquests, alongside ratings of 1 to 5. I'm unsure if the rating was his opinion of the date or his performance! Maybe it was best not to know. I wondered about Ande's family and if there were any contact details to give me a lead on whom to get in touch with and tell of my discovery. There were also 1966 and 1967 diaries but the latter was only half full. I guessed that was up to the point of his death. Buried at the bottom of the drawer amongst some private papers, was a photograph of a young man of about 30. Was this Ande? It was much more difficult to research a person before the dawning of the Internet.

The first thing Roger did when he arrived at the studio the next day was to inspect the tapes. "I wouldn't want to be the one who mangled all this material if it's as good as you say it is," he said. This took up most of the morning because a couple of the tapes had snagged a little and he had to make sure they were fit to play. They sounded remarkably fresh and I would not have guessed from the music that they dated back to the mid-sixties. They were the sound of a singer/songwriter and if these recordings had become widely known at the time they may have ushered in the singer/songwriter era a lot sooner. We reviewed all the recordings that day and concluded that this body of work needed to be made available to the public.

The biggest problem was: whom did it belong to? Ande had owned the studio and it was his work so we had to find his family. I went through all the diaries and there was no mention of other family members besides his sister Sarah Smith, whom I had seen in the newspaper cuttings at the library. We were simultaneously the curators of this beautiful body of work and detectives as to whom it belonged. Roger set about making notes on how many songs were on each tape and giving each a working title from Ande's comments throughout the recordings. The 15 analogue tapes had 3 or four songs each, which meant up to 60 songs' worth of material. There was enough for 4 or 5 decent albums alone.

In the meantime, I looked in the London phone book and began phoning every Sarah Smith. It was soon apparent that this would be a fruitless task because of how many Sarah Smith's there were and not just in London. Roger suggested we tell the music press of our find and the search for this work's rightful owner. Even though Ande had been a successful producer, there were no apparent clues from those he had worked with. Nobody could remember him discussing his family. All thoughts of recording any more material with Saliva or even Advent was put to one side until we found this elusive lady, and the days and months went by as we continued to clean up what little blemishes remained in the recordings and add the orchestration to these songs in the manner most had been recorded in.

It wasn't until 1980 (and in fact, I think it was mere days into the new decade) that Sarah Smith contacted us from Saskatchewan, a Canadian province where she had lived since 1970. She had been alerted through friends who read in the local Music Express magazine that we were looking for her concerning her late brother Ande. It had taken over a year for the story of our search to reach Canada, but though she knew my name, she had to find out how to contact me. She bought an imported copy of NME and wrote a letter asking if they could get a message through to me, and that's how one day I got a call from Fred Williams from the magazine to say he was coming over with Sarah. He was after an exclusive interview with Sarah and I, and to listen to her brother's work.

After Sarah arrived, Fred, Roger and I sat down in the studio and I played her some of the finished songs. I told her the story of how we were led to find all her brother's hidden work and asked if she knew her brother had any thoughts of becoming a musician. Sarah said he had written lots of poetry when he was young and wondered if he had used that in any of the work? She loved what he had recorded and got quite emotional to discover just how talented her brother had been. They had lost contact in the Sixties when she had the urge to go to Canada and had only heard of Ande's death in the early Seventies. Her parents had moved to the UK from Eastern Europe after the war but both died young and Sarah did not recall them speaking of any other relatives. She had intended to keep travelling but met a man in Saskatchewan and ended up marrying and divorcing him a few years later.

What did we intend to do with the recordings? she asked. We explained that the reason for searching for her was that we could not proceed with the release of the music till we had permission from Ande's family to do so. We could release them through PMSL records and royalties etc would all go through to her. Our interest was in getting this great music heard. When we released the first album in 1980 the sales went through the roof. Everybody wanted to know the tragic story of Ande Krick and hear the music of a man so cruelly denied success. Sarah had stipulated that Roger and I were to share in the profits made from record sales and to this day, I don't need to work anymore due to the continued interest in Ande's work. Five albums were released in the Eighties, and then the inevitable greatest hits compilations.

I had countless interviews and appeared on TV just as often, till one day an interviewer said, "aren't you the guy who wrote *The Centipede & The Slug*? I hear it's currently running off-Broadway." That was news to me. With Andre's posthumous music career now getting the attention it fully deserved, I felt I should get back to my own. Advent and Saliva had been in self-imposed hibernation. The latter had passed its sell-by date, and Advent was keeping a low profile because punk bands like mine referred to Prog groups as dinosaurs of Rock. It was time to get back in touch with Advent and find out about the stage show. The trouble was the band were none too keen on reforming because most of them had moved on musically and were working on other projects. It was time to record a solo album.

I spent two weeks locked away in the study just writing music and not speaking to anyone, other than the man at the corner shop who sold me my newspaper every morning. It was at this point that I got a call from one of my close friends to come and meet him at Edmonton Rovers FC

Match Of The Day

From an early age I supported my local football team, Edmonton Rovers. They played close to the Great Cambridge Road, the main route north of London. I would go to many of their home games with John James in our pre-Toe Tappers days and when I didn't have a gig.

When you are a football fan, you form a bond with a team and tend to stay with them for life. Edmonton Rovers were never going to win the F.A. Cup and would never reach Division One, which was as high as you could go in English football before Sky TV came along and changed our beautiful game with their wads of cash and players with inflated egos. A game that used to belong to the working man, and now you need a mortgage to take out a season ticket at Manchester United. Not at Edmonton Rovers. Rovers always bumped along at the very bottom of the Non-League ladder.

They played in the Poseidon League, which consisted of clubs within London and the surrounding areas of Essex and Hertfordshire. In those far-off days, there was no pyramid system where a non-league club with ambition could reach the Football League through successive promotion. Players were part-time, and the majority had day jobs that had to fit around their football activities, or was it vice versa? None of Rovers' players ever progressed to the Football League, but it was said that Fred King, a former goalkeeper, had a trial for Orient F.C.

I never had a problem getting into their games, even with no money, because I knew where the holes in the fences were. They should have been paying me to watch them; they were that bad. Rovers played their matches at a communal sports arena and the pitch was surrounded by a dirt athletics track that had seen better days and was tinged with clumps of grass here and there. The pitch was bumpy and always needed a good cut and during the winter, it became a quagmire. There was a main stand running along one touchline and a terrace on the other side, covering 300 or so hardy souls.

My visits grew infrequent as touring took me away from my hometown, but I still tried to catch their scores from John Brackley, a friend who used to go to the games regularly. Rovers did okay in the Sixties and I used to sponsor some of their games when I could, but come the Seventies they were facing financial hardship and were on the point of folding. Then my friend John who had now become their programme editor convinced me to come along to a game because I had not been for five years and this may be the last game they ever played. I was shocked to see the club could not afford a proper kit and that the main stand's roof had caved in. John explained that the club was in debt and that the club would fold if they could not pay off the £3,000 that the bank was demanding by the end of the following week.

I was invited into the boardroom before the match for what I thought would be just a drink and nibbles. Club Chairman Bob Tidy suggested that I could have a place on the board of directors and save the club with an injection of cash as Elton Johnson had done at Watford FC. I explained that I would not be a saviour of the club as he hoped I would be. Edmonton Rovers would never make it to the Football League on my money. Still, I could certainly pay off the immediate debt and a little more out of my pocket, plus I could play a concert to raise funds for the club. The roof would have to be fixed and new kit provided for the team and improvements made around the ground to make supporting the club a little more agreeable. I left the club in high spirits that evening, even though they had lost 5-0 to go bottom of the league.

Over the next month, my attendance at the club resumed as I took an interest in how it was being run. Years of neglect by its previous owners had left the club struggling to survive. Bob Tidy had tried to keep control of thc club's expenses and was known to be a cautious man when it came to spending money on the club for fear of running up debts, but his thriftiness had also meant the club missed out on acquiring up and coming local players who went on to have successful careers when all it would have taken to sign them on was an envelope with a wad of notes stuck into a top pocket of the parent as an incentive for their son to sign on the dotted line. Ah, the good old days before players had agents to advise them.

Our team manager quit soon after I joined as the club continued to haemorrhage points at an alarming rate. We needed to find a new manager with an eye for a good player. A man who was crafty with his dealings and was a good man manager. Greg Boroge was the name that kept coming up time and time again. Boroge was between jobs after parting ways with his previous club after a disagreement over wages. I agreed with Reg that we should at least meet Greg and see if he was interested in the challenge of Edmonton Rovers. He had a reputation for taking on clubs with average reputations and turning them into title challengers. Maybe he could turn Rovers into an average side? The three of us met at a Little Chef on the A10 just outside London one cold Saturday morning. Greg was there a good half an hour before us and said he had a thing for punctuality and discipline, which he expected any team of his to adhere to. He also had a thing for the Little Chef early morning breakfast and wanted to make sure he had finished up before we arrived.

"I expect a player to adhere to my work ethic of training, punctuality, persistence, level of focus, and overall dedication to the responsibilities of being a footballer," he said. "Oh - and they'll all have to get haircuts as well. I saw them last week at the Hendon game, and the side looks like a bunch of hippies from the Sixties. No offence, Charlie, but the centre-forward looks like a woman and plays like one too." Greg had already been checking the Rovers out. That was a good sign.

We told Greg that we were not a rich club and did not have a history of success, but the challenge we were setting him would be to build the club from the bottom up in his image. We would provide him with funds for players where we could, though the level of football we were playing at would not require the investment that the likes of Liverpool FC would need to sign a new player. With his contacts within the game, we could turn our season around and dream of winning trophies the year after.

Greg signed a two-year contract and was eager to get to work. He said to ready ourselves to register a whole list of players he was going to bring into the team. He wasn't joking, because there were five new players for the next game, including a goalkeeper built like a brick outhouse, a central defender resembling a tank and two wingers like whippets. We won 2-0 and our supporters went home happy for the first time in ages.

They were even more pleased when the roof to the main stand was fixed and attendances grew on the back of free admission for under 16's at selected matches and cheaper beer inside the ground after 2 pm. We finished the 1979/80 season in a respectable (for us) 15th place just below mid-table. After the final match, Greg gathered the players together and said he had big ambitions for the club the following year which included winning the Poseidon League for the first time and a run in the F.A. Cup. Things were on the up for Edmonton Rovers.

I was still writing new material for my next album. I planned to unveil some of my new work to an unsuspecting public when I played a fundraiser at the ground that summer. A temporarily raised stage was built in front of the main stand, and 3,000 fans gathered on the covered pitch to see me and bop along to a selection of my old Sixties hits and some of my more current ones. I even had calls to perform *The Centipede & The Slug,* but my scratch band were not familiar with the complexities of those numbers. I had gone back to using some of the drum recordings from the Umbooko people but in a rock beat, and very soon after, I released them on my first solo LP. Adam Ant used the same rhythms to far greater success and Paul Simon also incorporated them into his *Graceland* album. The rascals.

Apple called me one night at the football club to say she had some concerning news that could not wait and when I got home, she told me that my recording days were on hold for the immediate future. When I asked her what she was talking about, she said that she had been re-reading the tea leaves and the message she was getting was that it was unsafe for me to enter any recording studio for the next year. I didn't tell her that this was a load of nonsense but from the look she was giving me, I could tell I would have to tread very carefully around this problem. Apple had proven her predictions to be very accurate in the time I had known her, and besides, I was scared of getting on her wrong side! Roger Magneti was running the studio well. I figured there was no need to test Apple unnecessarily, so I would check in from time to time and ensure everything was running smoothly.

Much of my spare time was being taken up at Edmonton Rovers as the club prepared for the new season and I was involved in preparing the ground in readiness for the first fixture. Plans were already underway to extend the main stand, add facilities big enough to host events, and bring in some extra revenue for the club. That season Edmonton Rovers fared well in the FA Cup. They breezed through the qualifying round and made it to the 1st Round Proper. In the Poseidon League, they finished top for the first time in their history. Rovers attempted to apply for promotion to the Isthmian Premier League but it was to be some time before a recognised promotion and relegation system was established within the leagues, so for now it was a case of a job well done by the team and see you all again next season.

It's Music, But Not As We Know It

One evening in early 1981 I was watching *Top Of The Pops*. You could be forgiven for thinking that's all I ever did with my spare time, but even though I was fast approaching my 40th birthday, I still liked to keep up with the music scene. The current sound was Synthpop and I noted many duos of this type of music. No guitars and drums - it'll never catch on, I thought. Who is ever going to want to listen to music with no guitars? It's as though Rock & Roll never happened!

When Donna Summer released *I Feel Love* in 1977, David Bowie said that it pointed the direction that music would head and, though he proved to be correct, I wish he had got it wrong. I prided myself in being there at the beginning of most of the Sixties and Seventies musical genres but this one was passing me by.

In 1981, Japanese machines such as Yamaha, Korg and Roland made synthesizers more affordable. They came with strange names such as 'Odyssey', 'Polymoog' and 'Prophet' and were produced by exotic, elusive manufacturers such as Moog, ARP Instruments, Inc,

EMS and Sequential Circuits. Groups such as Kraftwerk, Space and Giorgio Moroder had hinted at what soundscapes were possible. When Gary Numan & Tubeway Army released *Are Friends Electric* and took it to No 1 in 1979, it opened up the floodgates for the likes of Depeche Mode, OMD, Yazoo, Soft Cell and Human League to dominate the charts.

Now that I had gotten my solo LP out of the way, I felt more inclined to see if I could record some new material in a group setting and though I couldn't see Advent wanting to get involved in this new sound I knew a man who might.

I called Keith Howells to come out for a few beers and a chat. It had been a while since we had gone out drinking but we had kept in touch since the Advent days. Once we finished our usual gossiping about the characters in the music scene and who was doing what to who, we turned our attention to music in general and what had become of rock music. As well as the current synth sounds dominating the airwaves, hair bands were prominent, and you couldn't get away from Adam Ant. I told Keith that he could make better music than the whole lot of them and even beat them at their own game by taking on synth music by showing them how it was done.

"Charlie Caine, are you challenging me?" he said, "because I fancy a challenge."

"You'll have to swap your piano for something a little trendier," I told him. "Do you need a singer? I can do that because I can't play synths."

Keith explained that he could program a keyboard to play automatically, and I had to pretend to play chords. We decided to name the band ZX81. It was an updated version of the ZX71 that Keith had invented/created with Clive Sinclair ten years earlier. I figured that it would be okay to go back to the recording studio now so we locked ourselves away for three days at my studios until we came up with a few decent songs. We knew it wouldn't be easy, but we were professional musicians and ought to be able to come up with something half-decent. We released our first single on the PMSL label, where we got a one-year contract. Once Reggie had stopped laughing at our songs, he said it would never sell because where were the guitars and drums? What would happen if there was a power cut at a concert and we couldn't play anything? But he was willing to sign us out of amusement.

We released our first single *Syntax* to an unsuspecting public in March, and within a month we ran into trouble with Clive Sinclair, who took exception to us using the name of the new home computer he had released the same month. It was a coincidence that both Clive and Keith chose to revisit their past and based the name of their latest project on something they had taken part in all those years ago.

We agreed to meet Clive in Cambridge in the Baron of Beef pub, where we had a full and frank discussion about resolving the matter. We then spoke with my publicist Joyce who came up with an unusual suggestion that Clive liked where we would keep the duo going as ZX81 but would advertise Clive's new home computer on our records and clothing, and Clive would use our music in his games consoles to give us extra publicity. We must have seemed such strange bedfellows - two musicians in their late 30's and at the latter stages of their music career and an entrepreneur and inventor.

Why would we need help to publicise our work after our experience in the music business? We were not as confident as Clive of our product, though he was laughing for the same reasons Reggie thought our project amusing.

He wasn't laughing when young bands started name-checking ZX81 in interviews and hanging out with us after shows. And boy, could we drink those upstarts under the table. We had 25 years of after-show drinking, and these youngsters were probably still in their nappies when we started. The tricks we used to play on them, like writing amusing messages on their foreheads - but nothing mean. We would call a cab and get them dropped off at their hotel or their Mum's house. Things like that.

While I had Clive's attention, I asked him if he could come up with a little something for my guitar. I currently plugged it into a pedal board, the pedal board plugged into a guitar amp. The guitar amp had a microphone that captured all the guitar sound and effects, which fed into the P.A. Could he come up with a more straightforward method of making me sound better?

"Fuck off", he said. "I'm an electronics genius, not a roadie!"

ZX81 were invited onto The Young Ones, a BBC comedy show that featured an up-and-coming band each week and first aired in 1982. Only two series were ever made of the show, but it opened the doors to alternative comedy in much the same way as Monty Python's Flying Circus had in the late Sixties. Keith and I went to the studios to see what the show was about. Clive came along too but left quickly when a bottle prop was smashed over his head as we performed. He decided he didn't want to be associated with a bunch of dirty, smelly students. We performed *Syntax* and took part in a small sequence with Rik Mayall where I pushed him down a flight of stairs during a skit in the show, but the sequence was shelved when Clive said he didn't want his brand being linked to the show. It remains to be seen if the elusive unshown 13th episode we featured in will ever make it onto a box set when the Young Ones is reissued on DVD and Blu-ray.

Aside from this hiccup, the arrangement with Clive worked well, and we became known as the two middle-aged men who were taking on the youngsters at their own game, pretty much like I had done with the Punk rockers a few years before. Very soon, Clive was sponsoring our *Syntax* UK tour and appearing on TV interviews with us. Whilst Clive discussed the latest advances in home computing and microchips. I used to chip in (get it?) that the only chips I preferred had vinegar on them. In addition, we would provide musical entertainment for each show.

Joyce then came to me with a request to present an Outstanding Contribution To Music award to Billy Shears at the end of the year, for which Earls Court had been booked. I was hesitant to say yes, but then she said I had misheard the request: would I like to present an entertainment awards ceremony *with* Billy Shears? The answer was still going to be no, but when I heard who was up for an award and who might be present I couldn't say no because Chuck Berry was rumoured to be coming to collect a lifetime achievement award.

Me and Billy Shears in the same building though. That was always going to be a recipe for disaster. In later years there was the Sam Fox/Mick Fleetwood Little & Large car-crash of an event at the 1989 Brit Awards that was broadcast to a gobsmacked audience. On that particular night, guests were coming on to the stage at the wrong time, errors were made with the winner announcements, and the icing on the cake was a specially recorded winner's acceptance tape by Michael Jackson that was forgotten. If you watched that show, you have a fair idea of what also went down with Billy Shears and me. The height difference didn't help because Billy is nearly a foot shorter than me. Sam Fox and Mick Fleetwood reminded us that height difference doesn't look right on television.

The only saving grace of the night was the event was pre-recorded for broadcast later in the week due to our reputation for fighting. In fact, I'm still searching for a clue as to why anyone would think it was a good idea to put the two of us together. Most of the cursing and such were censored, though I have been told that a full transcript of the night's proceedings is available online if you want to do a little sleuthing after reading this book.

What happened on the night? Well, it started off reasonably well because we had both been warned that many people had staked their reputation that we would work well together on this occasion because of who was attending. I, for one, was happy to be on my best behaviour, and as long as we both kept to a well-rehearsed script and avoided off-the-cuff remarks, there was no reason why it should not have been a successful night. In the audience were our music peers, and I sensed they were waiting to see how this on-stage pairing would pan out.

As the event wore on, I noticed that Billy was beginning to miss a word or two as he read from the autocue. I supposed that some of the words were new to him so he was just reading what he recognised. After a while, I could smell alcohol on his breath and experience told me this was bad news as he was a mean drunk. There were nervous conversations coming from off-stage as the show's producers could see the show falling apart. At a break in the show, I challenged Billy:

"Are you drinking?"

"So what if I am, Caine?"

"Get a grip on it, Billy. Let's not screw this up."

"Screw you. I'm off to the bar for a top-up."

He was not around for the next section of the show, which was the Best Song of 1981. I was just about to read the nominations when Billy suddenly appeared from stage left, knocking me over in his haste to get back on stage. There was stifled laughter as I got to my feet, and I had the urge to push back but thought: no, I'm better than that, and it was just a drunken lunge. I was so determined to meet Chuck Berry and tell him of my walk to see him play in Luton over twenty years ago that I let it go.

"Billy, thanks for rejoining us. Why don't you read out the nominations for Best Single of 1981?"

I laughed to myself because I knew what was coming next. On the shortlist was Depeche Mode with their *Just Can't Get Enough* single. In the rehearsals, Billy had been struggling to pronounce the name of the band, and with his intake of alcohol, I was expecting to be entertained. Instead, he swished the letters around in his mouth and spouted out "Deepish Moan" to a startled but amused audience. Human League became *Human Leg,* and

Adam & The Ants somehow metamorphosed into *Ad Men & The Rants.* By this point, the crowd were laughing themselves silly. They thought it was all part of the act.

One thing about Billy is that you don't laugh at him because he doesn't have a sense of humour. As I wrote, he's a mean drunk, and he was staring out into the audience, ready to have a pop at anyone who was continuing to laugh at him. The first person he saw was a well-known radio DJ laughing, and I know he would not want to be identified so I had better not reveal his name. Billy quickly reminded the man of his attempts at pronouncing Duran Duran.

"Who are DURRRRAN DURRRAN? And, oh yeah - Chic... CHICK???? How long have we got to go through all your gaffes?"

The DJ turned bright red, and I quickly distracted Billy and asked him to announce the nominations before he started ripping into everyone in the front row. The International Artist Of The Year award went to Michael Jackson, who accepted it via a recorded message section, so at least Billy didn't get the chance to botch up the presentation. While the show went to a break, I spoke to the producer and voiced my concerns that my co-presenter was drinking heavily. Could he find someone to step in and take his place as I could sense trouble brewing. He said to keep going, and if Billy looked like he was about to say something offensive, his microphone would be turned off.

Shears' biography laid bare the details of his evening:

"Yes, I was drunk. Drunk and bored. I hadn't expected the show to be so scripted. We were stopping and constantly starting

for each new category, and all I wanted to do was to get the thing done and get to the pub. At one point, I went to the toilet via the dressing room for a quick top up of my hip flask. When I returned, Caine had already started running through the nominations for the next category. It's said I pushed him over in my haste to get to the podium, but I tripped over his ego. I've never been keen on Depeche Mode's music, and yes, I do have trouble with my words from time to time, but then the front row started smirking at me and I let them have it both barrels."

The show continued to go downhill when the wrong autocue notes appeared on the screen. Not our fault, then, that the top TV Drama Show of the Year went to Metal Mickey, and Best Children's Show was awarded to Dallas. I could see the funny side, but Billy was steaming up and accusing the producer of making fools of us. The DJ was trying to hold a smirk back until Billy went and stood in front of him on stage, pointing and shouting, "Don't make me come over and tell you off again..." For the first and only time, I went over and defended him and said that it was actually quite funny, and had the whole crowd laughing when I repeated the mistake back to Billy.

The show went for another break, and no co-presenter came onstage with me when it returned. Billy was back in the dressing room, snoring his head off and in no fit state to continue. It was left to me to continue through the show on my own and I did an excellent job of this because the autocue was still coming up with conversation designed for the two of us, so I had to improvise.

The producer suggested that if I were to perform a song to keep the audience entertained, it would give him enough time to correct this problem. I went on stage and performed a ZX81 song with my acoustic guitar and when the show resumed, I excused Billy's absence by saying he had been taken ill. I believe this was the first time I had been on TV with Billy Shears and we hadn't fought. The fallout from the show was that Billy had blotted his copybook by getting drunk and it would be years before he was back on TV. Nevertheless, my calm handling of the rest of the show would have positive consequences for me in the future. The chance to get ZX81 out to a broader audience helped as well.

We continued our successful partnership with Clive. Despite his arguing that I could have at least plugged his product during the awards show. We would get a perfect chance of that the following year when The Tube TV show was due to begin airing on the newly created Channel 4. The band and Clive were asked to do a feature to be shown on one of the early shows, and we were trying to come up with something witty that didn't seem like advertising but was just that. We suggested something futuristic as the show's opening theme. They liked that idea, so I was trying to figure out how to get a subliminal message in my song, singing "ZX81" into the background. That didn't work because the program chiefs spotted it as soon as I played it. "Oh no, you can't do that these days" they said. "Can't Mr Sinclair just talk about future technology or something?" He could, but how would they edit a thirty-minute section down to a minute? I made some off-the-cuff remarks about Clive and thought nothing of it.

Two days later, I had a phone call from an irate Clive who said the partnership was ended. When I asked why he said it was because I had been talking about him behind his back. But when I said it was a pity we had to end this way, he said "We? WE? - I'm only ending my association with you!. Keith has agreed to continue working with me as ZX81."

Kicked out of my own band. That was a first for me. Keith came over the next day to apologise, but I wished him good luck. He said he was looking for a new singer who could play as well as me. Our paths would cross again in a few more years, but ZX81 never had the same success without me. Clive went on to manufacture the Sinclair C5, described by one critic as 'a motorised coal scuttle.'

Billy Shears phoned me to boast how he had just received a letter from Buckingham Palace saying he would be awarded an MBE. I was green with envy, though I didn't show it. He said he could now add three letters to his name, and I always did when I thought about him. 'TIT.' The next day I was being interviewed, and in the middle of the conversation, Shears' name came up, and I happened to seethe as I mentioned his award. The interviewee was unaware of the award and then I thought I should not have mentioned the award. Oh dear, what have I done? A week later, Billy contacted PMSL to say he had received a dressing down because I had revealed his award before it was officially announced.

Do They Know It's Live Aid?

In 1983 I met Cindy Swallows at a newspaper award ceremony in Central London. Cindy was a page 3 model, known for stripping topless for the benefit of the seedier elements of the tabloid press. She was twenty-five and the latest in a long line of models titillating male readers with provocative poses. Her real name was Beryl Davis but she was advised to change it by her agent to amuse and provoke, so adopted a more amusing moniker based on the fact that at the time she was dating a prominent horny ornithologist who admitted to being more interested in studying birds of the non-feathered variety. They parted with no egrets.

Of all the Page 3's, Cindy was the prettiest and most popular. By a twist of fate, we were allocated seats together in the front row because I was being presented with an award that night (though I had to pretend I knew nothing of this beforehand). It was a lifetime achievement award or something similar. An endless stream of meaningless trophies were doled out to a bunch of TV soap stars out for the night and making the most of a free bar. Cindy gave me a huge smile and introduced herself, though I was well aware of who she was.

A very wise man once told me that a smile from a pretty girl seldom ends in climax, though you would be a fool not to pursue her. Was it from a film? I don't know. I was immediately smitten with Cindy and asked her about her work; she already knew a lot about me and asked if I had come to the ceremony on my own. She liked a drink and was partial to a Dirty Banana and reeled off a list of Cocktail innuendos, some of which she drank that evening. I decided to try and stay moderately sober and see what the evening would bring.

At the interval I was the soberest person in the building and Cindy had been to the bar several times. On the fourth occasion, she did not come back. I was on the point of putting my coat over her seat because I thought she was probably propping up the bar with her girlfriends when I looked up, and there she was on stage, reading out the names for the Lifetime Achievement Award. *That's me!* I thought. After reading a long list of nominations, she finally got to mine and gave me a wink.

She announced me as the winner, and I bounded up onto the stage to collect my award. As was her way, Cindy was wearing a revealing strapless dress that left little to the imagination. She gave me a peck on the cheek and whispered, "see you later" in my ear as I headed back to my seat. *In my dreams,* I thought as I walked back to applause. She wasn't kidding, though, because when she sat down next to me, she made it quite clear that she was available for a little late-night fun after the show. She was a big fan of my music and wanted to get to know me better. I assumed that she was squiffy and played along with the joke, but we got to her home, and she invited me up for coffee. She had heard the story of *Charlie's Cracker* and asked if the stories were true.

Well...

We were hardly out of each other's company for the next month. Apple and I had an open-ended relationship, but she was extremely jealous of Cindy. When they met for the first time, Apple was extremely catty and made disparaging remarks about Cindy's clothes, hair and figure. She finished with, "and I bet they aren't even real," to which I responded that they were *VERY* real.

My male friends were congratulating me on my luck, and even I felt as if I had won the Pools. A man in his forties with a blonde model on his arm was the stuff of dreams. After two months, I was still living the dream, though my social life was in a whirl as Cindy loved the nightlife and was forever taking me along to nightclubs and gatherings with her girlfriends. After three months, I started to flag as I tried to keep up with this energetic woman. She would kill me if this continued, but what a way to go. I no longer had time for my friends, and my music began to suffer. No longer was I in the papers for my music abilities; I was now on the front page of the tabloids stumbling out of nightclubs with Cindy, who had an unnerving habit of looking fresh as a daisy while I looked dishevelled and drunk as a lord. There was a fifteen years age difference between us, and I was trying to remember what I was like at twenty-five.

I was also in the process of recording my third solo LP. The first one titled *Charlie Caine* was released in

1980 and sold well, but the expectations were too high, and the songs were not as good as I had hoped. The fans were not ready for the Umbooko beat. My second effort was released after I exited ZX81 and had more of a synth-pop flavour. I was quite proud of *Bells & Whistles* and it sold moderately well. My third solo LP was recorded whilst I was in the middle of my whirlwind affair with Cindy. She often came into the studio when I was recording, but I found her presence to be distracting as she often wanted to give me advice about songs to record, and just when I was at my weakest point, we recorded a duet that often gets featured on the worst songs of all time lists.

My friends were getting worried about my health. I was burning the candle at both ends, but I could not see what my new lifestyle was doing to me. Then one day it all came to a head after a particularly energetic night with Cindy, followed by having to rush off to PMSL headquarters to discuss future projects. I felt unwell all through the meeting and then collapsed on the way out. I had indigestion and a temperature, but this quickly became chest pains, so I was rushed to the hospital and diagnosed as having suffered a minor heart attack. I thought that kind of thing happened to men in their sixties, but here I was in my early forties concluding that I would have to make drastic lifestyle changes. The most telling thing about the whole episode was that Apple visited me while I was in the hospital, whilst Cindy could not visit as she had a critical fashion show to attend.

I abandoned recording my LP (it was not until 2010 that it was finally released, titled *Cindy Incidentally*) and Cindy and I broke up soon after. It had to happen or she was going to be the death of me. My doctor told me to take things easy and to avoid dating racy models in future. I had no band to tour with and took to watching daytime TV to while away the hours. This was the worst thing I could have done, and I became a couch potato and put on lots of weight when I should have been adopting a healthier lifestyle. It would take me a long time to get myself back into shape.

Bob Geldof called me one day in November 1984. We had not spoken for a while, but we chatted about my current health problems, Cindy, the night I fought with Billy Shears on *Top Of The Pops* and how he had dragged me off him. We talked about football, and I mentioned how Edmonton Rovers were doing very well in the FA Cup again and invited him along to a game, saying I would leave some tickets for him at the gate. He then came to the point of the call and told me that I was expected to be in Notting Hill the next day, where there would be a gathering of assorted celebrity pop musicians to record a song to raise money for anti-famine efforts in Ethiopia. Male egos and pop princesses were to be in attendance. He knew I had not been in a studio for a while but shut my protests down with some well-chosen industrial language and a few idle threats. What could I do?

"Caine, you owe me a favour" he said. "Be there bright and early or I'll finish the job Shears started!"

I went home and thought about what Geldof had said. I was embarrassed at what a mess I had become and resolved to get myself back into shape once I had kept my promise to Bob. I arrived at the Sarm West Studios bright and early the following day. In an ominous sign, the receptionist didn't recognise me, even though I sang a few lines from a Highwayman hit to jog her memory. "Oh yes, I know that one. My Grandad sang that to me when I was young", she joked. She showed me through to a side room where a few other musical celebrities had gathered to natter and pick at some nibbles on a table. Bob Geldof was nowhere in sight - apparently, he never got out of bed before midday.

Across the room I saw Billy Shears and wondered how long it would be before our orbits crossed, and we were thrown together. Maybe Geldof had a mischievous plan up his sleeve? I felt for the monkey paw around my neck, and I couldn't help but feel nervous because a lot had changed in the music world, and I was beginning to feel my age amongst the pop tartlets in the current charts. I hardly recognised anyone. I saw Macca, the Status Quo boys and 'Spill' Collins and teased him mercilessly about his beer-carrying prowess. By this point, Phil had ventured out from behind the drums and was conquering the pop world with his Genesis chums, though I did tell him that I much preferred his band in the Prog Rock days with Steve Hackett and Peter Gabriel. I moved over to talk to the Status Quo twins, and Collins dropped a plate of food on the floor. Priceless!

I had offered up some lyrics for the song, but when Bob arrived, he said that had all been taken care of and started issuing sheets of paper with the words printed out for us to memorise. I had hoped that with the seriousness of the occasion, I might at least be able to occupy the same room as Billy Shears and not have a competitive edge but right from the onset, we were at each other, trying to get the better lyrics and the better camera shots. While Shears was recording a couple of lines to see what sounded best, I was making faces at him through the recording booth to put him off, and he went to great lengths to put me off my stroke too. In frustration, Geldof put the two of us together to see how that would play out and he was complaining it was the wrong key for him.

If you listen carefully to the 12" version of *Do They Know It's Christmas?* you can hear us very low in the mix, so although we did not get an official line to sing in the single version, we were both in there somewhere. When it came to the video performance, I stood behind him and pulled faces but that part was edited out.

Come the Eighties, music was now being sold in a new format. CDs were a recent phenomenon, and even I had invested in a CD player. People say vinyl sounds warmer, but I wanted to be in on the new fad. Cassettes were far too fiddly for me when the tape mangled itself up in the machine. I used a Betamax recorder to tape most TV shows, including the Band Aid performance. I was also busy recording every single music show of interest for future viewing but unlike Bob Monkhouse, who was taken to court for the sheer amount of product that he pilfered from the BBC and ITV for his private viewing over the years, everybody laughed because I had been left with so much recorded work on my Betamax tapes but nothing to play it on once my machine broke. I threw the lot away, not knowing that if I had kept them all I could have done a deal with the BBC and given them my Betamax tapes for transfer to VHS as they were recording over their copies of shows. *Do They Know It's Christmas?* went on to sell in the millions and was the biggest event I had been involved in to that point. Then came Live Aid.

The following May, Bob Geldof came back to me with his plans for a *global jukebox of concerts* as he put it, and he wanted me to get back together with Advent and play a few songs at Wembley Stadium. I said, "That may be difficult as some of the band now live in the States and I'll never be able to convince them to come over to Wembley" and he responded, "Well that's perfect because the States is where we're planning to do a show, possibly in Philadelphia. I'll pencil you in for that venue immediately!"

What could I do? Bob is a very persuasive character! Then I remembered my flying phobia and tried to backtrack on my promise, but when I called him, Bob said that Wembley was fully booked and the only chance I had of performing at Live Aid was in the States.

Apple suggested I try hypnotherapy to beat my fear of flying. It was certainly worth a try because I couldn't continue being scared this way. I had rejected hypnotherapy before, but now I was desperate. She spoke with friends, and they suggested an experienced man who had worked with many celebrities. The way I was taught to overcome my fear was that there would be a trigger phrase said to me which would immediately relax me. I said that the words that usually calmed me down were "Do you want a drink?" but that was too familiar a phrase, and it would have to be something a little more obscure in case it was accidentally said to me at the wrong moment.

Soon after, I was invited to referee a charity football fundraiser for Live Aid, but I had to turn it down because it was on the same day as the concerts. However, many musicians who were too old to rock but young enough to kick a football around were persuaded to turn out for Rock Stars FC. the morning of the concert at Edmonton Rovers FC. I was able to provide the opposition for the team to play because the lads at Rovers were more than willing to rub shoulders with rock royalty.

I had already planned a celebrity side that I thought would be a winner. Demis Roussos would be in goal of course, with Ozzy Osbourne and Meatloaf like a bat out of hell on the wings, Rod Codpiece and Elton Johnson would have to work it out between themselves who would be the opposing captain. Then I heard 'Spill' Collins would perform at both Philadelphia and Wembley and had a great idea of my own to do a double of both football and music performance.

Bob heard of my football match and said it would be much more fitting to play at Wembley instead, but in a ghastly mix-up, I thought he meant moving the game to Wembley FC, not understanding that he now wanted me to perform at both Live Aid events. He asked me not to forget my outfit on the day, which I thought was a reference to my referee's kit. We all turned up at Wembley FC by coach with the team and musicians at 11 am that morning to a locked ground. The result was some frantic phone calls to an irate Bob, who was so incensed at the mix-up that he cursed me and said they might have to resort to filling in my slot with Cliff Richard and then he went on to swear live on TV. We all hot-tailed it back to Edmonton for the game because there was no other match arranged there that day.

After the game, I went by helicopter with Phil Collins to Heathrow Airport for a Concorde to NYC and then by helicopter to Philadelphia for my reunion with Advent. He was amused at my hypnosis and wondered if he could be taught how to calm down the people in his life that were putting him under pressure. I told him it wasn't a pleasurable experience getting on the plane or even the helicopter being piloted by Noel Tidy-Beard, but once I had heard my trigger phrase, all the tension and fear dropped away from my body. I felt so relaxed and lucid that I answered every question he asked me, including what I thought of his solo work. Lousy move that - I would be going home on my own!

I wasn't expecting much from Advent's performance because we hadn't put in practice beforehand. We went on after the Thompson Twins, so I didn't feel under too much pressure. We certainly weren't as bad as when Phil joined up with Led Zeppelin and his car crash of a performance. We had just enough time to say hello to each other, but like Woodstock, we were straight into the music after an introduction from Billy Shears by satellite from Wembley. He wasn't performing but seemed just a little too pleased with himself that night, and if it were not for the calm feeling I still had from the flying I might have had a few things to say to him.

As we ended our performance and came off stage, there was a buzz about the place as if something shocking had taken place. The thing is, I had very little memory of performing or of what had happened. It was like musical amnesia and I was quite perplexed because the more I tried to remember, the less came to me. The band looked less than happy, and I would have asked them what was wrong, but I was too tired to even stand.

Shears' autobiography *Shear Delight* picks up the story of what happened:

'My attempt at nobbling Caine's reunion gig with Advent couldn't have gone any better had I tried. Phil Collins was chatting to me on the video link about crossing the Atlantic by Concorde that afternoon and in the process, he mentioned how Caine had been put under hypnosis shortly before the plane took off because of his fear of flying. I asked how, and Phil said that he was not at liberty to say, but if I thought of song titles by Wham then I would be on the right track. I immediately wrote down a list of their most popular titles and by the time it came for the live chat link I was to have with Advent I was ready."

"Hi, Charlie!"

"Yeah, hi Billy, how are you?"

"Not bad... haven't seen you since last Christmas. How are you doing?"

"I can't complain Billy. How's the autocue? (he laughed)"

"Do you enjoy what you do these days?"

"What's that?"

"I wasn't getting anywhere with my guesses, and went through most of the Wham back catalogue before I accidentally hit paydirt when he tried to embarrass me with a joke about my getting an Elton Johnson thatch. I told him it was just a careless whisper. The glazed eyes told me I had him in my pocket.

I asked him if he was tired from his flight, and he said something incoherent about wanting to sleep, and I said that maybe he ought to lie down for a bit and get ready for bed. The band sensed something was amiss with Charlie and kept glancing over at him and signalling (are you okay?) Then, right before the first number, he rambled about Bob Geldof, an argument they had that morning, and an offside goal. His band tried to cut him short by launching into the first number.

Charlie continued to talk and sing before sitting down on stage till the song ended. One of the stagehands bought him a guitar to play, hoping it might focus him more, but he just absentmindedly strummed along during the next tune. The first catcalls from the crowd began, and the band huddled together and decided to play an instrumental. This was the more agreeable of the three numbers they performed that night because Charlie took no part in it. He was fast asleep curled up in a ball!'

I was mortified when I saw the resulting footage of my performance. I couldn't understand how I had been put into a trance till my interview with Billy Shears was shown, and I heard his line of questioning. I wasn't aware of my trigger word as much as the fact that it was a song title of George Michael's. I had to face the press afterwards and explain my performance, excusing it as having too many sleeping pills on the flight over.

The press had a field day with headlines such as *Sleeping Beauty* and *Wake Me Up Before You Go Go.* I can laugh about it now, but I believed my career was in tatters.

Arriving back in the UK, there was more depressing news. Unknown to me the Poseidon League had been making behind-the-scenes checks on Edmonton Rovers' registration of players after a tip-off from one of our disgruntled ex-players. He had complained about unfulfilled wage promises, which unearthed a whole catalogue of other irregularities including, but not limited to, bribing referees with cash, concert tickets to shows and general match day shenanigans. Greg Boroge was the innocent party to this as he knew nothing of the back-handers to match officials and the concert tickets were traced back to some of the ex players, but mud sticks as they say, and he was sacked. After an urgent board meeting, I was given the heave-ho as well because I was deemed to have been complicit in these affairs. My only connection was to provide many concert tickets and T-Shirts for free to the players. Edmonton Rovers folded a year later and the ground is now a shopping complex.

The Number Of The Beast

Fourteen years after writing *Centipede & The Slug,* and five years after the show had moved to Broadway and beyond to become a Worldwide hit, I was still living in its shadow. It was a juggernaut out of control, and whilst I couldn't control its speed, I could at least control its direction.

In 1986 when the script for the film was shown to me, I already knew whom I wanted as Director: Ken Russell. Anyone who can control Oliver Reed has to have a good handle on the tiller, right? Ken wasn't available, so my next choice was Russ Meyer. Russ wasn't too keen either because there were no large-breasted women in the script, even though I tried hard to rework a part for Cindy after he sent back a rewritten script that would surely have us in trouble with the censors. I tried Franc Roddam of *Quadrophenia* fame, but he also turned it down.

In desperation, I turned to a little-known director known for art house films because having thought about what we wanted from the film, it could not be sugar-coated in sentimentality. Oh - and when I write *we* I am referring to Reggie Cramwell and PMSL Productions Company, who had signed the exclusive rights to the film. I didn't know PMSL were into film production either. I wondered whom they would get to take part in the film?

Many well-known names were discussed, and options mulled over but the most significant decision was when we ripped up all plans to make a live-action film and agreed it would be animation-based. It was too problematic to make humans look like insects, but in the 21st Century, with CGI it would be relatively straightforward and believable. We cast many big-name actors and actresses for speech parts, and I was at my recording studios to advise and make helpful suggestions along the way as to how I thought the voices should sound for the soundtrack.

We were not after Daley Twins quality animation because that would have taken years to produce, nor were we looking for Roobarb and Custard-style animation. Daley Twins animation films could take four years to make, and we were looking to have the film completed in half that time. It was decided that some music needed to be re-recorded to fit in with the film. Some of the original songs were too long for the animation sequences, so the original Advent members were invited to my studio. Some were hesitant to attend after my Live Aid escapades, but Keith convinced them that what had happened was not my fault and that it would be good to have a proper reunion away from the cameras and prying eyes.

Keith had wrapped up his partnership with Clive and ZX81, so had some free time. I asked the others what they had been up to since we last met. Like me, they were all pushing into their 40's, and whilst these days bands can and do go on into their 80's when they really ought to retire to their pipe and slippers, back in the 1980's there was no benchmark with which to measure how long a career in Rock music may last.

People were looking at the Beatles, the Rolling Stones and the Fifties rockers and seeing that with the majority of acts, the best and most creative time of their careers came in the first ten or so years before burnout occurred. After that, nobody knew how long the creative bubble would last or when the fans would move on to something new. I was wondering if I still had a future in music, but for now, it was interesting to see how my friends were getting on.

Greg Jones was managing what we would now call a boy band, and I teased him mercilessly about the fact he had given up music for this. He told me there was lots of money to be made making music for teenage girls, and I couldn't argue with that. So some nights, he would go out to see a live band and sit in with them after the show and talk about the old days of Advent.

Brian Blessing had hung up his bass and was now working behind the scenes at a church. He played occasional charity concerts to raise money for a new church roof, so he had indeed turned into a rocking vicar. Dave Dunn had saved all his money and invested it wisely. He was now a multi-millionaire and was happy to do session work when he got bored of sitting on his yacht or needed a break from the easy life.

I hadn't seen Frankie in a while, but he was still in the music world. We drifted in and out of each other's lives, but music and Mum were reasons to remain in touch. We got into the habit of going to Walthamstow

Stadium on a Saturday night to watch the greyhounds because Mum told us how Dad used to work behind the scenes at meetings before the war. Dad sounded like a bit of a gambler and would be known to win big money regularly and knew all the tricks of the trade in how to give your dog a better chance of winning. He would hear all the reasons why a particular dog was the favourite. The first one was the name.

"Names make no difference whatsoever if your dog comes first or last" he used to say. "The colours they are running in or the sex or even the colour of the greyhound, be it brindle, black, red, fawn or white also have no bearing on the outcome."

He talked of a friend who used to watch and see what greyhound defecated before a race, and he would bet on that one. Again, no certainty that he would win. There was only one way of giving your greyhound a better chance of winning: if he was joint-favourite, you gave the other dog something to eat or drink before a race. You didn't have much of a time frame to do it because owners were very wary of the cheating that was going on and hardly let the dog out of their sight. Some dogs were highly strung and easily distracted before the race started.

Frankie and I used to talk to the owners and trainers at the meetings, and there was one particular character we chatted to more than most, whom I'm going to call Dave for reasons that will become clear. Dave worked part-time at Walthamstow Stadium for most of his life and was a butcher by trade. In the evenings, he would help set up the track before a meeting and then ensure the traps were in good working order. Dave always gave us good tips, and we provided him with concert tickets, so it was a win-win all round.

As time went by and we got to know Dave better, he let us in on a few tricks of the trade, such as how to look for winners. He talked of greyhounds that favour the inside rail, finish well, and not forgetting that greyhounds under the age of two fare better. He also discussed things that will help your greyhound NOT to win races. There were raised eyebrows at this revelation, but Dave explained that this was to manipulate the odds when your greyhound has slower races. When he or she has favourable odds to win a race, you can lay back on what you were doing and bet big to win. He loved greyhounds but was partial to making money on something he enjoyed doing.

I asked if he owned any greyhounds, and he said that it was nothing like owning a regular dog because they have to be trained and looked after correctly. You need a person to look after them on a day-to-day basis, and he was too busy with his work to train them and spend time with one.

"Have you ever owned a dog?" he asked.

I told him I once had a girlfriend with one of those yap-yap dogs. The thing was crazy and would never shut up.

"The dog was pretty cool though, right?" He answered.

People always seem to steal my punchlines.

The next time we met Dave, he told us of a conversation he had with a syndicate he knew who owned a greyhound and would we be interested in joining forces? We explained we were only in it for fun. He said most owners have a realistic expectation that their dog would not win most of their races. Competing and being involved in a race was the exciting part. Dave's a very persuasive person, and we met his friends very soon. They invited us to come and see their dog race the following week before committing to anything. When we saw Nervous Nerys for the first time, I didn't know what to say. She was highly strung and not unlike the character from *Only Fools And Horses* that she was named after. Any loud sound would make her jump, and she didn't seem like anything I would want to invest in so we turned the syndicate down. Fast forward to six months later and Nerys was winning races all around the country. Every time we saw Dave he would give us that *I told you so!* look before moving on.

Get the Led Out

Apple and I had known each other for 20 years in 1987. We hadn't married, even though I had asked her several times. She kept saying we would never find the time, even though I wasn't in an active phase in my professional life. We maintained an open relationship but were never both on the same page when one of us was ready to commit. Apple had her projects, including a clothing/perfume business that kept her occupied. I was pleased for her because she wasn't dependent on my money. I did notice that she was involved in some very long chats on the phone with a person or persons unknown. When I asked her out of curiosity who she was speaking to, she was very vague and distracted with her answer, but I just assumed it was business matters under discussion and did not question it further. This went on for three months and I said nothing but couldn't help but feel a pang of curiosity over the matter.

It all came to a head the night of a charity concert when I was asked to step in at short notice when Billy Shears had to pull out of the event. Apple said she would come along as well, which surprised me as she had stepped up her work schedule and we were not seeing much of each other in the evenings. I was asked if I could say a few words before the concert started, and I thought, why not? so was explaining to the audience how things can go wrong with live events and the unexpected can and does happen. Prophetic words from me, and I have to write that I had no inkling of what was about to happen next. The stage curtain was drawn behind me and I could hear some goings on. The audience did too, and there were a few gasps and excitable sounds as I introduced the first act, which was going to be a boy band big in the charts at that time. A man stepped out from behind the curtain and the audience gasped again. It was Eamonn Andrews.

Eamonn Andrews was the host of *This Is Your Life*, a TV show that had run since 1955. His job was to surprise unsuspecting celebrities by turning up unannounced with a red book which contained the particulars of that week's victim's life. Eamonn was an Irishman known for his radio work for the BBC and for presenting TV shows *What's My Line?* and *Crackerjack!* He was also a keen boxer and writer.

This Is Your Life was a show he saw in the USA in 1952, and he was so impressed by what he saw that he badgered the BBC until they initially programmed it for a monthly, then fortnightly and finally a weekly run. The show's premise was that famous names and family members would be introduced and would say a few funny words or recount an amusing moment they shared with the subject of the show, culminating in a long-lost family member coming on at the end for the big finale

Apple and I used to watch the show and always commented on how the intended victim could not have known this was being planned. I looked around for his intended victim and realised with a jolt that it must be me. Now I understood all Apple's secretive phone calls and late nights working. Unknown to me, she had been arranging most of the guests with Joyce and her connections to the music world.

I felt so mean to have doubted Apple and could see her grinning from where I was standing. I had gone from doubt to affirmation and what followed was the best night of my life. First, the stage had to be set up to record the show, so I paused to go backstage, relax, and think about who Eamonn might be bringing on and who might be in the audience. What usually happened was that Eamonn's victim would be taken to the TV studio to record the show, but because we were in a theatre, it was deemed suitable for the recording, and the original audience remained. What skeletons would be coming out of my cupboard?

Eamonn could see I was nervous and said to relax; there was nothing to worry about. I settled into my chair and the familiar theme tune began. I remembered my childhood and wondered if any of my chums would be coming on to say what a rascal I was at school. I remained seated as Eamonn gave a brief introduction, described me as a musical genius with a flair for the unpredictable, and described my early years at school.

The night's first surprise was when George Turpin came on and talked about the Foot Tappers' school fire that got me expelled in 1958. I fully expected Leonard Skinhead to come on and give me a whack with the ruler for not finishing my homework on time. John James followed with tales from the record shop soon after, though thankfully, he never mentioned my scratching Cliff Richard's records. Instead, a soundbite was played of him recounting the first song we wrote together. It's the one where we took five hours trying to think of rhyming words. He dressed as a highwayman for the show, which got a lot of laughs.

One of my favourite memories of the show is of Mick Oz bounding onto the stage with a giant rubber reptile and doing a *Crocodile Dundee* act. You would have thought it was Paul Hogan doing his film part, he was that good. He recounted how he found me knocked out in the jungle and set me on the path to recording my first solo album.

Advent all came on together to tell the story of how I attended Woodstock, got kidnapped, escaped to play with the band, and returned to the UK. A light-hearted attempt was made to explain away my Saliva years. I'm very proud of what I recorded with the band and defended them stoutly, but I had a wry smirk when Elvis Presley was mentioned. This was where Phil Jones and John James asked Eamonn if he wanted to hear us play a number. He was momentarily taken aback till we started laughing.

I was in for the night's biggest surprise. It was a pre-planned moment between Eamonn and Apple because just as he handed me the book, she went down on one knee and proposed. I was momentarily stunned but recovered my composure to say yes. The wedding would not happen immediately but most likely in a year or so.

My appearance on *This Is Your Life* was not the last time I was caught unawares on TV. Later that decade, I was a victim of one of Noel Tidy-Beard's Saturday Roadshow *Wotcha Oscars*, which was his sly way of catching a celebrity unaware with a trick and then awarding him a trophy. Tidy-Beard was a victim of his own pranking because Apple told me he was trying to arrange to push me in my pond, and when push came to shove, it was I who caught him off balance and upended him into the pond of my Highgate home.

As the wedding date drew closer, I began to feel nervous. I'm not usually the type to dwell on things unnecessarily, so I was not sure why this should be. It was nervousness and sickness all in one and it started in my stomach and made me feel I was going to be sick, yet I could not induce myself to do so to make myself feel better. This went on for a month, and Apple suggested I see her doctor - Doctor Robert - and get checked out. I'm not the kind of person who hangs out in hospitals and wards and waiting rooms, but she told me not to be silly, Dr Robert was private and, dare I say it, provided better treatment.

And this is what I did. Dr Robert gave me an examination after we discussed my symptoms. I hadn't been to a GP or seen a health professional since my suspected heart attack, and he could not tell me exactly what was wrong but he took blood samples, gave me an examination and said he would contact me with the results. Could it be kidney stones? Probably. More would be known when the results of the tests came back.

Three days later, he phoned me to say I should come in to discuss the results. When I sat down, he asked me what connections I had with graphite and lead. I was a musician, right? Puzzled, I asked him what he meant.

"Mr Caine, I'll come straight out with it. Do you eat or chew on pencils and pens?" There was silence.

"Well, yes, I do. But not regularly. I nibble on the top of a pencil when I'm writing, and sometimes if I'm drawing in my journals."

"You need to stop doing that because though it's not a life-threatening habit, I believe that if you have been doing it for most of your life, then you need to think of your health and cut it out as soon as possible."

But it was true. I had been nibbling on pencils since an early age when I took up journal writing. I used to gnaw on 2HB pencils as they had the best taste, but my liking for pencils included but was not limited to graphite, solid graphite, charcoal, carbon-coloured pencils, crayons (very embarrassing as this coloured my teeth) grease pencils and so on. I was telling half-truths when I said it was not a regular occurrence, and when I couldn't find pencils, I tried pens. All this I kept to myself out of embarrassment, but I asked Dr Robert if the pencil habit would seriously affect my health.

"Just cut out the lead" is all he said.

I went home, and when Apple asked how things went at the doctors. I said it was just a stomach bug. She didn't seem sure about this diagnosis but asked what he suggested I should do, such as changing my diet or letting nature take its course. I said it was something along those lines and headed upstairs to look at my pencil collection. Could I be a pencil nibbler out of control? It was true that I kept my habit on the down low from the people who knew me, but it was also true that my addiction (if that's what it was) had escalated over the past few months. But I could stop if I wanted to, but not on this night. I had an extensive collection of pens and pencils in the room I referred to as my Man Cave. Whenever I was on tour or in new territory, I would go to an art and craft shop and pick up a pencil. My hobby of collecting pens and pencils of all shapes and sizes did not look out of the ordinary, and when I got home, I would devour them.

It's said there are seven stages of addiction, and I had passed through to the 5th stage by the time Dr Robert pulled me up on my usage. The stages of addiction are recorded as follows:

Initiation
Experimentation
Regular Usage
Risky Usage
Dependence
Addiction
Crisis/Treatment

Most are self-explanatory, and the risky usage stage came on when I started neglecting responsibilities such as work, attempting to hide their use and putting pencils in easily accessible places like in drawers where I could find them when needed. Of course, I didn't have to try too hard to hide them because pens and pencils are everywhere, right? I knew this habit would not kill me, but I was embarrassed to admit it had taken over my life and I was depending on charcoal and lead to get me through the day.

It all came to a head the day Apple came into the bedroom to find me munching down on a particularly colourful children's set of crayons. She sat next to me and asked how long it had been going on, and I said most of my life but increasingly more over the past few months. She guessed where the stomach aches and pains were coming from and said I had to stop now because it could only make me feel worse the longer I continued.

I let her clear the room of all she could find to make her feel better, but as I wrote earlier, pens and pencils are everywhere and it didn't take long for me to find another supplier. I became very secretive in my consumption as I crossed from dependence to addiction. Friends were asking why my teeth were blackened and I started eating liquorice to explain it away, though behind my back they were talking about my bad breath. I thought they were interfering, but they had my best interests at heart because someone had a quiet word with Apple, who knew what she had to do.

All of this had been happening for over four months, and I hadn't noticed the wedding discussions had stopped. Finally, Apple said we would have a weekend away in the country and get out and about on healthy walking activities. I reluctantly agreed but said I would also use it as a working holiday and used that as an excuse to bring a box of pencils along. We checked into a very agreeable hotel and, after unpacking, went downstairs to find something to eat. She ushered me into a meeting room and followed me, shutting the door. Ten or so of my dearest friends were in the room, and all had concerned faces. I could not understand what they were all doing there at the same time until they told me this was an intervention.

We Gotta Get Out Of This Place

"My name is Charlie Caine...

...and I'm addicted to eating pencils and crayons."

And just like that, I began my journey back to normality at the Teddy Fort Clinic. It took a lot of persuasion from my friends and a few tears until I was convinced this was the right thing to do. The intervention had shocked me because I could not see for myself what a mess I had become. The only positive I could see was that my addiction was not going to kill me and did not involve trying to smuggle illegal substances into the country through customs. If it wasn't causing me so much mental and physical illness, I could have laughed it all off and gone back home, but I knew I would soon return to my bad old ways and munch enough lead and wood to write a book!

The intervention was a frightening experience and my initial reaction was to bolt for the door, but I was stopped. Advent were all there, as well as John James, Reggie Cramwell, Apple, Joyce and Mum. I was afraid of what Mum would think of me if I ran away; and only that thought made me want to stay and get better. All present shared good memories of working or being with me and spoke sincerely about how I could beat this habit if I tried my best. They would support me now and in the future to get back on track. I felt anger that nobody had said anything to me about how bad I had become, but they had, and it was because I had not wanted to listen that I had not heard.

It was decided that I would go straight into rehab. Apple and Joyce had been making enquiries with the Teddy Fort Clinic. Was this an unusual addiction? Not as uncommon as you may think. The clinic dealt mainly with drug and alcohol abuse, and even sex addicts. I had been booked in for a six-week stay, with the option to extend it to twelve weeks, depending on my progress.

As soon as I arrived, my belongings were searched for signs of contraband pencils, recreational drugs, and booze. I was given an intake assessment where they questioned me for an hour about my lifestyle choices and asked me to fill in some questionnaires to help them tailor a plan of action to treat my addiction. In the past 30 days, how many times did I eat lead, wood, and plastic? Did I drink or smoke on any of those days, and was this causing me to cut back on activities I enjoyed? Did it affect my job at all? Had I been arrested for any drug offences, needed to be hospitalised at any point?, and how would I rate my overall health? How satisfied was I with my life?, and was the addiction affecting my relationships?

I was asked to be as brutally honest as possible and felt quite exhausted at the end of the interrogation. I was then shown the room where I would spend some time. It was a basic affair with a television, chair and bed. It looked to me as if this encouraged guests to spend their time outside their rooms and away from self-isolation and pity. This was not the case because the room I was to occupy after this night was not ready for me to use it. A rich rock star was taking his time checking out that day, so I was given the current one till he had gone.

After showering, I went downstairs to the meeting room where I was further briefed on what was expected of me during my stay. There were 15-20 other patients like me at any time in the compound from all walks of life. Everyone was to be treated equally, with no favouritism given to celebrities. We were encouraged to mix and get along with each other, thereby helping the healing process together. Tonight, I would eat on my own, but in the morning, I would meet everyone else at breakfast. I said I felt I was going to be laughed at when I told everyone of my addiction, but I was reassured not to worry because there were a lot worse things that I could have become addicted to. And anyway, there were strict codes of conduct that forbade finding humour in anyone else's situation, but there would be plenty of time to have fun in the future.

The following day I was out of bed bright and early. This was more down to a bright and cheery "hello campers!" style intercom announcement at 7.30 am than a need to get up and about early. A rap on the door told me it was time to go downstairs and meet the merry crew on the good ship Teddy Fort. On the way to the breakfast area, I passed by many doors where I could hear the occupants grumbling about being woken up so early, toilets being flushed, and the sounds of breakfast TV, not unlike being in a Travelodge. I was shown where breakfast was served and asked for a fry up. My guide laughed and said there was a strict menu that everybody adhered to, and the serving would begin when everyone arrived.

One by one, everyone came and took a seat. I noticed there were single tables, so I sat on my own because I didn't feel like talking to anyone at the time. I didn't see anyone I recognised, but then I wondered if anyone would know me. There were fifteen of us in all and a wide range of years from a woman in her early twenties who had more than a passing resemblance to Kate Bush to a couple who, I guess, must have been in their fifties.

A young orderly began serving breakfast, doling out fifteen bowls of cereal and glasses of orange juice and said we could go and help ourselves to a light and healthy breakfast if we wanted more. I wanted more. I asked if I could have a coffee and was told that coffee was not drunk by guests.

"What about tea?"

"No."

"Alcohol?"

"No!"

"Coke?"

"Sugar or narcotic version?"

"Sugar."

"Both are banned, sir. It's either fruit drinks or water in the morning. Take your pick."

The guests had been listening intently to my conversation. Finally, one spoke to me after the orderly had left and said, "Nice try, but they think any kind of stimulants are bad for us. What are you in for?"

"Lead and graphite addiction."

"Nice. I'm into solvent abuse."

After breakfast, we headed to a large meeting room overlooking the hotel grounds. We sat in a semi-circle with two members of staff who were there to oversee the session. They called for a hush and invited me in, and I made my nervous introduction. I had expected a few laughs and giggles but was surprised to get a round of applause after my tense opening.

Encouraged by this enthusiastic response, I continued to describe my addiction. Murmurs and nods of agreement followed until I blotted my copybook by saying how I fancied some 2HB. Silence from the gathering followed by a rebuke from a man I came to know as Corden the warden, for encouraging other guests to dwell on their addictions. "Try not to focus too much on what you are here for and what you are trying to forget during your stay," he said. "You'll find out more as we progress." Corden then asked the man I was talking to in the breakfast room to repeat the four rules they were taught in the sessions that formed the basis of their treatment. I have adapted them to fit my situation:

First, identify the addiction. What are you here for, and why have you let yourself get this far out of control? Why do you need to chew on lead in the first place?

Deal with the emotions they are causing. Don't deny the anger you are feeling about your current state. Let the anger out. A therapist was on site to discuss this on a 1-to-1 basis after the group session.

What are the trigger points? What situations trigger your addiction? For example, did being alone and with nothing to do bother me? Nervousness about my upcoming marriage was making me stressed too.

Substitute the thought. Consider what thoughts trigger your addiction and when you think of them, change the outcome to a healthier lifestyle. For instance, if thinking of writing makes you think of pencils and chewing them, think of what songs you have written with pencils and change the thought process to a more positive one.

The group session continued for two hours and was a lively affair. My new friend the solvent abuser was the most lucid of the lot. I heard afterwards that those trying to crack (if you forgive the pun) drugs were given a little each day to help them wean themselves off a little at a time, and my friend had been inhaling a tiny amount of glue that was administered by the warden. Oh good, that meant I might be given a pencil later, I thought, and I asked Corden about this. He said no. In my case, it was getting into the habit of not being around writing utensils at first, and if I felt I needed to have a pencil to write and couldn't control myself, then I should sit down and write on a computer screen.

"But I can't type. If I wanted to type, I'd have become a bloody secretary!" I wailed.

After lunch, I had an individual session with a therapist keen to discover why my habit, usually just a harmless 'tic' I had during quiet moments, had now raged out of control. What was going on? I had already discussed in my intake interview how I was under a lot of stress due to my declining (as I saw it) career and nervousness about marriage and all the arrangements to be made.

It was suggested that I use the gym during my stay, burn off a lot of excess energy, and get myself fit. Exercise helps manage mood swings, and it wouldn't harm me to lose a bit extra poundage before I left and went back out touring again. I was also advised to stick to a healthier diet, which would help with the stress and curb withdrawal cravings.

I sat out in the garden and went through the documentation I was given to read on my admission the previous day. I wasn't in the right frame of mind to go through it all and fell asleep. I awoke in time for the final meal of the day, followed by another group session and then an hour back in my new plush room in time for lights out at 10:30pm. All main lights, TVs and appliances were automatically switched off, apart from a bedside lamp, for using the en-suite facilities during the night.

The next day followed the same pattern, and so did the day after. I had stopped eating fried food in the morning and had become health conscious almost overnight, taking up my spare time with gym use, using the library to study, and jogging around the perimeter of the grounds three times a day. I said hello to everyone else in the meetings, but I wanted to get better as quickly as possible and kept to myself. I was constantly told to join in with the others in my spare time, but I was too focused on leaving. Besides, I was sure I was getting better, and by the time I knew them all, it would be time to go, so what was the point of making friendships?

After a month, I had a meeting with the manager and Apple. I was so pleased to see her and said I was feeling better and couldn't wait to leave. I told her of my lifestyle change and all the extra exercise I was doing around the grounds and she sounded impressed. I had hoped that I might be leaving, but she was there because the recommendation was that I should stay for another month as there was a possibility that I might let all my good work drop once outside and that I could return to my bad old ways. I was devastated.

I said goodbye to Apple, returned to my room, and sulked for the rest of the day. The following day I woke up feeling better and stepped up my exercise regime. In my dreams, I was going to get so fit that I could scale the walls and run for freedom before anyone noticed I had gone. Were there any trees I could climb to aid my escape? None were close enough to the walls, which were at least 10 ft in height. I was even looking out for a shed where I might find a ladder and make good my escape in the early hours of the morning. Maybe I should become a steeplejack and scale the walls with ropes, or I could have pole vaulted over the wall had I been an athlete.

One morning I was running my usual route when I noticed something white on the path ahead. I picked it up and it was a letter. I stuffed it into my tracksuit and continued on my way. Once I had completed the morning session, I returned to my room and remembered the letter. I opened it up and immediately noticed my name written in pen.

The letter was from Keith Howells. He explained that Advent were now big in East Germany and beyond the Iron Curtain. We had been invited to go and play a series of concerts at the end of the year and would I be interested in going?

The band wanted me there, and if I agreed, they would get me out of rehab and make arrangements to travel to Eastern Europe. They had been in touch with Apple, and she was against it, but if I acted now, their plan could be put into action. If I was in favour of the plan then leave a piece of my clothing in one of the trees the next day where I found the letter. That was odd because Apple never mentioned anything of this interest from East Germany when she visited me recently.

I wanted to get in touch with Apple and ask her about this, but I was not allowed to make private phone calls, so I decided I would escape with the band and make my excuses to Apple when I saw her outside. This was the cure to my addiction because playing music once again would give me something to focus on, and I would be too busy and tired for the silly habit I had got myself into. Another thought occurred to me: how was Keith able to place the letter where I was going to run? He must have heard of my daily route and took a chance that I would see the letter before anyone else. Very risky.

The next day was a Wednesday and on my morning run I left a black sock in one of the trees close enough to where I saw the letter, but far away from the pathway for it not to be seen unless it was being looked for. I couldn't relax for the rest of the day and was absent-minded throughout the group and one-to-one meetings. Eventually, I excused myself as not well and went back to my room. I had to think about things because I didn't want to make it obvious that I was up to something. I went back downstairs after an hour and told Corden I was feeling better and was able to take part in the quiz night that was held every Wednesday evening.

The following day on my run I didn't see a letter and was concerned that somebody else may have picked it up. The sock was gone though, so I hoped a plan was being put into place. On Friday morning, I found another letter from Keith, which went into a bit more detail. It said that on Saturday evening I would need to make my way to the wall near where the letter was placed. No time was given but I would know the signal when I heard it so had to go about my nightly routine and not make it obvious that I was listening for a signal.

No other information was given, so I spent the rest of the day trying to act as normal as possible and wondering what the signal would be and when I would hear it. I was listening for the sound of an owl hooting and a stepladder against my window, but I wasn't too keen on trying to climb down from the Third floor. 9:00 pm came and went and I was just wondering if the plan was off or if I should try and get to the meeting place when I finally got the signal because the fire alarm sounded. At first, it didn't occur to me that this was the signal, but as I started for the door, I knew this was what I was waiting for.

I grabbed my coat and made my way through the fire exit doors and down to the bottom of the stairs which led to the back of the building. There were three of us standing at the fire exit and I remembered I had to get to the wall. I slipped into the shadows and dashed down the path from the building. I heard the hoot of an owl... hmmm...

"Over here!!!!"

Keith was waiting for me and signalled to get over quickly. I looked for a ladder but couldn't see one and asked him how we would get over the wall.

"Don't be daft man. There's a gate behind the bushes over there."

I could still hear the sound of the alarm going off and make out figures near the building. Keith showed me to the gate, which had been forced open to allow him in. To think I could have escaped at any time I wanted! He had parked his car close by outside the hotel grounds and we had to keep in the shadows and make a run for it as the fire engines came screaming past. Keith had pushed the alarm button and then dashed in the gate to collect me. As we drove away, he laughed about how he had always wanted to set off an alarm and had now ticked it off his bucket list.

The Wall

When Apple heard of my escape, she immediately cancelled all the wedding plans. She refused to speak to me on the phone and went on a holiday with her family without letting any mutual friends know where she had gone. I had not envisaged this happening and was taken by surprise. Sure, I expected her to be mad at me for a while, but I knew I would eventually be able to win her around with my charm and wit. In a way, our split solved my health problems because the nervousness regarding the wedding melted away. The press had been unaware of my rehab stay and went to town with headlines such as *Charlie Loses His Marbles* and *2B Or 2HB, That Is The Question.*

Joyce did as much as she could to put out some positive press releases, but really, I had become a figure of ridicule in the way the British press like to build up celebrities and then knock them down again when they get too full of themselves.

The Centipede & The Slug animated film had come out to rapturous reception in 1988, particularly in the German Democratic Republic (GDR), aka East

Germany. In a nutshell, the East German people were not in a good place under an oppressive Communist regime and saw their plight against the state reflected in the themes of the film (good vs evil/right vs wrong). By word of mouth and over a year, Advent had unwittingly brought the East Germans together and the songs had become a rallying cry for freedom. Officialdom had tried to block our music from being heard but the wave of rebellion had turned into a non-violent call for action that could not be stopped.

Copies of our LP were smuggled into East Germany and played at secret meetings across the country. The demand for our music was so great that there was a plan to ask us to visit Berlin and play our music to the masses. When PMSL records heard of this, they immediately saw the potential for a quick profit and were repackaging our back catalogue for the German market and encouraging us to tour and promote the product. They hadn't banked on me being in rehab with no time frame as to when I might be released. That's when Keith had his bright idea of springing me out of rehab and back on the road again.

We couldn't fly to West Germany (as Germany was known then) until we had band practice because I wasn't going to have a repeat of Live Aid. I was to be hypnotised to be able to fly, though not with such an obvious trigger phrase as *Careless Whisper*. We practised for a solid week before feeling good enough to perform live. We booked the flights, and off we went!

The tour of West Germany began with some warm-up gigs before I took part in a live radio broadcast from Cologne. I was met by an elderly presenter named Zelda Schmitt, who I discovered was partially deaf. We debated current music as much as possible with a person whose interest in music probably ended with Louis Armstrong and the Swing era. The subject turned to women in music, and I offered the opinion that Suzi Quatro was an excellent vocalist as well as a musician and that she had a super bass. We chatted for ten or so minutes before it was time for me to leave.

There were a couple of TV performances to fulfil, which I was looking forward to doing. Crowds followed us everywhere, and reporters asked what we felt about the current political unrest in the GDR. I, for one, was not going to fall into the trap of getting involved in a controversial soundbite or a slip of the tongue, so left that line of questioning to the other band members. They quoted the usual spiel of looking forward to playing in front of our fans for the first time in West Germany. We would be playing *Centipede & The Slug* in its entirety because that's what the fans wanted, and we would be in full costume for selected shows.

We had a full guided tour of Hamburg and did the whole tourist thing to see where the Beatles had performed before they became famous, most notably the Indra Club, the Kaiser Keller, the Top Ten, and the Star Club, which had burned down a few years before our visit. I took photos in front of the remaining buildings and wished we could have gone inside and played a number or two. We played on a TV chat show and there were more questions afterwards about the political situation, and once again, I was at my tactful best. The guests on the show were close to coming to blows with their opposing views and verbal posturing and didn't need any of my help.

A couple of days after my Cologne radio interview I got a call from one of the daily newspapers to say that there was a storm brewing over my controversial interview with Zelda Schmitt, and did I have anything to say regarding what I had said about Suzi Quatro? I asked what they meant and was told I had made a sexist comment about Suzi. My radio conversation comments had been transcribed and syndicated around West Germany, and in a terrible error, my words about Suzi's super bass had by way of a typo error been quoted as Suzi's *superb ass*. It took a lot of explaining to get out of that escapade.

We travelled on to Berlin. A city that David Bowie and Iggy Pop had called their home a little more than ten years ago, and where from 1977 to 1979 Bowie had recorded what became known as his *'Berlin Trilogy'* of albums: *Low*, *Heroes* and *Lodger*. An open-air concert had been arranged near the Brandenburg Gate for this, the finale of the tour. It may not have had as many attendees as Woodstock or Live Aid, but neither of these shows would have the same political impact as the concert we played in Berlin on 9th November 1989 because that was the night the Berlin Wall came down.

The band did not know that one of our songs, *The Garden Wall* from the *Centipede & The Slug*, was the call for the East Germans to take to the walls and strike a blow for freedom and unify East and West. The thought occurred to me that we had been hired to play so loudly that nobody would hear the sound of pickaxes and hammers pounding on the walls, but the East German guards were casual bystanders to the destruction going on around them. After the concert we relaxed backstage, talking to fans and guests and were invited to a party to celebrate the wall's demise. By this point the band had consumed too much alcohol to be able to say no and mean it.

We arrived at a mansion where a party was in full swing. I froze in horror because three or four border officers were dressed in official dark green GDR uniforms with '*Grenztruppen der DDR*' in white lettering on their left arm. Where were we? Our guests had driven us into East Germany and we were without official documentation and feeling slightly apprehensive. But we need not have worried because the uniforms were souvenirs taken from guards that night and try as I might, the prospect of taking one home appealed to me. I asked if I could have one as well. I collected such items from around the world, sometimes sneaking them in my luggage or by bribing a member of the crew to sneak it through customs. I even bought back an authentic Zhongshan suit (or Mao suit), a style made famous by Chinese Communist leader Mao Zedong.

The GDR uniform would be a challenge because if I wanted to take it back to the West, I would have to do so myself. The wall might have been in the process of being dismantled, but all it took was an overzealous border guard still manning his post and with an itchy trigger finger and it would be bye, bye Charlie! I managed to coax one of the uniforms from its owner with a small bribe and tried it on. It fitted perfectly. The feeling of power became too much and I didn't want to take the thing off, so I hatched a plan (still under the influence of alcohol) that when we were driven back, I would get in the car boot still in my GDR uniform and smuggle it back that way. The plan backfired because the car was searched by a guard who had us all arrested on the charge of kidnapping and impersonating a GDR official. Explain that one away, Charlie Caine!

I had been in a few scrapes before, but this was going to top the lot. A diplomatic incident involving the British Embassy was sure to follow. Maybe the band would be released when they discovered who I was and I would be the only one in trouble. We were locked up to be interrogated, then taken to who knows where before they shipped us off to Russia to work down the coal mines or something: you know the way the imagination runs wild on these occasions. We might even be taken to the Berlin Stasi Prison which I heard was just as brutal. The reality was nothing of the sort because we were taken to Unter den Linden, the British Embassy, to a much classier do than the last one we had attended. We were given a slap on the wrist and told we couldn't go around dressing ourselves up and embarrassing our hosts.

News of our escapades were leaked to the British press over the next few days. It was claimed that it was just a publicity stunt to get our names back in the papers again. When I returned to the UK, I was summoned to 'clear the air' talks with Apple at her place, where we tried to resolve our differences. Things escalated into a shouting match and it was at the point that she started throwing the crockery at me and shouted out she was pregnant at the age of forty-two.

She said she couldn't trust me anymore and accused me of seeing other women since announcing our wedding plans. Sure, there had been partners in the past, but since splitting with Cindy after my suspected heart attack, I had reined in the wilder side of my life. I didn't have much choice because I felt I had been given a second chance and was not about to blow it. Touring had been much easier since the demands were not so great, and I was away from home far less than before.

Apple said that we were through and I was trying to process the idea of being a dad whilst simultaneously trying to dodge her best china. She then ran out of dishes and threw more insults instead, and when she ran out of insults and swear words, she collapsed to the floor. At any point, I could have just made for the door to get away, but that would have been me not facing my problems again. I told her that I was returning to the Teddy Fort Clinic and that I would stay and finish my treatment this time. I didn't expect her to believe me; I know she didn't. I said that when I came out, we would then have a proper discussion over where our future lay and also that of our child. How did she feel about being a Mum? A piece of broken crockery launched at my head told me precisely what she was feeling.

I Wanna Be (Elected)

Just before I was due to return to the clinic, I had some devastating news. Mum had been involved in a terrible car crash, and the driver had left the scene before the ambulance and police arrived. She died on the way to the hospital from multiple injuries. She was Seventy. I fell to pieces and couldn't cope for some months with the anger and the sadness I was trying to deal with, plus the breakdown of my relationship with Apple.

Mum was a proud woman and didn't need our help because she had her friends in Edmonton and didn't want to relocate or start elsewhere. We cleared her house and I found many items relating to my music career. There were even quite a few scrapbooks detailing my press coverage, both good and bad. I smiled when I looked back through all the Saliva and Elvis Presley scandals.

I returned to the Teddy Fort Clinic after Mum's death and spent six months getting myself together and learning how to deal with losing the two ladies who were the most important part of my life. When Apple visited me, it made me feel worse because we had nothing left in common. She was bitter that she could not spend as much time concentrating on her own business because of her pregnancy. We fought and shouted at each other until Corden the warden told her she should leave as her behaviour was detrimental to my health.

After the birth, she announced she was moving out of London and selling up her business. She would keep in touch so I could see Lyric (a boy born on my 49th birthday!), but she needed time alone. I accused her of running away from her problems which did not go well. She accused me of turning the argument back on itself, and I started laughing.

I didn't see her for a long time, even though I tried to keep in contact and said I would provide financial support. Apple was self-sufficient, now a millionaire and needed no help. Eventually, she got back in touch because Lyric asked who his Daddy was and wanted to know why he could not see him. We arranged to meet twice a month and when she saw how much Lyric enjoyed our meetings, she agreed that I could have him stay at my place as well. I was eager to get him into music, but he was more into playing *Sonic the Hedgehog* than attempting to play music. Early days though, as he was only five.

One night I was sitting on my own, flicking through the TV channels and unable to find anything worth watching. I was so bored I began watching *Question Time*, a political programme on the BBC where the audience, members of the Government, press, and leading figures discussed the issues of the day. I would never entertain shows like this because I was not politically motivated, but the episode I watched caught my interest because it featured a member of the Official Monster Raving Loony Party (OMRLP).

The show host was having difficulty controlling the conversation's flow. It sounded as if the less serious the OMRLP representative behaved, the more cheers he got and the more fun for everyone involved. Why couldn't politics be more like this and not so staid and stuffy?

From what I already knew, the OMRLP was formed in 1983 by an old pal of mine, Screaming Lord Sutch, born David Sutch, who sadly is no longer with us. Every time the General Elections came around, I avoided the news like the plague and never saw the fun his party got up to in the build-up to election day. Nobody ever stood for the OMRLP in Highgate where I lived. Too stuffy and full of Conservatives and Liberals for my liking.

The tabloids were full of the show the following day, and I correctly surmised that the only participants who benefitted were the OMRLP. I contacted David through his party headquarters, congratulated his party representative on an entertaining performance, and asked David if he remembered how I was invited onto his *Radio Sutch Show* in 1965 with the Highwaymen. We discussed music and swapped stories, and then he asked me a direct question: he was having a fundraiser in London for the party at the weekend and wondered if I was free to come along and sign a few autographs and sing a few songs afterwards. Sure I would!

I met up with David at a local pub for a few drinks before we headed to Croydon Town Hall for a gathering of OMRLP members, curious onlookers and assorted press members out for a few soundbites from

David. There was surprise when I arrived and began to mingle with the crowd, and I guessed they were wondering what my involvement would be. Sutch introduced me as his good friend and said with a chuckle that I was the entertainment for the night but not to ask me any controversial questions, what with my previous record. Red rag to a bull!

"Charlie, what do you make of John Major and his policy on crime?" asked the first hack. "Well," I paused for good effect, "crime could be halved if they bought back hanging... did you hear that last record by Jason Donavan? Now that's a crime against music if ever I heard one."

"Are you saying we ought to hang Jason Donavan, Charlie?" I heard shouted above the din. "That's probably too harsh even for Jason," I responded. "Maybe just send him to jail for crimes against music instead."

Sutch stepped in and changed the subject to talking about the OMRLP and its policies and cleverly steered me away from any controversial statements. Afterwards, he joked that I would be a useful candidate but was probably a little too right-wing in solving the political issues of the day. I told him I had joined the OMRLP at the half-time interval for a laugh. Sutch put on a serious face and said that this was no joke to his party, then burst out laughing when I took his words too seriously. He said that if I was serious about taking a more active interest, I should read the documentation I was given upon registration and contact him when the time was ready.

When I got home, I looked at the paraphernalia I had been given. I flicked through random pages and read:

Stand for the Official Loony Party

Information To Potential Candidates

Please remember we are a registered political party. If you are standing as a candidate, you are representing the OMRLP. Don't do or say anything that could reflect poorly on the party. We are loonies, not nutters...

It looked like I had got off on the wrong foot there. I could see why Sutch stepped in when he did. I should have changed the focus back to the OMRLP and quoted the official party line on crime that *Capital punishment will be opposed because it is unfair to Londoners*. I went through an A to Z on party policies.

Education: *kids will be made to sit closer together on smaller desks to reduce school class sizes* or, *Environment*: wind farms will be created nationwide, where breaking wind will be encouraged.

I finished off my cup of cocoa. The days of living a rock star lifestyle had passed me by since those wild nights out with Cindy. Nowadays, I settled down in front of the TV before falling into a deep sleep. My dreams are usually quite vivid, but unlike Keith Richards I have yet to create a song such as *Satisfaction*, where he woke up to play a few chords from a dream into a tape recorder and went back to sleep again.

In my dream, I was walking the streets of Highgate at night when I came up to the Gatehouse pub, which at that point in 1996 was closed down and even had squatters occupying the premises. It served over the years as a music hall, cinema and even a meeting place for the Sisters of Mercy cult made up entirely of (you guessed it) women. Paul Simon had played at the pub in the Sixties before he became a big star. In my dream, the Gatehouse was no more because the huge 'M' overhead told me it had been turned into a giant Mcdonald's drive-in, and cars were queuing down Highgate Hill to Archway just to get a tasty burger and fries. I was thinking, why had Burger King not got permission instead? I went and ordered myself a Big Mac and noticed a door leading to an entertainment venue upstairs where Advent were playing that night. I walked in, and the band told me to hurry up and eat because we were due on stage in ten minutes.

I awoke. What a crazy dream! That morning I walked past the Gatehouse to get my morning newspaper and looked in through boarded-up windows, and thought how much better it would be for me if there was a fast-food outlet in its location. What a delicious thought.

A week later, I was watching *Question Time* again and what are the chances of me seeing that twice in a row? I called up Sutch and told him about the dream. He laughed and asked how seriously I wanted a fast-food chain in Highgate. The villagers (as I disparagingly called them) would have a hissy fit if one landed on their doorstep. "I know," I said. "Do you think the OMRLP could field a candidate on that policy?"

"Oh no," he said. "We've never had a serious policy in our life! Maybe you should stand as an independent where you can raise the issue as a local and whip the community up into a frenzy?"

As luck would have it, P.M. John Major called a General Election in March of the following year. The Tory Government had turned on itself after a series of scandals rocked the party. Tony Blair, as Labour Leader, focused on transforming his party through a more centrist policy platform, entitled 'New Labour,' with promises of devolution, referendums for Scotland and Wales, fiscal responsibility, and a decision to nominate more female politicians for election through the use of all-women shortlists from which to choose candidates.

Meanwhile, in the Hornsey & Wood Green constituency, the Fast-Food Party promised a drive-in for Highgate on every available vacant street corner premises.

I was ready to put my plan into action because I had spent the Winter of 1996 plotting what I would do if a General Election came soon. The first thing I did was register the Fast Food Party, with advice from Sutch, and once I was on the list of candidates standing in the Hornsey & Wood Green constituency I asked my friend, a local printer, to create thousands of flyers for me which I was going to hand out and get stuffed into letterboxes around Highgate. The hard work was about to begin.

The campaign trail began on a wet morning in March. There were six weeks till election day on 1st May, and I intended to speak to as many constituents as possible. I stood outside the Gatehouse with a self-made placard or two proclaiming the virtues of a fast-food chain in Highgate. The first person to approach had a huge scowl on his face as if he had been chewing on a wasp and refused to look at me or engage in conversation when I said hello. This was the general reaction for most of the morning, though I did notice that the younger generation was more than willing to discuss my views.

Most people laughed at me and said there would never come a time when a drive-in or similar was allowed in the area. Others told me to give up on the idea because mysterious forces were at work behind my back, trying to rid Highgate of my presence. My campaign was going nowhere fast until the local newspaper picked up the story. From there, I was featured on London local news with a live TV interview. And then, things got very interesting because I was approached by a new burger chain franchise looking to create a buzz for themselves and asked if they could use my campaign in their advertising and on their products to get a foothold in North London. I told them I didn't mind because my only objective was to shake stuffy old Highgate up, so sure, go ahead.

This dramatically increased my profile awareness, and to increase it further, I employed local youths to go around the immediate area stuffing leaflets through doors. They would benefit if my plan came through and agreed to help. I was only working to a half-mile radius. An odd quirk of Highgate is that it touched on the borders of Islington, Camden and Haringey. Still, I was concentrating on the High Street to do my campaigning and carry out my mischief-making.

I was going home after a particularly fruitful meeting and had taken a shortcut through Pond Square and up the steps to the High Street when I was stopped by an burly gentleman coming the other way. I stepped aside to let him go, but he stopped and spoke to me. He knew who I was because he introduced himself and said "Mr Caine? Don't underestimate the strength of opposition to your plans. The Highgate Elders have taken an interest in you." He thrust an envelope into my hands and was gone before I could question him further.

Who were the Highgate Elders? I thought, and why would they be interested in what I was up to and who was the man on the steps? I opened the letter when I got home and pulled out a piece of white A4 paper filled with printed information and some newspaper cuttings.

The letter informed me that up until recently there had been cult meetings in the area of Highgate by a group calling themselves The Highgate Elders, and that up until my interference, they were meeting in a disused building (the implication was that it was the Gatehouse) on Monday evenings but now I had got the address in the public eye they had to meet elsewhere. They were said to be planning to gain ownership of the building for their purposes. The newspaper cuttings were instances of hauntings or paranormal sightings in the local area, and funnily enough, these were happening in nearby pubs.

I did a little digging around for information and the only thing I could find through my local contacts was that in the past, the Gatehouse building had indeed been a Sisters of Mercy Cult headquarters but no more. I was also told about the ley lines that crisscrossed the country and fell in direct lines through Highgate. Ley lines are imaginary lines between religious sites and places of significance and are said to attract paranormal activity. I had heard of ley lines before because one was said to be close to my recording studio and Apple said that it was probably a factor in us getting in contact with Ande Krick in 1978. Was it possible that my stirring-up interest in a disused building in Highgate went deeper than local resistance to chicken wings and greasy burgers?

My interest in the Highgate Elders and finding out who they were and why they were against my plans were now more important to me than my campaigning. Were they still meeting on Mondays because I was curious to see what they got up to. On the other hand, this could be a trap to get me to attend so they could turn me into a frog or a toad or something! It would look good if I were to play the *Slug* LP again.

Fate took a hand, though. The following week marked my campaign's third week, and I had been invited to attend a public meeting in nearby Hornsey with all the other candidates. The interest from the press and local news was such that there were camera crews present. They need not have bothered because a couple of the major parties had made excuses and pulled out of the event. They didn't want to share a stage with me and had cold feet. Still, the Labour representative for the night was quite a charming man and did not resort to the name-calling that these meetings usually became. He told me after the meeting that he had needed a drink before going on stage because he had been urged to represent the Labour Party at short notice, and public speaking was not his forte. But, of course, Labour was always going to win the seat and could have sent a donkey along that night and people would still have voted red. But I digress.

After the meeting, a few of us decamped to the nearby pub, the Railway Tavern, for a few hours at least. Alcohol loosens the tongue, and I was hoping that I might find some information on my opponents that I could use to my advantage, but all the alcohol did was make me very sleepy, so I closed my eyes for a moment.

I had another of my vivid dreams about being at the Gatehouse. Instead of it being a fast-food franchise it was now deserted. The atmosphere was not too dissimilar to that of a horror movie. Highgate itself was deserted, as though everyone had left town in a hurry. I could hear my name being called throughout the dream and the calling was from within the Gatehouse. I walked into the darkness, and the voice grew louder. A semi-clad young female appeared in front of me and I thought this was going to be interesting and stretched out contentedly, only to wake and find that I was strapped to something by the chest. I was in darkness and could not remember when I had left the pub or when I went to sleep.

The sound of a man clearing his throat close to my ear made me jump as much as possible, given that I was tied to a chair.

"Ah, you're awake," said a male voice. "I wondered if I'd given you too many sleeping pills."

I tried to wriggle free but could not.

"They aren't tight knots. I could set you free if you promise not to get violent, okay?"

I nodded. He untied the knots and turned on a light.

It was the Labour representative.

"I'm still feeling very sleepy," I said. "Where are we? Why did you need to drug me and not just invite me over here at the meeting?"

"We're in a cellar close to the village," he replied, ignoring my comment. "I have some people who want to speak with you."

I froze, not just because it was so bloody cold down in the cellar. I was going to come face to face with the

Highgate Elders. Who knows what kind of cruel acts they would perform on me? These cults were into dark arts, or so I had heard.

I could hear footsteps coming down to the cellar. I braced myself and looked towards the steps leading upstairs and was surprised to see two elderly men dressed in suits enter the cellar. I had been expecting them to wear robes or hoods or something similar to hide their identities but they were doing nothing of the sort. Instead, they introduced themselves as Mr Smith and Mr Weston, obviously waiting for me to make a wisecrack or something and then came to the point of this impromptu meeting.

"Mr Caine?" said Smith "I suppose you are wondering why we have bought you here tonight?"

"Not at all" I replied. "I'm used to being held against my will in a cold, damp cellar. It happens to me all the time!"

Weston chuckled. "We've been taking great interest in your campaign, Charlie, and want to help you."

"Hang on a minute. Are you Highgate Elders?"

"Yes, we are Charlie. Why do you ask and what were you expecting from us?"

I told them that I thought the Elders were set against me and that I had already been warned that they wanted the building for themselves for their Monday night meetings. I was told that this was nonsense because they had changed venues to elsewhere on a Tuesday and anyway, Monday night was *Coronation Street*, and the Elders never missed that. They wanted to help me because they were keen to make sure the Sisters of Mercy were denied bidding for the Gatehouse in future and that they would rather see a fast-food franchise in the area than another local cult in competition with them.

While I had the chance, I asked what the purpose of the Highgate Elders was and what they stood for. Weston answered that they wanted to prevent undesirables from living in the borough by creating scare stories about the Elders, but I responded: wasn't a fast-food outlet going to encourage more outsiders to Highgate? Smith said that everyone who moves into Highgate is vetted by the Elders, who have connections with the estate agents. They had even vetted me in the past and I made it through because I was an artist. They liked my *Slug* album too.

"What is this help you are going to give me?" I queried.

"We have connections with the electoral system" one replied. "It only takes a genuine slip in counting."

I told them that if I was going to win the seat of Hornsey & Wood Green I would do it fairly and squarely. "Well, we can provide some financial assistance if that is what you require to keep your campaign going, print posters, grease palms etc. How much do you need?"

They gave me £2,000 and assurances that it was a gift and would not need to be repaid. All I had to do was discredit the Sisters of Mercy enough to prevent them from getting a toehold in Highgate. When I got home, I put the money in a teapot and thought about my next move.

A couple of days later, I was in Crouch End having a working supper with an employee I had taken on to help run my campaign and keep me organised. The pub became busy when a bunch of women came in and it was obvious that this was a hen party or something similar. Being the generous chap I am, I went over and said hello, told them I would buy them all drinks and we all got drunker and louder. Once again I fell asleep and heard voices giggling my name and felt I was being lifted gently and carried for quite some time before settling on something soft.

"Wakey, wakey gorgeous" I heard in my ear.

I woke to semi-darkness and I was lying on a bed. "Oh no, not again!" I moaned. "Twice in a week. What do you want from me now?"

More giggling came from close by, and the first voice replied, "aren't you the lucky one!"

My eyes adjusted to the light and I made out the forms of six ladies. Maybe things were on the up after all! One introduced the group as The Sisters of Mercy, so I asked where I was. I was in the disused Gatehouse and anticipating... well, I didn't know quite what to expect but it had to be better than the Highgate Elders and a cold cellar. The group leader was a blonde named Denise, and I'm only assuming she was the leader because she did most of the talking. The conversation went along the same lines as two nights previously. Denise was dead set against the Elders getting the current premises to themselves and was looking for me to use my influence to scupper their chances. She said she could support my campaign financially to the tune of £1,500 and said it was a gift. I said I would see what I could do.

I got home and put the money in the teapot. £3,500. That's a lot of money for doing nothing. If the Highgate Elders and Sisters of Mercy had done their homework, they would have seen that a well-known chain of pubs had already bid for the place, which was as good as accepted. Sure, my Fast-Food Party was never going to win, so I kept up pretences for the next two weeks until the election was over. I amassed 525 votes, and the Hornsey & Wood Green constituency was won by Barbara Roche with an increased majority. The result was that whilst a fast-food chain was never in question, Wetherspoons took over the premises and renamed it Upstairs At The Gatehouse, where they put on performances and music and provided me with a cheap hot breakfast until they moved out in 2015. I like to think that my campaign encouraged the pushing through of the chain, though it probably would have happened anyway, though not quite as soon.

Takin' Care Of Business

At the turn of the century, I received a call from Joyce James entirely out of the blue. I hadn't seen her for a while, but she told me that the BBC had just contacted her. Joyce was occasionally approached with offers of work for me. She wasn't my official publicist any more but kept me informed if my name was mentioned in a work capacity. The BBC wanted to know if I would come down to Television Centre and have a screen test for a show they had commissioned which was due to start production. They remembered how I had fared when sharing presenting duties with Billy Shears (which seemed like an age ago) and thought I might be what they were looking for. I was unsure if I could handle such an undertaking but Joyce said she felt I was capable of the project.

The show was going to be half interview and half talent show. It was named *The Wow Factor!* It sounded a load of old pish, but I needed to do something with my Saturday nights rather than sit around drinking beer in front of the TV and eating crisps in my underpants. I failed the audition but, in the process, came up with an idea for a show which was to be *Rock Band*, a Saturday night family show where two teams comprising of up-and-coming musicians vied for a record deal over six weeks. I was the host of the show and got to judge how each team was faring and generally kept the show ticking along. Special guests came on each week to educate the audience concerning a particular style of music and its history.

I had accidentally made myself the front-runner for the job by coming up with the idea in the first place. It was more of a joke when I said that there had never been a decent show based around Rock music and when I was asked what it would involve, my ideas were deemed good enough for a pilot to be made with me at the helm. For that episode, we had Phil 'the spill' Collins leading one team and my good mate Keith Howells the other. I thought it was a great pilot. Everyone was enjoying themselves and having a good time.

When the show was viewed by the producers, they thought it was coming across as too cosy and felt that there had to be an element of tension to the show. Lemmy from Motorhead was being considered because he was always very outspoken right to the end of his life, but when he pulled out at the very last moment the producer shouted out in desperation, "call for Billy Shears!" I begged and pleaded that they reconsider, but there was not enough time to get Phil back, so I was outvoted. That's why, for the first series of *Rock Band*, it was Billy's band Splinter, paired against Keith's band Anvil.

I have to say that he was actually on his best behaviour and probably realised that, just like me, his days in the musical spotlight were over, and he was approaching his sixties with no other career to fall back on. I was fortunate enough to have money from my *Centipede & Slug* and Ande Krick nest eggs and was only doing this show out of boredom, but Billy threw himself into the challenge of motivating his team and found he had an easy rapport with Keith. Each show was an hour long and was just long enough for Billy to stay focused and not go off script. We filmed six episodes which were scheduled to be shown later on in the Summer, and at the very last one, when I came to judge the winners of the show, I picked Anvil as the best band and Billy didn't even react.

In his biography, Billy Shears wrote: *"When I got the call to go on the show at the last minute I nearly refused. But I bit my tongue because if I blew this one, I would have to give up on my last chance of TV stardom, so I just got on with the gig. I went into the show thinking I was going to hate working with Caine but had to give him some grudging respect as he was the consummate professional. I think that like me he was trying hard to make it work. I couldn't believe it that there was no bar for a quick drink but thinking about it, that's probably why I was able to make it work."*

When the show aired it was an instant success. Remember, there were no shows of this type around at the time and I hold my hands up and apologise for being partly responsible for the copycat music shows that were to follow and fill up prime-time weekend TV. Another longer series of *Rock Band* was quickly agreed on and the show was extended with live elements to it where the public got to vote on their favourites. A new section was added to the show with a guest music celebrity sitting in on a practice session to jam with each band in turn, bouncing off ideas about song writing and how to structure songs. Occasionally the bands would go out to play a gig at a pub and see how the audience reacted.

Rock Band ran for five series, and whilst none of the bands went on to have successful careers in the music world after leaving the show, a couple of band members became VJs introducing music on satellite TV. I was pleased the show got such high ratings in a world where kids wanted to rap or be DJs rather than rock stars, but the writing was already on the wall for rock music; the schedules were filling up with a variety of junk music shows catering towards boy bands and singers with auto-tune turned up to 10.

In May 2005 Reggie Cramwell died. He was 85 and I was saddened to hear of his passing. Times had been hard for Reggie and the label, since the days when their artists could be counted on to shift LPs in their millions. He had approached me a few months earlier to see if I wanted a senior role in PMSL but I had politely declined his offer as I was still busy with *Rock Band*.

I still had my recording studio but I hardly visited any more. It was being rented out to PMSL records because they couldn't afford their own premises. At a well-attended funeral, I was talking to PMSL executives about the affairs of the label and one in particular, John Martin, was keen to discuss the future of the label without Reggie at the helm. Like Reggie, he offered me the chance of a role within the record label, but I had not had a decent holiday for a few years so again declined the offer. John was a persuasive fellow and wouldn't take no for an answer. He invited me to come by his office the following week so we could discuss matters further - not that I had anything else to add to the discussion. I had a week to think matters over and decided I would visit John and see what he had to say. What did I have to lose? John was pleased to see me. He offered me a drink and came straight to the point.

"Charlie, I know you already said you are not interested in a role at PMSL, but I think you are well suited for one I have in mind. With Reggie gone we need an experienced man to bring the label out of a rut." He paused. "You are that man, Charlie."

I looked at him in surprise. "Are you serious? I mean, what experience do I have for that position?"

"You have a wealth of experience, Charlie. You've learned a lot since you signed your first contract." He showed me a piece of paper. "And here it is!"

I took the paper and read "2 loaves of bread, cheese, a bottle of wine..."

"Sorry, wrong paper. Try this one."

I laughed and took the other piece of paper. It was double-sided with the details of the Highwaymen's contract on it. I couldn't believe we had signed such a paltry deal. No wonder Reggie got to ride around in a fancy car.

"I would be looking for a much better contract than this one, John" I said in all seriousness. "Add more digits to this, and I may become interested."

A week later, I was sitting at my desk at PMSL Records. This was a turn-up for the books, I thought. I spent the morning looking around the offices, drinking copious amounts of tea and going through the many files of bands that the label once had on their roster. I looked at how measly the contracts were and how quickly bands would leave after their contracts expired. Things hardly changed when Reggie was promoted to the head of the label, and Advent was the golden egg that kept the label afloat.

I read through all the files and found Reggie was a serial hoarder. He would not throw anything away that had a signature on it in case it was needed later; some letters he kept for sentimental reasons. A lot of those records I boxed up to be put into storage, never to be seen again. I was left with files and letters solely relating to those who were currently signed to PMSL Records.

After a few days, I began looking at the back catalogue of the label to see what recordings they had amassed over the years. I was surprised to see that PMSL Records went back to 1945 and was originally a record shop that liked recording home-grown talent and then selling their records at the shop. This worked well, with the records being pressed by a local manufacturer and this financed a larger building where better recording equipment was used.

There was a treasure trove of old master tapes I was sure had not been heard since their original recording - material that would fit just right on an anthology set of PMSL Records. I also saw that the greatest hits of their artists were not fully utilised. I remembered there had been one for the Highwaymen long ago, along with an Advent compilation. Why didn't Reggie see that these were released regularly? I went through lists of recordings and could see what needed to be done: box sets, compilations, anthology series, live albums, the lot. I told John that I would start the ball rolling and come up with an anthology set for the Highwaymen, with lots of unreleased tracks and detailed information on recordings, together with some of my souvenirs that fans would be interested in. This package would be released on CD and LP. He thought it was a great idea and immediately set the commercial team on to it.

The PMSL Anthology Set was a great success, outselling all other rivals box sets and compilations, so there was great anticipation as to how the Highwaymen collection would fare. I need not have worried because the band was still very popular in Europe because of my connection and sales were such that once again, there was talk of another tour. It had been fifteen years since my last visit but I just wasn't up to the job and wanted to keep up the excellent work with the label.

One day I was in a nostalgic mood and decided I would look at the Advent recording contract, but couldn't find it, no matter how hard I looked in case it had been misfiled. I called John and asked him if he knew where it may be and he was just as baffled as I. Could it accidentally have been filed away when I cleared out the cabinet with all the redundant contracts? I had not seen it then. Finding the Advent file became my No 1 priority and I made it the day's task to be found.

All the office assistants were looking for it and even the tea lady got involved. I then remembered the Ande Krick episode and was tapping on all the panelled walls of the office to see if I could detect any false sound in case Reggie had a secret drawer. A month went by and I forgot about the lost contract, and it wasn't until I was reorganising my office that I struck gold. Late one afternoon I had enlisted a couple of lads to move my desk nearer to the drinks cabinet and they had just lifted it when I heard a cracking sound. Oh great, now I need a new desk. I said my thanks for their work and they left. I opened the drawer to take out my briefcase to go home and discovered that not only had the desk drawer been broken but I could see inside a cracked and concealed lower part of the drawer a folder. My Advent folder.

I searched the folder as soon as I got home and recognised Reggie's writing on a letter addressed to me. Either he knew I would be searching for this folder in his office or he had written it but knew he would never send it to me. Why would he have written a letter rather than tell me what he wanted? I opened the letter, four pages hand written and opening with 'Dear Charlie,' very informal. I read it through once, scarcely believing what I was reading. I read it again just to make sure I wasn't dreaming.

In the letter, Reggie wrote that he was my father and the story I was led to believe of my father dying was to stop me from asking questions about where Dad was, who he was and why I couldn't see him. Reggie had met Mum through his music, that was true, and he had always wanted to marry her, but Mum wanted someone to settle down with and not to have to share him with his musical ambitions. There were so many questions I would have asked and now I was denied ever knowing why Reggie (Dad) had never told me all of this in the living years. I was angry and sad with Mum for never telling me the true story either, but most families have a secret and this was mine.

Celluloid Heroes

I was getting to see Lyric more often now that Apple and I had made our peace. He was as musically inclined as I had been at his age. He already had an acoustic guitar and was using all the rock star poses while practising in front of the mirror.

We were checking out MTV one afternoon when an Advent video from *Top Of The Pops* came on and Lyric was commenting on my flares in a lightly mocking way. I asked him about the music he was listening to and told him that when I was his age, I witnessed the birth of Rock & Roll. He had to look it up on Google before coming back at me with questions about Elvis, Chuck Berry and the like. He was confusing Little Richard for Cliff Richard so I had to put him right on that score. I went to the front room, picked out 10 CDs, and gave them to him, saying that if he was serious about his music, then give them a listen. They were all guitar-driven of course and he had a good knowledge of current bands but I believed he needed educating on the history of rock music and I should have been doing so long before. He took the CDs away and, in a few weeks, he came back asking for more. I must have lent him 50 over the coming months till I had the idea of just buying him an iPod and putting my entire collection on it for him to listen to.

Another eventful night in my career came when I took part in the Eurovision Song Contest. They hadn't forgotten about me in Eastern Europe, even in 2011 when I was in self-imposed musical retirement. I was asked by the German Eurovision representatives if I was willing to take part in the pre-show for that year's contest. Germany had won in 2010 in Oslo so were due to host the event. Dusseldorf Arena was chosen as the venue for the contest and this was Germany's first hosting of the show since unification so I wanted to be involved as I had a connection to that eventful night in 1989.

I had watched the show on and off for many years since being a judge in the 1974 Brighton contest when ABBA won and became global superstars. I said I was probably too old to be a contestant but wouldn't mind being a technical adviser or mentor.

I travelled to Germany to discuss ideas, and I was asked to do a skit after all the contestants had performed their songs to keep the audience and TV viewers entertained. I was also going to introduce each song with a ten-second video, dressed in the competitor's national costume and doing something amusing. These were the sections that Terry Wogan and latterly Graham Norton found so funny each year.

I was backstage getting ready for my performance. It was going to be a duet with presenter Greta Schmidt and I was looking forward to it, though I had been told there would be a surprise element to the show and I was waiting for a sign that it was time to move to the green room where I could prepare, and have a talk with Greta. There was a knock on the dressing room door and a funny little man entered and said his name was Mike and that I was to follow him to another part of the arena. After going down a maze of tunnels he motioned to me to enter a room and by now I was ready to sit down because all the walking had left me feeling quite tired. It certainly wasn't a green room. Three chairs, a wooden table and what light there was came from a lamp in the middle of the small room. A figure that I thought I recognised was sitting at the table but I could not put a name to him until he spoke.

"Hi, Charlie."

"Oh! Hi Hal, what are you doing here? I didn't know you were into Eurovision, or are you performing on the show?" I laughed.

Hal didn't find that funny.

"Do you remember our plans to become famous with our band Mike & The Magic Mushrooms and how you abandoned us when you went off after Woodstock?"

"That wasn't altogether my fault, Hal" I responded. "I'd been drugged by a couple of hippies and only just managed to escape their clutches."

"Do you hate hippies, Charlie? By the way, this is Mike. Say hello Mike."

The reunion was taking a sinister turn and I was looking for a way out of the room. I know what the two of them wanted but I wasn't going to wait to find out. I wondered if I was going to have to fight my way out of this situation. Normally I couldn't fight my way out of a paper bag - or at least that's what they used to say at school. I knew I could take on Mike easily because a breath of wind would probably blow him over, but Hal was a different matter.

I was due on stage in five minutes and knew everyone would be looking for me. The quickest solution was one I used at school to get away from bullies, so I stood up quickly, flipped the table up and towards Hal and made a dash for the door. Hal was too slow and I made it out into the corridor and began to run in the direction I thought led back to the stage but I must have gone around in a large square because I soon found I was back where I had escaped. They were both closing in on me so I made a dash for another door, pushed it, climbed up some steps and found myself on stage in the middle of the German national anthem. I rushed across the stage, closely followed by Mike and Hal and security bods, bringing unexpected gasps of surprise from the crowd who must have thought this was some kind of comedy act

In the aftermath of the show, Hal and Mike were charged with attempted kidnapping. They had been at a pot-smokers convention in Germany and Hal, still holding a grudge about his failed attempt at stardom, had concocted a half-baked plan to kidnap me and hold me to ransom until I organised a recording contract for his Mushrooms. I could see he had not thought things through. They were arrested and held overnight but I bailed them both out the next day and got them back to the airport and home. So much for hating hippies.

After this, I gave up on making music. I may as well have done so because I signed a deal to provide soundtracks for Daley Twins Studios. These were lean years spent making music so bland I felt it was going to put me to sleep. I wanted to add an element of rock to the songs but kept getting told: oh no, that wasn't what the films were all about. They had to be family-orientated so no controversial lyrics.

I complained that they should have signed up Barry Manilow if they wanted something uncontroversial. The songs were to be no longer than three minutes in length and with heart-warming lyrics. And also, no choruses. I couldn't get my head around that until I tried to come up with a Daley Twins song with a chorus. There also needed to be a key change in every song and a sped-up ending. All trademarks of your regular Daley Twins animated films.

I worked on three or four of these films, getting constantly reminded to stick within the boundaries of what was acceptable to the brand and getting no job satisfaction. I grew to hate the job of creating music that meant nothing to me and was trying to find a way to escape my contract of four pieces of work over two years. My wicked sense of humour got the better of me, and I decided to add a subliminal message to some of the songs. Nothing too serious at first, just backwards-taped low voices saying "Daley Twins are holding me to ransom to produce crapola on an industrial scale," and layering it beneath a nonsensical soundtrack featuring ponies, sea creatures and mermaids.

I was ratted on by the sound engineer who listened to the recorded multi-tracks one night and isolated the offending soundbite. I was summoned to the Daley Twins Headquarters for a dressing down and made to promise I would never pull that stunt again.

2012 and Lyric was growing up fast. For his 21st birthday and my 70th, I was planning a surprise. It was more of a surprise for friends and family, because unknown to them all, we were going to get together and play a gig for them all. Every Thursday night for two months, whilst all the nonsense of recording for Daley Twins was going on, I met up with Lyric and the band he had formed. We practised a few rock & roll standards such as *Johnny B' Goode*, some Led Zeppelin and punk numbers. We were ready to give a great show.

The night of the party I was all geared up and couldn't sit still because of what was planned. We blew everyone away with our surprise and Lyric and I joined together on stage afterwards and I wished him a happy birthday. He then provided a surprise that I had not seen coming, because as he pointed behind us a plume of mist formed and as the curtains pulled back, I could see all of Advent were in theatrical dress, and strains of *The Garden Wall* began.

Sneaky Lyric had insisted that we practise this particular song every week as well as a couple of others from my past and now it made sense. I was all ready and warmed up and Advent showed those upstarts how to hold an audience captive. It was to be the last time we all played together. The next day I went back to the studio and told them in no uncertain terms where they could stick their ponies, sea creatures, mermaids and woodland creatures.

That was the last time I saw Keith Howells alive. He was to die on stage a few years later, playing with his new band The Keith Howells Project. Keith loved his synthesizers and keyboards so much that he began to stack them around him, one on top of each other until he had fifteen of them on different levels in a semi-circle at the last count.

This was beginning to create a problem as he had to figure out a way to get to any one of them at a particular moment. It was a health hazard as he was boxed in on three sides from above and sometimes, he never came out of his play area and would have stayed in there all night just playing if he could. The only members of the audience who could see him were those on the balcony.

On the night of his death, he was playing an open-air concert in Germany. The gig had nearly been cancelled due to inclement weather. Being the consummate professional he was, Keith knew he couldn't let his fans down.

The official cause of Keith's death was suffocation, caused by his Mellotron and three keyboards collapsing in on him. He died for his music but I think that is the way he would have wanted to be remembered. His funeral was held two weeks later and as befitting for a keyboard player he chose Procol Harum's *A Whiter Shade of Pale,* Henry Francis Lyte's *Abide with Me* and Judee Sill's *Jesus was a Crossmaker* as his music but revealed his sense of humour with *Always Look on the Bright Side of Life.*

I currently spend my time doing voiceovers for video channels playing the hits of the Sixties, Seventies and Eighties. Last night for instance I was introducing the Top 30 pop songs from the Seventies and hint, hint an Advent song was in the mix. Sometimes I cross paths with Simon Crisp and we nod and say hello.

These days up and coming band's name check us and use us as a point of reference, saying things like "we're going for a theatrical angle like Advent," or "we want our songs to last the test of time like Charlie Caine's." There are so many Advent tribute bands and I was always tempted to go along and see what I must have looked like live because some of these bands do a very good theatrical show with all the costumes. I eventually went along to a show in Edmonton incognito but sitting in the front row a band member recognised me at the end of the show and I was invited up to the stage to play an encore number.

Every so often I get invited to fill in on a rock radio show while the host is away and I use my connections to call in favours and get my music friends to come in for a chat and to play some great music. I accidentally created the *Unplugged* MTV shows well before the TV version came along when I invited a lot of my folk friends to come along and play some numbers on a radio show.

In an unexplained turn of events, I was the victim of an electrical shock that could not be explained away and called time on the show soon after. I appear on the occasional TV chat show but my appearances are not nearly as controversial as they used to be. Billy Shears and I do occasionally get together and whilst the animosity is not there, we still get very competitive when remembering the old days and who had the better band, the biggest hit singles and so on. We call it a draw most of the time.

Of the four biographies written about me. Two of them were published shortly after 1991 and covered most of what was known about my life up to that point, and the others were just a lot of gossip cobbled together and a muck-slinging exercise of rumour and lies. I've taken a back seat concerning my music career these past ten years. Many bands and musicians don't know when it is time to hang up their guitars and put their plectrums and drumsticks down, continuing to regurgitate the same old tunes till they are called up to the great gig in the sky. I was never going to let that be me. I was hopelessly out of touch with the music scene as Acid, House, Rap, Grunge, Brit Pop and goodness knows what else flashed by. It all sounded all too formulaic for me to take an interest.

Apple and I never quite reconciled but we became friends again. We see each other from time to time when Lyric has a show but I've never wanted to overshadow him by appearing in the crowd and stealing his thunder. I like to go and watch with a baseball cap pulled firmly down but how many 80-year-olds do you see at a rock concert? They tend to stick out a mile, don't they?

While writing this book I received a letter from Buckingham Palace. I don't know who was more surprised when I got news saying I was going to be awarded a Knighthood in the New Year's Honours list. I was flattered and surprised. A visit to Buckingham Palace to meet the Queen - I hope she was not going to be too mad at me for what happened during the Jubilee celebrations when I was with Saliva. The award was being made for 'services to popular music' and along with the letter came a list of instructions as to what I would expect on the day and what was expected of me. Such information as when to bow and how to approach her. Don't speak to Her Majesty unless spoken to and so forth and so on. I was going to have to go and get suited and booted because the last pair of shoes I wore were platform shoes when I was with Advent.

Epilogue

Charlie submitted a lot of extra material for me to use, which was helpful because his journals became increasingly erratic and difficult to decipher after 2000. He started writing the journals in 1960 because they helped him remember where he had been, what he had done, and who he had met in his career. As part of my job, I have to research the information I am given to make sure it is factually correct. Whilst a lot of details in Charlie's journals were easy to corroborate and confirm had occurred, there were lots of oddities that didn't match up.

Some of the more recent journal entries were just downright fantasy. Either Charlie was making things up to make the book more exciting or he was losing his marbles and needed help. When I approached Apple about my concern for Charlie's health, she expressed surprise when I mentioned a relationship between them. It was true that they had a close physical relationship that lasted while they were in the commune but only for a couple of years. After that, they were just very good friends and nothing more. Furthermore, Lyric wasn't even his son. I decided to dig deeper and this is what I found:

Charlie went to Graceland one evening but on his own. There were no journals to confirm this so I contacted John James and Dapper Dave who he claimed had been with him. They said meeting Elvis in person was never mentioned by Charlie but he did get into an altercation with security. He never made it beyond the main gates before being turned away, so impersonating a Beatle was another fact we can dismiss.

He was never on Pirate Radio with Simon Crisp but provided zany commercials in Kenny Everett's style. He only met Cindy briefly and they never had an affair. Cindy thought the idea of her and Charlie as an item to be hilarious and said I could publish it for a laugh. I could go on picking holes in Charlie's account of the facts but it is, therefore, open to conjecture that some of Charlie's recollection of his past and events after 2005 should be taken with a large pinch of salt. So why publish the book I hear you ask? Well, if anything it makes for an amusing story.

I talked to Laura Norder, author of *My Way, Or The Highway,* which was published in 1991. She described Charlie as a regular kind of guy when they met to discuss his biography. I asked did Charlie have problems remembering his past. She explained that Charlie answered all the questions she threw at him and seemed clued up with everything. I wondered if the death of his Mother and discovering Reggie was his biological father may have affected him more than could have been realised.

Apple spoke to Frankie, and Charlie was admitted to a private psychiatric hospital suffering from BPD (borderline personality disorder) after this book was completed. His deterioration was gradual but was already obvious when he finished working on *Rock Show*. He spends most of his days talking to the other patients about his career and how plans are progressing for his next tour with Advent. He has visits from friends from time to time who come away feeling sad at how he had deteriorated over the past five years. When Joyce saw him just before COVID reared its ugly head he asked when Keith and the band were going to help him escape to East Germany and play a gig to bring down the wall.

Frankie told me that Charlie is not ready to leave any time soon.

Discography (recommended works)

With the Dandy Highwayman

1964 *Stand & Deliver* debut single and LP
1964 *Hey Girl* single
1964 *Wouldn't It Be Good?* single
1964 *Rocking With The Highwaymen* LP
1964 *In Your Room* single
1964 *What's Your Name?* single
1965 *Highwaymen For Sale* LP
1965 *Hold On* Single
1965 *This Is The Place* single
1965 *On The Road Again* LP
1965 *Talking 'Bout You* single
1965 *Hey Mr Postman* EP
1966 *Let's Take A Trip (Far Away)* LP
1966 *The Colours Of Your Mind* single
1966 *Linda in the Shop with Donuts* single

With Advent

1970 *Arrival* LP
1971 *The Coming Of Advent* LP
1972 *There She Goes* single
1972 *Centipede & The Slug* triple LP
1975 *LOST* LP
1975 *Earth* LP
1985 *Centipede & The Slug* Soundtrack

With Saliva

1976 *Gob On You* Single
1976 *(Let's Have A) Glue Sniffing Christmas* single
1977 *Churchill Is A Punk Rocker* single
1977 *Gobbed On You* LP
1977 *We're Sorry, Elvis* single

Andre Krick
1980 *The Legacy Recordings* LP Set

With ZX81
1981 *Syntax* single and LP

Solo
1980 *Charlie Caine* LP
1982 *Bells & Whistles* LP
1984 *Cindy Incidentally* LP (Released 2010)

Soundtracks
Too many to mention.

Acknowledgements

I have always wanted to write a book, but about what? Always write about what you know, or so it is said, and seeing as I am an avid music fan it was just a matter of time before a story line formulated in my head and I wanted to get it onto paper. There have been a lot of spoof music stories such as Spinal Tap and the Rutles, and using these as a benchmark I thought of devising a character whose life I could tell from start to finish and fool around with the history of music in the process.

Writing a book was harder than I thought, or should I write that the first chapter was the hardest? It took two years of frustration and false starts before I decided in mid-2022 that the best way to continue was to sit in the kitchen and allocate a couple of hours each night (and some wine) to write a minimum of 500 words at a time. I had a framework for what I wanted to write but never knew how much fun I was going to have once the process was in full flow. The wine probably helped with my positive mood and there were times when I would write a paragraph and start laughing at what I had recorded so I knew I was doing something right.

I have read a lot of music biographies in my time and most of them follow a process of having a great start and middle, but tailing off a little as the subject gets to old age and loses their creative spark. I didn't want Charlie to finish on a low so was toying with an idea of making him an MP, but that was never going to happen as I know little about the political process to develop the storyline. I eventually decided Charlie was going to make his mark in television and be responsible for kick-starting the crazy world of talentless performers that clog up Saturday night TV. At least I can blame someone for that now.

I kept my writing habit a secret in much the same way Charlie kept his pencil-nibbling from his friends until I had 100 pages in the bank, and then took the step of showing what I had written to my sister Sandra Whelan, who became my proof reader and general advisor throughout the creation of this piece of work. At this point, it became a family affair, with my brothers David and Ian Avey offering up amusing anecdotes and writing ideas. Ian was the first to read the draft all the way through and was able to quote verbatim the Rubettes quote after learning it word for word in the Seventies.

Throughout the book I managed to weave in a few family stories for my own amusement. The incident with the powdered milk happened to me on the way into Calais in 1982 with my late aunt and cousin. I also wanted to get a little of my footballing past recorded in the book, so followers of the late, great, Enfield FC and Enfield Town FC may spot a much-admired name buried in the football chapter.

My thanks go to Graham Venning and his idea for the Umbooku people and also his Michael Caine impressions that gave me the idea for my main character's name.

Thank you also to Kim & Marco Maiolatesi for their friendship and Friday night chats and encouragement.

I would also like to give thanks to work friends who spurred me towards the end as I stalled with getting a cover designer and finalising how I would get published. I decided to create the cover myself and self-publish. If you find any factual errors or typos whilst reading the book then do contact me because I can update it with the sequel!

Neil Avey
February 2023

Printed in Great Britain
by Amazon

17813720R00169